DEAD AND BURYD

Book I of the Out of Orbit series

Chele Cooke

Copyright © Chele Cooke 2013.

All rights reserved. No part of this publication may be reproduced, distributed or transmitted in any form or by any means, including photocopying, recording, or other electronic or mechanical methods, without the prior written permission of the publisher, except in the case of brief quotations embodied in critical reviews and certain other noncommercial uses permitted by copyright law.

Publisher's Note: This is a work of fiction. Names, characters, places, and incidents are a product of the author's imagination. Locales and public names are sometimes used for atmospheric purposes. Any resemblance to actual people, living or dead, or to businesses, companies, events, institutions, or locales is completely coincidental.

Cover Design © Mia Holappa 2013
Book Layout © BookDesignTemplates.com 2013

Dead and Buryd / Chele Cooke. -- 1st ed.
ISBN: 978-1-4922030-7-0

For Moa

*For helping bring "Out of Orbit" to life.
Without you, this would still be "buryd"
in the depths of my laptop.*

Days that Came Before

"Grandda'," the young boy asked, pushing his blanket back impatiently and gathering his stuffed toy horse up in his arms. "You tell me a story?"

Lyle lifted his head, looking away from the knife and half-carved wooden block in his hands. A small, tired smile slipped over his lips, and he gave a gentle nod. It was already a long way past the boy's bedtime, but he could hardly blame him for being restless. The heat had set in, and the thick air remained uncomfortable long after the sun had set.

Pushing himself up from his chair, Lyle moved over to his grandson's bed, fixing the blanket neatly across the end before he sat down. The bed was low and it made his joints ache to sit on the soft mattress, but the boy would only complain if he remained on the other side of the room for the story.

"Which story would you like?"

The boy thought for a moment, nuzzling the horse's soft flank as he blinked sleepily.

"Ships!" the boy answered finally, sitting up.

Reaching out and leaning across the bed, he gently pushed his grandson back down onto the mattress and brushed his dark brown hair away from his eyes. If he was going to tell him a story, the boy could at least pretend to try to sleep.

"You had that one last time, Brae," he reminded him.

"It's my favourite."

Lyle rolled his eyes. He was sure that he'd told Braedon the story of the ships the last half-dozen times. Just like his son, Braedon's father, his grandson never tired of hearing the tale of their past.

"Alright," he answered with a slow nod.

He leaned away from Braedon, placing his knife and the block of half-whittled wood down on the floor before looking back at his grandson. With his son, Halden, working long hours so often, it was a regular arrangement that he put Braedon to bed. Lyle didn't mind. In fact, he rather enjoyed it. The young boy was almost as enthralled with his stories as his own children used to be. Though they were both grown now, no longer needing stories at bedtime, when they even came home at all.

"Long, long ago, Os-Veruh was a beautiful and rich planet," Lyle began, smiling back at the grin spreading across Braedon's face. "The Veniche people lived in one place, they had everything they could ever want, even if they sometimes complained that they didn't."

Braedon rolled onto his side, knees drawn up towards his chest as he hugged the horse tightly and turned it in his arms so that the toy could hear the story better.

"Men fought for more, to see more of the skies. So they spent years building big ships that could float on air instead of water."

"Grandda', you forgot the men who look up!" Braedon whined.

Frowning, Lyle shook his head.

"I was getting to it," he answered. "Os-Veruh had everything, from men who examined the deepest oceans, to those who looked at the furthest stars in the night sky. One day, one of the sky watchers saw something. He saw a shooting star heading towards Os-Veruh. The Veniche people panicked. No one knew whether the meteor would hit the planet or sail past, but the sky watcher said it would collide with them, and they had to believe him.

"The big sky ships were almost ready, and all the people argued and fought over who would be allowed onto them. Men argued using their power and their money, claiming that those things made them more worthy of saving. Others asserted their intelligence and skill, saying that those things should be what mattered."

"Like Gianna?" Braedon asked.

"What?" Lyle asked, thrown from the rhythm of his story by Braedon's sudden question. In the times he'd told his grandson the story, he'd never asked that before.

"With the med'cine."

Lyle reached up and scratched his cheek. He had to admit, he didn't know. He'd never stopped to think about which skills would have been prized above others back then. He could only imagine that the people on the ships would have needed medicines and medics to administer them.

"I guess," he agreed finally. "Yes, probably."

"Good, I want to save her."

A quiet chuckle came out in a breath as Braedon nodded resolutely and settled himself back against the pillow. Lyle blinked, the interruption having dragged his thoughts from the flow of the story.

"Where was I?"

"The arguments."

"Oh, yes, I was," Lyle agreed. "The arguments and battles over who had places on the ships continued until the final days, and then one year before the meteor was set to hit the planet, the ships took off with as many people as they could carry."

"Into the sky to search for new places," Braedon said with an enthusiastic nod against his pillow.

"That's right. The ships went in all directions. Each ship carried a machine that could talk to the others even over millions of miles. If one ship found another planet, they could tell everyone else."

"But the meteor didn't hit us!"

Lyle frowned, pursing his lips as he looked down at his grandson. Halden and Georgianna, his own children, had not jumped ahead in the story every chance they could. Then again, it could have been that he just didn't remember. It had been a long time ago. Halden with his bright green eyes and dark hair like his own, Georgianna with her honey-gold curls that were always in a mess. He missed them as children, hanging on his every word like Braedon did now.

"No, it didn't," he said. "The meteor went straight past Os-Veruh, colliding with the planet that circled between Os-Veruh and the sun. That planet was destroyed, broken into thousands of pieces which would become meteors of their own.

"The Veniche who remained on Os-Veruh were relieved, and celebrated that they had been saved. However, as the days and months passed, they realised that things were not the same. They were travelling closer to the sun than they had before. They realised that the other planet had been keeping them away from the sun. The people began to suffer: some were killed and others driven mad by the heat. Some people fled north where the heat was less, hiding inside their buildings and creating tunnels under the ground to escape the sun.

"Next came the freeze as the planet moved further from the sun again. The snow froze everything it touched, and people ran south to escape as much of the blizzards as they could."

"I don't like the freeze," Braedon complained in a small voice.

"No, many didn't," he answered. "But families banded together, set on helping each other through the worst of it."

"Tribes! Tribes!" Braedon chanted, his dislike of the freeze forgotten as he pushed himself up.

Lyle reached out and settled the boy back down before he continued.

"Yes, Brae. All across the land, families joined together to share their skills, forming tribes who travelled together.

"The Kahle, one of the biggest tribes, had two settling grounds, Adlai in the north for the heat, and Nyvalau down south for the freeze. The Kahle built up these grounds, creating sturdy homes and even tunnels in Adlai to escape the sun."

Braedon was getting sleepy, Lyle could tell. After looking after the boy for most of the heat while his father went off to find work, he was getting pretty good at telling when the youngster was ready to doze off. The tight ball he'd curled his body into loosened a little, and lifting his weight from the bed for a moment, Lyle tugged the blanket out from underneath him and draped it over Braedon.

"It was decided by the elders of each tribe that a ledger would be kept," he continued, setting back into his spot at the end of the bed. "When people joined in love, when children were born and people died it was written down, so that, like the Veniche before them, they could remember the past."

"Grandda'," Braedon mumbled. "Who has our ledger?"

Lyle smiled.

"I do, Brae," he explained. "I'll show it to you tomorrow."

"Okay," the child yawned. "Finish the story."

Lyle wasn't entirely used to being ordered around in the telling of his bedtime stories, especially not by four-year-olds. However, being his only grandchild, he let Braedon off with a lot of things he knew he shouldn't.

"For generations, they lived this way. Travelling between the two grounds, the Veniche people lived in peace."

Braedon rolled himself further onto his stomach, burying his face into his pillow.

"Then the Adveni came," he mumbled through the material.

"Yes, Braedon," Lyle said as he got up from the bed. Leaning over Braedon, he smoothed the blanket across his grandson's small body and kissed him gently on his temple. "And then the Adveni came."

The Quarter Run

He made each turning the same as he had the last time. He'd been warned against it and told to take a different route through the buildings on each journey, but he liked the routine of a well-trodden path. He liked knowing exactly where the blind spots were on a journey and where he had to be extra careful. The sprawling training grounds were best avoided entirely. There were too many eager young Adveni who wanted their first capture. He knew the routes that caused the least problems, so while it made it easier for others to follow, he took those every time.

High above, the sun made a slow progression towards the horizon. In the Adveni quarter, the polished stones of the buildings shone like the sun themselves in the suffocating heat. The buildings' occupants were as deadly as the close, mid-heat sun. Perhaps more so, as it didn't take days for an Adveni to kill. It took moments, minutes, or hours…

depending on their wishes.

Sweat clung to his skin, his shirt plastered against his back. At his wrists and neck, the skin was already turning pink, and he could only count himself lucky that he knew a good medic to ease the burning flesh when he returned home.

The building stood halfway along the perfectly laid Adveni road. It was easy to spot amongst the other buildings. The design was similar, its colours uniform with the rest of the street, but this building was larger, more impressive, and slightly more terrifying for what waited inside.

He lengthened his stride, making brisk progress down the road towards the building. He wouldn't be going inside, he never did, but it wouldn't change the fact that he didn't have long. Pass offs had to be made quickly and without fuss. With their situation, they couldn't risk being caught.

He was almost opposite the building before he could look up into one of the front windows, able to spot the sky-blue shirt hanging behind the glass. He smiled, stuffing his hands into his pockets as he turned towards the house, making his way through the gap between the buildings.

The contact he'd been coming to see was a drysta, a slave to an Adveni, so he wasn't able to venture far from his owner's house. The drysta was already outside by the time he rounded the back corner of the house. He stood against the wall, a cigarette hanging from his fingers, and a fresh bruise blackening his cheek. A collar shone around his neck and numerous small scars snaked out from underneath it. He glanced up. At the sight of his visitor, he grinned.

"I wasn't sure you'd make it."

"When have I ever let you down?"

The drysta tilted his head to the side as he rubbed his hand against his shoulder, ash dropping from the end of the cigarette and sprinkling down into the grass.

"You got anything for me?"

A brief shake of his contact's head as he leaned forward, glancing through the back door which stood open just enough to warn them of an approach.

"No, he's been in a particularly bad mood," he said, pointing towards his eye. "I've been keeping a…"

The low thud of a footstep cut him off, and the drysta quickly stood up straight, turning to peer in through the gap. They both listened, expecting the steps to fade into the other sounds of the house, but they came closer, and seemed to multiply.

"Go!"

He didn't need to be told twice. Turning on his heel, he made his way back around the corner to the gap between the buildings. The door was wrenched open so hard that it smacked into the wall. Though he knew that only one Adveni lived in the house, he heard at least four men pour out through the door.

"Who was here?"

The drysta's howl of pain seared through the air as the only answer.

Breaking into a run, he didn't need to look behind him to know he was being followed. The drum of footsteps evened out into a constant beat against the pavement. If it had been any other situation, he might have laughed that the Adveni were so well trained that they couldn't even run out of unison.

Another scream of pain echoed between the high walls. Even through the percussion of footfalls, he could hear the drysta claiming he didn't know anything, that it had been no one. He rounded the corner, guilt following at every turn.

The wide street was the worst place to run from an Adveni. He knew that if even one of them chose to stop running and aim a weapon, he would be dead or captured in an instant. He had to get into some of the narrower streets, or somewhere he could try to lose them, instead of listening to them slowly close the gap.

Launching himself around a corner, his shoulder collided with the wall. His shirt caught on a rough patch of brick, tearing through the material and scraping the flesh beneath as he pushed off the wall and sprinted along the thin alley.

A shot smacked into the pavement by his foot, bouncing away in the glare of the evening sunlight. It was a warning shot, an order to stop. The next one would not miss.

He couldn't be taken in alive. He knew too much. He'd never fully considered his ability to withstand Adveni torture, but he wasn't about to risk finding out. At least he'd learned something from the shot: they were firing metal, not copaq bullets. They were aiming to kill.

The road was taking him further through the Adveni dwelling quarter. There were so many roads to take. He didn't usually come this far into the quarter. He hadn't memorised the routes. Tall buildings obscured his view and disorientated him. The footsteps were getting closer as he hurled himself into an alleyway. High walls threw him into the shadows.

Blinded by the harsh sun as he came out into the next street, he squeezed his eyes closed. He didn't care where he put his feet as long as it was away from the Adveni behind him. He blinked and shook his head. The glare of the sun on his left blazed across his eyes. He was heading north, further from the city, he knew that now.

A shot nicked his shoulder with a sizzling burn. He gritted his teeth and pushed harder. For a moment, the briefest soaring moment, he gained some ground. He ducked into the next alley he came across. His eyes widened at the sight of a metal fence at the opposite end. A bark of gruff laughter followed him along the tunnel. Through the blood pounding in his ears, he could hear that the footsteps had slowed. There was no use in running. They'd caught their prey.

Through the bars of the fence, he could see the open plains of the northern land. He'd reached the outer ridge of the quarter. There would be no protection, and given time, the heat would be as ruthless as the Adveni behind him. There was nothing for it. Time was not to be argued with, and he had run out of it.

He didn't break stride as he hurtled down the alley. It was no different from jumping onto a horse, right? Hands up, swing your leg over, and hope you went high enough. There was no stirrup. It would be a big leap. The Adveni realised what he was doing. Two of them pelted after him as the other took aim. He didn't slow as he ran straight at the fence. Grasping the top, he launched himself up, the top bar of the metal digging into his stomach as he swung his leg over. The shot blew off the heel of his boot as he swung his other leg over the fence. Pushing himself up from a stumbled landing, he set off running from the Adveni, into the merciless sun.

1   Buryd in the East

The eastern Mykahnol pillar loomed over Lyndbury Compound, onyx bricks towering into the sky, sending a long shadow sprawling over the large, oppressive building. The sun had barely hoisted itself above the mountains, but the sky was already such a clear, bright blue that it could only mean another blistering day.

    Georgianna Lennox brushed her long, blonde hair away from her neck, sweeping it high onto her head: a mess of waves and curls that she tied haphazardly into a knot with a ribbon. The dirt track from the end of the tunnel to the gates was already giving off waves of heat under her leather boots. The dense, heavy air stuck her clothes to her skin. Grasping her leather bag to her side, her brown-eyed gaze settled on the building up ahead. She let out a deep sigh, and trudged towards the gates.

She had promised to spend the day below ground helping the Belsa rebels with any medical emergencies that came in. However, she'd not even reached the hidden tunnels before her tsentyl device had beeped, informing her of an emergency within the compound walls. Changing her route, she'd made her way through the eastern tunnel instead, heading out of the city. There were multiple entrances along the line, but most Veniche people didn't use this particular tunnel, driven off by the knowledge of what waited at the other end.

The Adveni had built it when they first claimed dominion: a large compound they had named Lyndbury. While criminals of the Veniche tribes used to be marked for what they were and sent on their way to live alone, far from those they would rob or hurt, the Adveni had a different method. Instead of sending the criminals away, they would lock them up, keeping them all together in the compound.

The creation of Lyndbury had sent outrage spiralling through the people. Who were the Adveni to lock a man in a single place, especially through the volatile seasons of Os-Veruh? At times, Georgianna could almost understand it. A man who committed murder should be kept away from others and not given any opportunity to commit his crime elsewhere. However, the Adveni did not offer that. Instead of keeping criminals away from other people, they locked them all in a building together, and let them do as they pleased so long as they never left the compound walls.

One group of Adveni had been tasked with guarding the

compound. Specially trained and working with ruthless efficiency, the Guards of Lyndbury were infamous within the city. The Veniche of the city described the inmates as being "buryd alive", after the compound's name, Lyndbury: though your life was over and there was no escape, your body remained alive.

The Veniche people might not have considered it so bad if the Adveni were fairer about it, punishing those who committed crimes the Veniche agreed with, but the common opinion was that the Adveni punished crimes without understanding them. They didn't look at the starving family of a thief, nor did they care for the claims of five other victims when they said the man a woman stabbed to fend off an attack had also attacked them. There was no justice, only punishment. Even those who refused to bow to Adveni rule and register themselves were labelled as criminals and sent to the compound. Those sorts, however, never stayed inside the walls for long. Instead they were sold off in the drysta yard as slaves to whichever Adveni would pay the highest price.

Georgianna hated going there. She detested the sight of the inmates burned by the sun when the Adveni forced them outside into a fenced yard while the sun was high. She abhorred looking at the women, locked in the cell block with morally lacking men who had not seen a woman in so long that their urges overcame them. She heard her brother's pleas that she stay away, that the Adveni would, at some point decide she was no longer useful and lock her in there as well. Whenever the tsentyl communication device she had been given lit up, however, she answered it, because she knew that no one else would. The Adveni didn't care if a Veniche man died in the block in a fight over food. The body would lie in the block until count if the Adveni wanted. It was only her continued service that meant that someone saw fit to call for a medic at all.

Turning towards the compound, Georgianna brushed an errant lock of hair out of her face, and walked the last couple of hundred yards towards the high metal gates looming in front of her.

Inside the gate, two Adveni men stood watching for her approach. She was not even ten feet from the metal fencing before one of them pushed the gate forward to allow her entrance.

"In the block," one of the men explained bluntly. "Edtroka will take you."

Georgianna glanced at the other guard and nodded politely. Without so much as a word, the guard, Edtroka, turned and began walking away with long, purposeful strides, leaving Georgianna to hurry to keep up in his wake.

Georgianna had met Edtroka many times before. He was the first guard to take her through the routine of being let into the block. He showed her the items she would not be permitted to take inside and showed her how to work the Adveni tsentyl device that would let her inform them that she was ready to leave. His Veuric at that time had been broken and difficult to understand. Over the two years since her first visit, however, his use of the language had improved dramatically. Unfortunately, Georgianna could not say the same for her Adtvenis.

"Do you know what happened?" she asked, struggling to keep pace with him.

"Fight," he answered, his thick Adveni accent clear through the Veuric words. "We found him this morning."

"And what are his injuries?"

Edtroka turned his head, glancing down at her with what she could only imagine was derision, though it could have been amusement, the way his brow quirked like that. Edtroka was always slightly odd. He wasn't cruel or insulting to her like the other guards would be, but he had never shown her any obvious kindness either, only unreadable expressions that he never explained, even when she asked.

"I thought you were the medic."

"Well, I am!" she answered. "But surely you've seen his injuries if you called me?"

The guard shrugged, and she wondered if he had not seen the injuries on the prisoner, not paid enough attention, or not cared enough to remember what he'd seen. He didn't pause as he led her through the drysta yard towards the doors, and though the sun was now high enough to make being outside uncomfortable in mid-heat, the Veniche people set to be sold as dreta were lined up along one side, a group of Adveni looking at them with interest.

The Adveni were easy enough to spot even though in face and shape they resembled the Veniche in almost every way. Yet most Adveni stood almost a head taller than the average Veniche, and were also built better, with broader shoulders and longer legs, making them faster and stronger. It hadn't taken long for the rumours to begin circulating through the tribes that the Adveni bred differently to them. Unlike the Veniche, who paired most commonly for love, the Adveni were put to numerous tests. If their tletonise—the Adveni way of referring to what the Veniche people knew to be the aspects of a person passed on to their children—did not pass these tests, they were forbidden from creating offspring. Georgianna had often heard the term they used for people with undesirable genetic qualities: Zsraykil.

Most Veniche didn't spend a lot of quality time speaking to Adveni, not when they didn't have to, but they all knew that the Adveni considered most, if not all of them Zsraykil.

The strength and skill of the Adveni was also due to their extensive training. Georgianna had heard, from a friend who, in the ways these things happened, had heard it from another friend who knew someone, that the Adveni were trained in combat from childhood upwards, until they were ready to take their nsiloq and become an adult.

Georgianna had been trained to fight too. Life on the trail could be hard and attacks from outcasts and animals were not uncommon. However, Georgianna was certain that the Adveni's combat training had probably gone further than a lesson from their father, a lesson which included instructing them to aim for the face if the attacker was female, to go for the groin if male, and if an animal, to run as fast as your legs could carry you, preferably screaming to get the attention of people nearby.

One drysta at the end of the line, a man in his early

twenties, caught her eye and opened his mouth to call out. Georgianna quickly shook her head as she strode behind Edtroka, though she longed to run and gather him in her arms. Letting the guards know that they recognised each other would not be a good idea: not when she knew that he had been a Belsa, and not when she knew that the Adveni had already killed his brother Alec for the same reason. She couldn't bring herself to remember that name, not now. If they discovered Landon's affiliation, he would not be heading for a life as one of the dreta, he would be heading for execution. The idea of being sold as an Adveni slave like that, like cattle, disgusted her, but she simply turned her head and looked in the other direction. The good she could do was not in stopping the system; it was in making sure that those within the system had basic care. She was a medic, not a revolutionary.

Once they were through the heavy metal doors that led into the compound, the guard Edtroka patted her down and had her empty out her bag onto a sturdy table. He looked through each item. Deeming that none of the objects were dangerous, or intended to be passed on to prisoners, he allowed Georgianna to pack everything haphazardly back into her bag.

The corridors through the compound were wide with clear visibility. Where corridors intersected, they opened into wide, curving mouths, offering little cover. For all the things she could fault about the Adveni, their knowledge of attack theory was not among them: within the compound there was nowhere to hide.

Inside were three blocks: one for those who would become dreta, personal slaves to whichever Adveni had enough money to purchase them, and two for the compound inmates. Georgianna was rarely asked to the compound to visit the dreta block. The Veniche inside were given far better care than the other inmates, in order to be in peak health for their new owners.

Georgianna had learned very early on that the compound inmates were sent into the block and left to fend for themselves. The only time guards went into the block was each morning and evening to carry out a mandatory count. During her time in the compound, she had heard many horror stories about men killed in fights after count and left in the middle of the block until the count the next morning or evening. Most of the time, when fights broke out in the block, there was no point in calling a medic because by the time she'd been contacted, the man was past saving.

The only time prisoners were allowed out of the block was once every other day when they were allowed into a yard kept solely for the permanent inmates. Personally, Georgianna was sure most of the inmates would have preferred to be kept indoors instead of being sent out into the burning heat, but they did not get much choice in the matter. It wasn't called being buryd for nothing.

As they approached the thick, red, metal door, Georgianna hitched her bag a little higher onto her shoulder and glanced at the guard. He seemed completely uninterested in her, and for a moment, Georgianna felt the familiar fear that once she was inside, she would not be getting out.

DEAD AND BURYD

The guard, Edtroka, pulled out a device and placed it against the lock on the door. She had seen it on every trip into the compound, and yet still had no understanding of its mechanics. He turned it, and a buzzing sounded from the lock. Next, he brought up a polished black card and placed it against a reader. Lines of a brighter blue than Georgianna had ever seen in the natural world slid across the panel from the spot where the card connected, and slowly, the door creaked and slid open.

"You know how to get out?" Edtroka asked.

She nodded. He asked her the same question every time he walked her to the block. Georgianna couldn't help wondering whether it was something he had to ask, whether he had once found himself locked inside, or if he just thought her stupid.

"I have my tsentyl."

Edtroka nodded for her to go in, and as soon as she had stepped through the opening, the door began sliding closed. It shut with a rusty groan.

* * *

It was almost an hour before Georgianna sighed, slumping back on her heels. She reached up, about to rub her fingers wearily into her eyes when she realised that they were covered in blood. Pushing herself up, she stepped to the basin in the corner of the cell, twisting the tap until tepid water spurted angrily from the spout beneath.

"Med, what you doing?" Owain, one of the inmates,

asked from his spot on the other side of the bars.

She scrubbed the stains from her hands, thinking of what to say. Owain had been rather vocal throughout, always asking questions, telling her the story of how it had happened. The prisoner, Jace, currently sprawled across the flimsy mattress, had gotten into a disagreement with Vajra and Ta Dao, two of the more powerful men within the compound. Though the guards ruled the compound, these men ran the block once the doors were closed. Jace had apparently refused to bow to one of their strict rules and his injuries were their punishment for his disobedience.

As soon as the lock had fallen into place after count, they'd come for Jace. They'd hurt him just enough so that it would be a long, painful death before he was found the next morning. Jace had not died before count thanks to the quiet help of a couple of the inmates, Owain included. However, from Owain's constant quiet chatter, Georgianna had realised that most likely, those who had helped Jace might be the next to receive a visit once the block door slid closed.

Once her hands were clean, she turned to look at Owain, frowning when she saw his hopeful gaze.

"There's nothing more for me to do," she answered. "I've done all I can for the wounds, but he was left too long. Infection has gotten in. I only have two options now, to give him drugs to make it easier, or see if he can fight it off."

Owain glanced both ways as Georgianna dried her hands on her trousers. For a moment, Owain watched Jace, a frown knitting his brow as he finally nodded.

"Give him the drugs," he said slowly.

"You don't..."

"Just give him the drugs!"

Owain's voice was stronger, rougher, and she knew better than to argue. While Owain had been kind to her during her visit, she had no doubts that he knew how to deal with those who weren't helping his friend. He had the look of a man who had been in the compound for a while. He probably knew what happened to those who couldn't fight off infection within these walls.

Finally, Georgianna nodded, crouching and digging into her bag for the small bag of pills she hated using most.

* * *

Walking towards the end of the cellblock, the door didn't budge as Georgianna pressed her thumb and middle finger to opposite sides of her tsentyl. Holding it tightly until the cube shuddered, the feeling of a wave travelled up her arm. She didn't know how it worked, or what the odd sensation proved, but she knew that it sent a signal to the Adveni on the other side of the door, telling them that she was ready to be let out. Sure enough, only moments passed before the thick red door began sliding open. Throwing a look over her shoulder, Georgianna caught the gaze of a beautiful blonde woman sitting on one of the upper levels, her legs dangling over the side. With her arms on one of the railing bars, her chin resting on her hands, she gave Georgianna a brief nod and smile. She'd been watching the entire thing from entrance to end. Any time she glanced out of Jace's cell, she had spotted the blonde in her position, her bright blue eyes watching from above, like a guard in the tunnels waiting for something.

She pursed her lips, blinked, and turned back to the waiting guard.

"You do your thing?" Edtroka asked.

Georgianna frowned and stepped out of the block.

"No," she answered as the door slid closed behind her and Edtroka came to her side. "He's dead."

2 Ships and Supplies

It was almost sun-high by the time Georgianna left the compound, once again searched by the guard to make sure she was not taking anything out of the blocks. No matter how many times she visited, the guards still didn't trust her not to break their rules. It didn't surprise her. They barely trusted any Veniche, and she wasn't really any different.

Walking back towards the tunnel entrance, she shrugged off her outer shirt, splattered with blood, and stuffed it unceremoniously into her bag. She knew the dangers of going bare-skinned under the sun, but as she was only going a short distance, she didn't see the danger in being a little more comfortable. There was next to no breeze, even outside the city, leaving the heat to lie dormant, baking from above and radiating out of the hard ground in visible waves.

It was a welcome relief when she stepped over the threshold and began descending into the tunnel, leaving the direct rays behind her and disappearing into the shadowed underground. The tunnel was deserted this far east, and as pity for those held fast in the compound began creeping up on her, Georgianna shook it off and began humming a tune her mother used to sing while doing chores. It wasn't that she didn't want to feel pity for the poor souls buryd, but pity would do them little good, and it would only make continuing on after the death of a patient that much harder.

By the time she reached the main line, she was singing softly under her breath, letting her arms swing back and forth as she walked. After a moment's pause, instead of turning right to travel north towards Belsa territory, she took the left turn onto the main line, joining the flow of people heading down underneath the Oprust district.

Up ahead, two Adveni in full military gear walked side by side, large copaq guns at their backs. While the men were walking slowly, far more slowly than the pace most in the tunnels would choose, nobody moved to slip past them and hurry onward. Even Georgianna found herself slowing her steps to keep a safe distance behind. It may not have been a crime to overtake and walk in the large space they had created before them, but nobody wanted to risk angering Agrah Adveni when it could be avoided by hanging back.

As the Veniche had learned in the first wave of attacks, the Adveni were a highly militaristic race. Trained from childhood to fight and work for a common goal, they joined one of the branches of their military once they had proven themselves by receiving their nsiloq mark, a painful design drawn into the skin over their ribs.

There were the Agrah, who fought best on land at close quarters with their enemy. The Nyrahby fought from the air in small ships fitted with powerful weapons. Those who commanded the bigger ships that travelled between worlds were classed as Tzelik, and then there were the Tsevstakre, the most dangerous of all. The Tsevstakre were the Adveni elite, their best trained and most skilled, ruthless killers. Georgianna considered herself lucky that she met any of them but rarely.

She slowed her steps further, letting people overtake her and slipping seamlessly back into the crowd. She couldn't risk taking an exit into hidden tunnels anywhere near an Adveni, let alone two attack-ready Agrah. She didn't plan on going back to the compound just yet. Giving such a wide berth to the Adveni, it took twice as long to reach the entrance to the Junkyard, home of the Carae. She took one last glance around before she began moving to the other side of the tunnel, finally walking along the wall before a single step sideways had her disappear through a hidden opening into a dimly lit tunnel.

The tunnel into the Junkyard was slim, just wide enough for a single person to walk comfortably. There were only two entrances to the Junkyard, one in the south-east and one in the west, both ending in these bottlenecked tunnels, preventing a swarm of attackers from any direction. It was a long walk through the small tunnel. The ground, uneven and off kilter, was difficult to navigate unless you walked it every day and knew the places to step. It wouldn't have been the first time that Georgianna had returned from the Junkyard with skinned knees and bruised elbows when she had relaxed and tripped on a hidden rock.

The Carae, like the Belsa, stationed guards in the tunnels that led out towards the main lines. However, unlike the Belsa, a Carae was more likely to shoot you on sight before giving you a chance to identify yourself, so when Georgianna felt she might be getting close, she raised her arms above her head and crossed her wrists, walking forward in slow and cautious steps.

Her effort to appear submissive and of no danger proved useless as a low buzzing sound culminating in five beeps rang out from her pocket. Before she knew it, a gun was placed at the back of her head, its muzzle pressing firmly against her skull. Georgianna jumped; she had no idea how she'd managed to walk past someone, and she'd not heard anyone following behind her.

Standing squarely and keeping her gaze ahead, she kept her wrists crossed above her.

"Get it out!"

She hesitated before she brought her right hand down, digging into her pocket and pulling out the tsentyl. Pressing her thumb to the panel on the cube, she let the low pulse hum out and swiped it open.

"What's it say?"

Glancing down, she realised she couldn't look down that far without moving her head, so instead brought the tsentyl up before her, the blue writing glaring out brightly through the darkness.

"Oh, look: Marshall Casey is top of the Adveni kill list," she answered. "What a surprise."

For a moment, there was silence, and figuring that the daily alert of the "Veniche at Large" list was nothing a Carae guard would be too surprised about, Georgianna slid the tsentyl back to cube form and carefully slipped it back into her pocket before her hand resumed its position above her head.

"Should know better, Georgianna!" the voice came from behind her again. "I could've shot your pretty head off without you ever realising."

She wanted to turn to see who was talking to her, but while the voice seemed to be amused at her predicament, she couldn't fully believe they wouldn't shoot her if she made a wrong move, not until she knew who it was anyway.

"Well, I do like giving you boys some target practice. Would you prefer it if I ran?"

The man chuckled, his amusement bouncing off the close walls of the tunnel. Despite herself, she smirked.

"Nah, you're alright. Guys might kill me if I shot the only pretty medic we got left to make them *really* feel better."

Georgianna coughed a short burst of laughter and shook her head a little.

"Aww, Taye, that's sweet."

The muzzle of the gun left the back of her head as the man began laughing. Sure enough, in amongst the laughter, there was the sound of the gun being slipped into a holster.

She turned around, coming face to face, or more chest, with a tall, slim, dirty-blonde-haired man.

"How'd you know it was me?" Taye asked, pouting mockingly at her.

"How many other Carae would suggest I start giving sexual favours for medicine?"

Taye rocked his head from side to side and the gaze of his hazel eyes travelled a very obvious trail down her body.

"I'd go with, I dunno, all of them?" he suggested. "Though, admittedly, most of them would probably just think it, not say it out loud."

"Well, how kind of them to keep their filthy thoughts to themselves, unlike someone I know."

Georgianna tried to give him a disappointed glare, but failed when a smirk curved her lips. Reaching out, she slid a hand over Taye's shoulder and pulled herself up to give him a tight hug.

"How've you been doing?" she asked against his shoulder, holding the embrace a moment longer before she let him go and Taye's arms slid away from her waist.

Taye shrugged his lithe shoulders and stuffed his hands into his pockets.

"You been this week?" he asked.

She knew she couldn't lie to him, not when he was always so kind to her, but Taye's hope, she knew, would slowly destroy him. Finally, she nodded.

"Just come from there."

Taye's eyes lit up through the darkness, and he reached out, grabbing Georgianna's shoulders and bending his head down to get a good look at her.

"How is she? Did you see her?"

"She's..." Georgianna paused, taking a deep breath as she looked back at Taye's hopeful face. "She's there. I didn't speak to her, but she looked the same as before."

Taye let out a relieved sigh and brought his hands up, cupping her face, fingers lost in the waves of her hair.

"You are my ship, Gianna!" he told her gently. "I swear, I don't think I'd be able to stay back if you couldn't tell me how she's doing."

Georgianna brought her hand up, resting her fingers over Taye's hand, curled around her jaw.

"Taye..." she murmured. "Nyah was buryd. You can't keep obsessing."

He shook his head violently and pulled his hands back from her face.

"No, she wasn't. She made a mistake! She'll be let out, and then things will be the way they were meant to. We'll be joined, I promised her!"

It was stupid to argue with Taye, Georgianna knew that. She'd tried telling him that he should move on, that the likelihood was that Nyah would be sold before she was released, a beautiful girl like she was, but Taye wouldn't hear of it. Any time the compound was brought up, he would get angry and start suggesting they find a way to get her out. Georgianna didn't want Taye to end his life on an impossible task. Sometimes she feared that he would commit some horrible crime just so that he could be buryd with her.

"Alright, Taye, okay! I believe you," Georgianna placated. "Let's, uh... You got time to take me down?"

Taye was still distracted, but he nodded just the same and waved her onward.

They walked in silence until they reached the Junkyard, passing by the tents and other motley shelters the Carae used for their homes within the tunnels. Taye called to one of the tents and a bleary-faced woman tugged the opening back, a blanket clutched to her chest.

"Got a sale. Will you take over guard until I get back?"

She didn't look happy about it, but she nodded and disappeared back into the tent to get dressed.

"What do you need?" Taye asked once they stood outside the fenced Junkyard entrance.

"Dressings, bandages, stitching thread, and a couple of needles, whatever you've got really."

"Wait here, I'll be right back," he murmured, unlocking the chains holding the fence closed and disappearing in amongst the stacks of supplies.

Georgianna knew from experience, when Taye had taken her into the stacks once before, that there was no rhyme nor reason as to how the supplies were stacked. Things were grouped together, so hopefully all the medical supplies would be in one place, but there was no method on how to find a particular stack. Georgianna suggested that perhaps that was in order to make it harder to rob from the Junkyard, but Taye had said that most likely it was because the guys who set stuff up in there were smoking something at the time.

Taking a seat against the fencing, Georgianna reorganised her bag to get ready for the new supplies. While Taye had said he'd be right back, it wasn't odd for him to take at least twenty minutes. Not only did Taye have to find his way through the maze of stacks, but also select the right supplies. Thankfully, these days, Taye knew exactly what she needed, so it didn't take nearly as long as it did the first few times she had come down to stock up.

When Taye returned, Georgianna had reorganised her bag twice and begun scrubbing the blood from her shirt with a bar of wrapped soap. She looked up from her position on the floor, hands covered in a thin lather of pink-stained foam, and grinned at Taye's laden arms.

"I grabbed you a bag of those Adveni drugs you liked last time," he told her quietly, lowering himself onto the ground next to her as Georgianna unscrewed the lid of her cantina and poured some water over her hands and the shirt to wash off the suds.

"Where do you get those?" Georgianna asked.

Taye smirked devilishly, taking Georgianna's bag and beginning to slot the supplies into it.

"I have my sources."

Georgianna laughed lightly and shook her head. Trust a Carae to keep his secrets. Don't reveal your sources, or something along those lines. It was like the Carae wrote the rule book on dirty dealings.

"I got a deal for you." he announced finally, holding up the last paper packet and waving it teasingly.

Turning away from the shirt, her fingers tangled in it as

she wrung the water out onto the floor beside her legs, Georgianna raised an eyebrow. From the name scrawled across the packet, Georgianna knew it was the one holding the Adveni drugs.

"I can pay for them, Taye."

"You will," he answered. "Just not in coin."

Georgianna didn't like the sound of that. She dealt in coin with the Carae because their deals were often things you really didn't want to get involved in. She'd known Taye a long time. He was Kahle, and they'd travelled together since they were kids, but he'd joined up with the Carae and she knew there were things they asked you to do that most people wouldn't agree with.

"I dunno, Taye…"

"Oh, come on, Gianna. For me, please? It's… It's not your kind of illegal!"

The desperation in his voice and the use of the nickname her family used for her almost immediately thawed her. Since Taye had joined the Carae, he had kept his distance most of the time, having explained once that he didn't want everyone in the Carae knowing that they were close. Apparently, being close to someone meant you held things over them, things that could be used for Carae purposes, and Taye didn't want that for Georgianna.

Everyone had an opinion on the Carae, even people who'd never dealt with them. Her own father had commented on them from time to time, grumbling about them being a band of criminals. He said that if they had been in a tribe, they would have been outcast for their actions.

Coming from every tribe and background, often when they had no other way to make money, the Carae had formed their own tribe, like the Belsa. Only, unlike the Belsa, the Carae seemed more interested in money than freedom, and were therefore looked on slightly less favourably by Veniche, and more favourably by Adveni.

However, as he claimed it wasn't "her type of illegal", she knew it was illegal by most standards, most importantly, Adveni. Georgianna did quite a lot of things that were, by Adveni standards, illegal, though she didn't find them morally wrong.

"What is it?" she asked finally.

"Just a delivery."

"Of?"

"It's... It's for Nyah,"

Georgianna let out a groan and shifted her body, looking away from him.

"Taye, they search me!" she complained. "Even if I wanted to..."

"You can, Gianna! I know you can! You have before!"

Georgianna stared blankly at the ground. He was right, of course. She'd made deliveries into the compound before when people were desperate: messages and small objects that meant nothing to the Adveni. Reaching up, Georgianna rubbed her wet hand over her face and groaned.

"I can't promise anything. But I'll consider it."

"'Gian..."

Georgianna shook her head even as Taye clutched at her hand. She pulled it back from his grasp.

"No, no Gianna-ing me, Taye Rann!" she said. "I'll think about it, but if it's dangerous, you owe me another packet!"

"You agree and get it in to Nyah, I'll give you five packets."

"Yeah, yeah, deliver them to me in Lyndbury!" Georgianna complained as she got to her feet.

This was going to be a mistake, she just knew it.

3 ABSENT FROM THE GUARD

Already late for her promised appointment with the Belsa, Georgianna hurried along the tunnel towards the underground settlement. The guard in the black line, leading in from one of the wider tunnels, had stopped and searched her thoroughly as she'd passed. She'd called in Georgianna's arrival via a tampered Adveni radio, and even after having received the all-clear, had been dubious about letting her past. It was only when she mentioned Lacie, the Belsa marshall's adopted daughter, that the guard had apologised for the inconvenience and sent her on her way.

The Belsa had been around almost as long as the Adveni had been in power. Forced into servitude by the invading race, many Veniche had tried to fight to reclaim their freedom and their planet, Os-Veruh. As more people died in the continued fighting, it no longer became an option to stay within their tribes. Those who fought joined together, tribal rivalries pushed aside to rebel against their conquerors. Even a decade after the arrival of the Adveni, the Belsa received new rebels each season. Veniche men and women who arrived in the city of Adlai and wanted to fight, or who needed protection that their tribe could not offer.

The darkness was strangely comforting, and it wasn't odd for Georgianna to feel safer in the dark tunnels than she did above ground. Up there, everyone could see her and could question her. Down on the lines, the people who needed to know her already did, and those that didn't know her didn't ask questions. No one asked unnecessary questions down here. It was safer if they didn't know the answer.

By the time the lamps began filtering light across the worn tunnel floor, Georgianna was in her stride. Moving swiftly and purposefully through the settlements, she smiled and greeted those she knew and nodded curtly to those she didn't. Though well-known, she would not dare insult those that she didn't recognise by snubbing them. The Belsa demanded respect; she knew that, especially as she wasn't officially one of them. She didn't train or stand guard. She was never sent out to scout Adveni movements. She was, to most of them, just one of the medics who occasionally patched them up.

The old tunnel car stood at the end of one of the collapsed lines, its sliding door held open by a broken knife blade wedged into the bottom of the metal run. From inside, a light flickered, and as she came closer, she could hear the low murmur of voices.

She barely paused between banging her fist on the metal shell of the car and heaving herself up through the open doorway. Standing up straight, she glanced both ways down the car until her gaze settled on the two men inside. One of them was already looking at her. His cold eyes narrowed for a moment, refocusing before a smile parted his thin lips, bringing a softer look to his square jaw.

"Marshall Casey!" she greeted with a cheerful wave, stepping further into the car.

Glancing briefly at the other man, the marshall pushed himself to his feet.

"Beck!" he corrected in a low, gruff voice.

Georgianna laughed.

"But you *are* the marshall! Always will be."

Beck rolled his eyes as he lifted a large hand and patted her cheek, plastering her wavy hair to her tanned skin.

"Whatever you say," he agreed with a reluctant shake of his head. "Looking for Lacie?"

She nodded, turning to look at the rest of the car. One portion was cornered off, a thick burlap sheet hanging from where it had been nailed into the ceiling some time before. Behind it, she knew stood a bed lashed together from old car seats and a trunk of clothes that belonged to Beck's adopted daughter, Lacie. Unlike the other times Georgianna had climbed into the car looking for her, the sixteen-year-old had yet to stick her face out from behind the makeshift wall.

Georgianna had once asked why Beck didn't have his

own section cornered off; it was his home after all. Lacie had explained in his stead that the Belsa marshall rarely slept long, and even when he did, he felt guilty keeping space to himself that he didn't need. Instead, he would sleep on the chairs used as his work space, covered only in a tattered blanket if Lacie saw fit to throw one over him.

"She's gone already, said she was heading over Medics' Way," Beck explained.

Georgianna knew that she should be surprised, but she couldn't say she was. Lacie spent a lot of her time in Medics' Way, especially recently. The arrival of a young man with injuries he had suffered from his Adveni owner had sparked interest in the sixteen-year-old.

Glancing past Beck, she looked at the other man in the car. His lips were split into a broad smirk, revealing a line of white yet uneven teeth.

"Alright, George?" he asked.

"Morning, Wrench."

Wrench shifted the strap of his weapon against his chest and glanced at Beck. Wrench was a large man, easily a head and a half taller than Georgianna and half again as broad. Beneath a tattered shirt, his chest heaved and he let out a slow, resigned breath. He reached up and rubbed his hand over his hair, cut so short against his scalp, that against his dark skin, he almost looked bald in the low light.

"We about done, Marshall?"

Beck nodded.

"Guess I should go make sure Lacie doesn't kill anyone," Georgianna teased, stepping back towards the door.

"Go easy on her," Beck chastised.

She nodded. It was the same advice Beck gave her every time she came to collect Lacie. Each time, she rolled her eyes and told Beck she wouldn't promise, though he knew from experience that Georgianna was one of the more easy-going people to help Lacie in her hopes of becoming a medic.

She'd already jumped down from the train car, heading out towards Medics' Way when she heard the crunch of his boots. Glancing over her shoulder, she smiled when she saw Wrench jogging down the line to catch her up.

"Everything alright, Wrench?"

"Oh it's nothing," he sighed as he fell into step with her. "Si was meant to take over the shift before sun up. Never showed."

"Do you know why?"

"Marshall says he ain't seen him, but thought I'd head over to Medics' with you and ask Jaid."

"Well, if anyone would know…" Georgianna left the suggestion hanging in the air. She knew Si's wife Jaid much better than she knew Si himself. He did sometimes stop by Medics' Way when he was off duty. He was always kind to her, Georgianna liked him.

"You coming from Zanetti's?"

"Compound."

Wrench wrinkled his bulbous nose into a grimace at the mention of the compound, but it was quickly replaced with a smirk.

"He was pretty sour when he got called in to take over

the shift down Guard's Sight," he answered. "Figured you may have been keeping him up last night."

"He been bragging?" she asked, shaking her head.

Wrench cocked his head to the side.

"Were you expecting him to keep your virtue intact?"

It was clear from his tone that he already knew that the answer was no. Keiran Zanetti may not have been the type to go shouting his business around the tunnels. However, that didn't mean he hid things, especially when it came to women, and especially not from Wrench. She knew the two had grown up together within the Nerrin tribe and their friendship remained strong, even after Keiran had been promoted to sergeant above Wrench.

When she didn't answer, they fell into a comfortable silence, their footsteps keeping them company on the walk to Medics' Way. She felt bad for the guys on guard duty. It couldn't be easy, sitting on your own in a tunnel for hours on end, with nothing for company except the darkness and the familiar rest of a weapon on your back. The guards were necessary, she knew that. They couldn't leave the entrances from the main tunnels unguarded, not when sweeps of the main tunnels by the Adveni were so regular.

The entrances into the deeper tunnels were hard to find from the outer passageways, even when people knew where they were. Branching from the walls of the main lines, yet hidden by bricks built up to look like any other section of wall, the smaller tunnels had remained remarkably private. However, sometimes people stumbled in and needed to be turned back. It was, admittedly, only luck that the people finding their way in by accident had never been Adveni. The guards would also help if the unthinkable did happen. Georgianna knew how far an echo could carry within the tunnels; the sound of gunfire would alert those down the line to the problem.

Luckily, apart from Si's mysterious absence, the day seemed calm in the Belsa tunnels. Beck probably would have said something if someone had been taken down to the Way for treatment. Though, she supposed she wouldn't really know the state of Medics' Way until she got there.

"It sure is odd," Wrench mused. "Si not showing up like that. Not like him at all."

Georgianna shook her head. She'd been working for the Belsa long enough to know that they rarely missed shifts, and Si was no exception.

"No, it's not."

* * *

Medics' Way, while still part of Belsa territory, was almost counted as a separate area of the tunnels. To get there from the main Belsa encampment involved going through another check point and into a less protected region. Not many civilians dared go into Belsa territory—not if they didn't have to, so the Way had become a neutral area to allow them safe passage for treatment if they couldn't find a medic out in the camps. Out of all the tunnels, Georgianna easily spent the most time there.

A wide tunnel running north-west to south-east, Medics'

Way used to hold one of the busier paths underneath the city. The actual section used for treatment was only short—a section of tunnel that had been blocked off by a cave-in a couple of years before, burying three tunnel cars.

The tunnel cars, now in various states of dilapidation since the arrival of the Adveni, had previously been used to ferry people and trade through the larger underground tunnels in the city. Pulled by horses, the large metal shells stood on thick wheels that rolled them along the line. When her father's work had been more productive, he had used the tunnel cars to move larger furniture from one place to another. Lyle Lennox didn't make many larger pieces for trade anymore, his body not being what it used to, but Georgianna remembered sitting just inside the sliding door, watching the people pass her by as her father led the horses along.

Since the arrival of the Adveni, all the cars had fallen into disuse and disrepair as a mode of transportation. With the air attacks and fighting above ground, many Veniche people had needed somewhere to hide from the onslaught of the conquering Adveni. They had taken to the tunnels, and the cars had been pulled into disused areas, to be used as shelter and storage. Those rebelling against the Adveni had quickly been referred to as "Belsa", which Georgianna understood to be an Adtvenis word for "rat". Despite the insult the Adveni placed upon the word, the rebels stood behind it, and within the space of a single heat, Belsa had been scrawled all over the city as a warning that the Veniche would continue to fight against the invasion.

Sticking her head in through the doorway of the first car, but not climbing up, Georgianna waved to Jaid, one of the other medics, noting that her cropped auburn hair was sticking up in every direction above Jaid's thin, pointed face. As usual when working on the Way, Jaid had set herself up in the car they used for simple injuries, where people could be treated before being sent home. She could always tell how busy Jaid had been during a shift by how spiky her hair had become. The older woman had a habit of running her fingers through it and twisting short locks around her fingers while she thought. Her moss-green smock was stained and two buttons at the hip had come undone. Apparently, it had been an incredibly busy shift. Jumping up from her position on the floor, Jaid came towards them and thrust out a sheaf of papers.

"You on for a while, Georgianna?"

"Yeah, planned to be here all day, but I got a call and…"

"It's alright," Jaid interrupted. "But I've got to head out for a few hours. Si's not come home."

She squeezed Georgianna's shoulder briefly and disappeared back into the car.

Georgianna glanced at Wrench, raising an eyebrow.

"So you've not seen him?" he asked, stepping forward to look into the car.

Jaid reappeared at the doorway, tugging a jacket onto her shoulders.

"You've not seen him either?"

Wrench frowned and shook his head.

"He didn't show up for guard's."

Jaid looked between the two of them as she chewed on her bottom lip. Reaching up, Wrench held his hand out for Jaid to grasp as she jumped down from the car.

"Don't worry," he assured her. "I'm sure it's nothing. He probably just forgot, you know how guard shifts are being changed all the time."

"Si doesn't forget things like that."

"Not usually, but if you're really worried, I'll help you look."

"Really?"

"Of course. Come on, let's go."

The sigh that slipped past Jaid's lips was not believable as relief, not while her eyes darted from Georgianna to Wrench and back again. Georgianna wasn't sure that she trusted the casual calm in Wrench's expression either, though he was far more convincing than Jaid.

"Good luck," she murmured.

She watched as Wrench and Jaid set off down the line, two hurried steps of Jaid's to match every one of Wrench's long strides. Shaking her head, she turned and ambled down the Way towards the last car where she suspected she would find Lacie Cormack.

4 Down the Way

Georgianna grasped the side of the open door and hauled herself up into the car at the end of Medic's Way. Inside, patients who needed more permanent care could get more peace than the comings and goings of the other cars. The lamps were turned low, and it took her a moment to locate the slim girl kneeling on the floor at the end of the car. She was bent over an unconscious man on a bed.

Georgianna held the papers under a nearby lamp and flipped through to the man's notes, reading them quickly. Out of all the protocols required on Medics' Way, the notes were the one Georgianna found hardest to complete. She was great at working in an emergency and even figuring out what to do if they didn't have the correct supplies, but by the time she remembered to make her notes for the next medic on shift, she'd usually forgotten what she'd done throughout the day. Luckily, where she failed, Lacie was brilliant at keeping track. Maybe it was a natural attention to detail, or perhaps an effect of living with Beck, who had notes everywhere. Either way, the girl was a wonder at helping her keep everything up to date.

"He spiked another fever," Lacie muttered, her wide blue eyes fixed on Georgianna through the murk of the low lamplight. "Miss Oaks gave him something to help him sleep."

Georgianna lifted her head, glancing away from the notes for a second. Lacie's round face gazed fretfully at her, her long, red hair pulled back and braided down between her tiny shoulders. The girl was much smaller than most of her age, an almost boyish frame that had yet to blossom fully with the flowers of her gender.

"How does he feel now?"

For a moment, Lacie hesitated. Her hand hovered above his forehead for a few seconds before she pushed back a fringe of unkept curls and placed the back against his pale skin. Georgianna found it sweet how Lacie could now dress wounds with relative ease yet still felt nervous checking a temperature.

"A bit better," she murmured, looking to Georgianna for confirmation.

She made her way over and, careful not to place her hand down too quickly and risk waking him, she pressed her skin against his own.

"Yeah, feels like it's going down," she agreed.

She glanced at the wound Lacie was redressing, a nsiloq

mark half uncovered, red and sore. Georgianna frowned. She felt a twinge of sadness every time she saw the young man, Jacob. From what she knew, Jacob had been sold as a drysta, a slave to an Adveni, not long after the Adveni arrival, and as a young teenager had been submitted to systematic abuse. She had seen a lot of torture over the years, she had healed a lot of different wounds, but this young man was different.

Jacob Stone was barely twenty-one years old, and yet he'd been beaten, whipped, and given five different nsiloq marks, a pattern drawn into the flesh by a laser of Adveni design. Every Adveni had a nsiloq, a test to prove themselves ready for adulthood. Georgianna knew it hurt more than anything, and she couldn't imagine how the young man had endured five before he snapped and made a run for his freedom.

It wasn't common for Veniche to be given a mark, not that Georgianna had seen. She'd heard stories whispered amongst the Belsa that the Adveni sometimes used the nsiloq to torture on an invisible setting. It caused the same pain and brought the same screamed confessions, but left no trace of ever being used.

That was not the case with Jacob. Every design stood bright on his flesh. Swerving lines of blue over his calf, a geometric pattern in red on the front of his shoulder, circles and spikes in red and blue on his torso, stretched over his ribs. The red designs reminded her of burned flesh when it scarred. The blue marks, on the other hand, shone in his skin. The nsiloq laser didn't put ink into the skin the way

Veniche marks did. It was molecular, or so she had been told during one of her shifts behind the bar at Crisco, where she worked, by a particularly drunk Adveni. The laser targeted the cells and changed their design, creating a change of colour in the skin. She hadn't really understood, not having had the technology to study the building blocks of the body, but she couldn't deny that the effect was beautiful. Well, it was beautiful when it wasn't forced on a young drysta because his owner wanted to hear him scream.

Reaching out, she kept her hand against Lacie's, stopping the girl from rebandaging the most recent mark. Against his almost ghost-like flesh, the design was an angry, dark red, the lowest setting on the nsiloq laser. The design was shaky, unlike the smooth lines of an Adveni nsiloq, and it was clear that Jacob had been held down while it was administered, probably writhing and begging to be released. Georgianna frowned and leaned closer. It wasn't bleeding; the laser didn't produce blood, but it was certainly causing the young man a lot of pain, even weeks after its application.

"Leave it open a while," she instructed.

"But, but it hurts him!" Lacie complained, looking desperately up at the older woman. Georgianna released Lacie's hand and rubbed her fingers into her eyes.

She wanted to be kind to Jacob and leave Lacie to wrap the wound, she wanted to be nice to all the patients that came through the Way, but she knew that even if she had to be the bad guy, it would help them more in the end.

"Just a short while, I promise."

Lacie frowned, looking between Georgianna and the

unconscious Jacob before nodding and undoing the bandage she'd been wrapping over the mark.

Checking behind her to make sure there wasn't a patient in the bed, Georgianna slid down onto it, dumping her bag next to her and slipping the strap from her shoulder. Lacie had been with her, training to be a medic, for almost a year. Most Veniche started training for their profession by their twelfth birthday, but Lacie's capture by the Adveni and her years spent as a drysta meant that, by Veniche traditions, she was a long way behind.

Beck Casey, the leader and marshall of the Belsa, had found Lacie, fourteen at the time, beaten half to death and starving in a back alley of the Oprust district. It had taken quite a bit of coercion, Georgianna had heard, getting Lacie to trust him enough to carry her down to the Way for treatment. Since that day he'd treated the girl like she was his own, and from what Georgianna saw between them, Lacie loved him as a father in return.

While the going had been tough in the beginning, earning the trust of a skittish young woman, she could not have asked for a more attentive student. Then again, it wasn't as if she had taken a student before. She didn't know exactly how well Lacie should be doing at this point. She'd been only sixteen when the Adveni invaded, only recently accepted as an adult within the Kahle herself, not in the position to take on a new trainee. Now, at twenty-six, Georgianna had yet to take on a new medic. She didn't feel safe bringing a young student down to the Belsa territory with her, and she couldn't have expected the student's parents to be okay with her affiliations: not until Beck had asked her to help Lacie in exchange for a few coins a week.

They managed about twenty minutes before Lacie broke down and begged that they dress Jacob's wound. Georgianna, unable to watch the forlorn look on the girl's innocent face any longer, nodded and allowed Lacie to redress the nsiloq mark. She didn't know what dressing or keeping it open would do, it wasn't often that she treated nsiloq marks. The Adveni had their own medics, their own systems, not to mention that they'd been dealing with the marks for decades, maybe even longer.

When the Adveni had arrived on Os-Veruh, in their big, impressive ships and with their fancy technology, it had been like something out of the stories her father used to tell her as a child. Almost everyone knew the story of the meteor and the floating ships, how they left before Os-Veruh's seasons changed. As her father also told stories about talking coyotes and bears, however, she had begun to wonder about the truth in the history as it had been described to her. Her father said that the story had been passed from one generation to the next for over five hundred years, but even as a child Georgianna had known far too much about how a story changed with each telling.

It had been just after her sixteenth birthday when they arrived. Scouts from within the Kahle tribe had travelled ahead to check the trail as they did every season, and returned with news that there were large shining clouds above Adlai. The tribe had travelled onward, wanting to see the phenomenon. When they arrived, it had seemed like all of her father's stories had come true. The Adveni, as they called themselves, used to call Os-Veruh home. Having found another planet to inhabit after leaving in one of the ships, they had flourished, but the desire to return to their home planet had always been great. Scouts had been sent, and upon seeing that their home world remained, they had come back, and they planned to stay.

Now—looking at the injuries of the young man across from her, seeing the suffering of the people within the compound every time she visited, forced to live by the foreigners' laws and serve their whims, living in the tattered remains of what had once been a challenging but understandable life for a Veniche—Georgianna wished they had never returned at all.

* * *

Sitting in front of a patient from the camps who had come in after a robbery, Georgianna had finished stitching the wound closed and smeared the yellow paste of the lutiner flower sparingly over it to speed recovery.

Unfortunately, robberies and attacks were more common now than they used to be, especially in the camps, where the Adveni presence was less pronounced. It wasn't as easy to hunt while in one place with so many others. The trail had been much easier for hunting, and by the time the different tribes reached Adlai for the heat, they had enough stores to keep most families relatively comfortable. There had always been robberies of course, by those who moved alone instead of with a tribe, or those who had been banished for committing a crime, but these days they seemed to happen every other day—more often in fact. As times became harder, more people began only looking out for themselves.

"I hope it's okay that I came down," Kael said quietly.

Georgianna glanced up from the bandage as she wound it tightly around his arm.

"Of course it is."

"I wouldn't normally. Keep to myself, you know? Don't like a lot of trouble, but this wouldn't stop bleeding and…"

Tying one end of the bandage to the other, Georgianna patted him lightly on the shoulder.

"There's no need to explain," she smiled. "You needed help."

Kael nodded as she turned away to note down his visit.

Georgianna had left Lacie in the end car with a collection of hyliha leaves while she treated him. While the leaves weren't useful for much more than easing a heat rash, Georgianna had given them to the young girl to practise making paste out of the herbs that could be collected. Hyliha trees grew everywhere, having adapted to the planet's altered seasons, so the leaves were ideal for practising on before moving on to some of the rarer, more useful substances.

"I don't have much," he mumbled shyly as Georgianna scribbled her notes.

Looking up, Georgianna glanced over her shoulder at the man and finally turned around to face him:

"Kael, don't…"

"I will make good!" he interjected before Georgianna could speak further. "I have some pelts drying. I'll bring one down!"

"That is far too much for a simple cut, especially when you already lost so much in gaining the wound."

Kael stared down at his knees, dragging his teeth over his lip worriedly. She sighed. She hated taking from people who couldn't afford it. However, it wasn't her supplies that she was using up down here. While she was happy to do the work for a bowl of stew or some other kindness that families could afford, the Belsa needed things they could use.

"Look," she blurted quickly. "I'm going to have to see you in a couple days anyway, to make sure that's healing the way it should, and take out the stitches. So, how about we trade then?"

Kael looked up, finally meeting her gaze. He nodded gratefully.

Georgianna returned to the last car once Kael had said his goodbyes and set off along the tunnel. She looked in to find Lacie keeping watch over Jacob, making her own notes in a small book. Either Lacie hadn't realised, or the two were keeping an easy silence, but Jacob was awake.

"How're you feeling?" Georgianna asked, moving further inside.

Lacie lifted her head, her gaze shifting to Georgianna before she looked at Jacob. He was curled in the corner of his bed, looking far younger than he was. The moment Georgianna had spoken, however, his expression contorted in panic. His wide brown eyes darted around the car, and he quickly pushed himself up. Pressing his back against the end of the bed, he hunched over his knees, pulling them tight to his chest.

She took a step back, chewing on her bottom lip. Even Lacie, who had been the closest to Jacob since his arrival, moved away from him, giving the terrified young man as much space as she could.

"I'm sorry, Jacob. I didn't mean to scare you."

Jacob shook his head violently, but didn't say a word.

With a single glance from Lacie, she took another step back.

"I'll... I'll be in the other car if you need me."

Lacie placed her notes next to her knee, but she didn't even look at Jacob or Georgianna again. She stared at her feet, hands clasped in her lap, perfectly still.

Georgianna climbed down from the car, wishing that every injury was as easily cured as Kael's.

5 FREED-UP TIME

Jaid took over on Medics' Way again in the late evening, having had no luck in locating her husband, Si. Georgianna could see the worry on her face and had offered to cover the next shift, but Jaid would have none of it. She claimed working on the Way would keep her mind busy, but Georgianna was sure that the moment Jaid was alone she would be imagining all the worst things that could possibly have happened to him. Then again, Keinah, the only other regular medic, wasn't in any state to go very far, with her pregnancy so far along. No doubt, if Jaid needed, she would be able to call on the mother-to-be.

Once all the notes had been handed over and the current states of patients explained, Georgianna walked with Lacie back into Belsa territory, leaving the girl a couple of hundred yards from the car she shared with Marshall Casey. She didn't need to walk the girl back; enough Belsa knew exactly who Lacie was that she would get help if she ever needed it, but she enjoyed the walk. The young girl was sweet and quiet, but always had interesting opinions on things when you got her talking.

Turning away from the tunnel leading to the marshall's car, Georgianna headed west through a smaller tunnel off the main encampment, away from the main bustle of people coming and going. It wasn't a long walk, which, after being out and about all day, was a relief. Georgianna had always been active, but some days it became a bit much, running all over the place.

Despite her work as a medic, helping people didn't pay much more than trade and favours. Most nights, once she'd finished whatever she happened to have on that day, she headed over to the Rion, an Adveni district filled with bars and restaurants. The Adveni were more accustomed to having purpose-built places to eat and drink, so they allowed a few Veniche to work in their establishments, pouring drinks and delivering food. Today, however, Georgianna wasn't expected to be at Crisco so she headed through the Belsa tunnels to one of the other places where she spent some of her evenings.

The shack, made of sheet metal stolen from an Adveni construction site, was held together with rope and strategically placed bricks. Despite its ramshackle appearance, it was surprisingly sturdy, something Georgianna had found out by accident when she tripped and fell into one of the walls.

Approaching the side where a thick canvas sheet covered the opening, Georgianna reached out and smacked her hand against the nearest section of metal.

"Are you decent?" she asked, shifting her weight. "Or alone?"

There was silence for a moment, in which Georgianna considered peeking inside. There was always a chance that he wasn't there. It wouldn't have been the first time she'd found the shack empty. Though before she had the chance to peer inside, or turn and walk away, the canvas was pulled back at an angle and a cheeky grin appeared in the opening.

"Have you ever known me to be either?" it asked.

A large hand came out through the gap and tangled itself in amongst the hair at the nape of her neck, pulling her in.

Georgianna barely had time to look around to confirm the answer to either of her questions before soft, warm lips found her own, drawing her up to meet them. She smiled against the kiss, her own hands seeking out the gentle slope of his waist before she carefully pulled herself back.

The lamp was lit, and it sent flickering light over Keiran's stubbled jaw and smooth skin. He looked down at her, grinning that charming, cocky smirk that had first made her notice him. He was so self-assured, with such easy going charm, that it was almost impossible not to like him.

"You're dressed, I'm disappointed," Georgianna chuckled.

A raised eyebrow met her comment, his smirk broadening as he teased his fingers through her long hair.

"Easily solvable!" he answered.

Leaning forward, Keiran placed a kiss gently against Georgianna's temple before he released her and turned around, retreating the couple of steps over to his bed and falling down onto it. Picking up a piece of paper from the upturned crate by his bed, he folded it a couple times and slotted it into his pocket before reaching out for her to join him. Georgianna indulged him happily, placing her bag down on the bed as she eased her boots from her feet and clambered over him to the other side of the bed. Placing herself against the wall, her legs resting over Keiran's, Georgianna reached out and tugged her bag toward her.

"Save any lives today, Med?" Keiran asked, resting his arms over her shins, one hand sliding her trousers up a little so that his thumb could gently stroke her ankle.

Georgianna shook her head.

"I was called to the compound," she explained. "Vtensu left it so long that by the time I got there, it was too late."

Keiran frowned a little, but shrugged.

"Better dead than buryd!" he answered.

Lifting her head, Georgianna glanced at him. His grey-blue eyes and tanned face, worn with work and age, still held the amusement and cheer that so many Belsa had lost somewhere along the way. He looked relaxed, as if he didn't have a care in the world, as if maybe the Adveni hadn't invaded and they were just two people in the mid-heat of Adlai. Looking at him like this, it was hard to believe that their world had changed so much, that Keiran had once been a hunter with the Nerrin tribe, that she'd nearly finished her training. Back then, she'd not even thought about Keiran

Zanetti; she'd barely known him.

Keiran, four years older than she was, was thirty. Had things been like they were before, he could have expected to have been joined by now. He didn't talk much about the old days though, except to regale her with stories of hunting with Eli Talassi, the Belsa everyone now knew as Wrench. She was sure that Keiran didn't like what had happened to their world any more than anybody else did. Yet he wasn't secretive that he was glad their joining traditions had fallen by the wayside in all the turmoil.

Thinking about it, Georgianna had to admit that she wasn't upset either at not being hounded to find a partner to continue the Kahle lines. She felt happy with the way things were between her and Keiran, something that would not have been looked on kindly if she were expected to join.

"You saying you wouldn't come break down Lyndbury if I were caught?" she asked, smirking at him.

"Oh, I'd come to Lyndbury," he answered, pushing himself up to lean forward and kiss her again. "I'd be first in line to purchase myself a George drysta."

Georgianna reached out and smacked him as he fell back against the cushion, laughing.

"That's not funny, Zanetti!" she chastised.

Georgianna suddenly wasn't sure that they should be joking about the compound, not after her trip over there and her conversation with Taye. Glancing at her bag, she thought about the packet of Adveni drugs Taye had given her. It felt wrong to have them. She'd not even agreed to make the delivery, and the drugs came with too many strings attached.

"I'd treat you well!" Keiran smirked. "You'd hardly have to get out of bed in the morning."

She gave him a disapproving glare, but Keiran grinned back at her and gave her ankle a squeeze.

"In fact, I think I'd demand that you never got out of bed."

"I'm sure you would," she answered.

Silence stretched out between them. Georgianna watched as he turned his gaze onto the ceiling, tucking his hand beneath his head.

"I saw Taye today," she said finally, slumping onto her side next to him and propping herself up on her elbow.

"Taye..." he murmured. "He's Carae, right?"

Georgianna nodded, reaching between them and picking at a loose thread in the blanket.

"We knew each other as kids."

"Oh yeah, he's the one with the girl in the compound."

Georgianna glanced over at him. She didn't remember telling Keiran about Nyah. They didn't generally share their lives much. He had his friends and she had hers. Apart from the people they both knew within the Belsa, she wasn't even sure how much their lives intersected. Though, with the Carae supplying the Belsa pretty regularly, it wasn't surprising that Keiran might know Taye. Maybe he'd even known Nyah before she was arrested.

"So, what did he ask for? A way to turn back time? A mass breakout of Lyndbury for his little girlfriend?"

Staring down at the blanket, Georgianna grazed her teeth

across her bottom lip. Keiran frowned, his pale blue eyes narrowing.

"George, you've got to be kidding!" he chastised. "What is it?"

"Just a delivery," she answered. "He wants me to take a packet in for Nyah."

Keiran's expression said it all. His lips pursed into a thin line and a crease formed above his straight nose as his brow knitted together.

"He's worried about her," Georgianna lamented. "It's been months."

"It could be years for all he can do about it," Keiran answered dismissively. "He should let it go."

"You don't think I've told him that? He loves her."

Keiran scoffed, but didn't answer. Georgianna pushed herself up further and looked down at him. She shouldn't be angry at Keiran. She knew it was who he was. He didn't want love and joining the way Taye did, but in Georgianna's opinion, he didn't have to be so cavalier about it.

"I'm worried about him, Keiran," she explained. "He's becoming more erratic. He wants Nyah out, and I think... I think if things don't change soon, he'll do something without thinking."

Turning his head to look at her, Keiran's eyes narrowed.

"What do you expect me to do about it?"

Georgianna shook her head. She didn't expect anything from Keiran. He'd never been close to Taye, and it wasn't like he owed her anything. The two of them were having fun, they both agreed that.

"Nothing, I'm just... I'm just worried about him doing something stupid."

Keiran frowned and went back to staring at the ceiling. He reached up, running his hand over his short, dark hair.

"As long as you don't do anything stupid, like getting caught sneaking stuff into Lyndbury," he agreed. "I do prefer you being a free woman. You getting yourself buryd would free up far too much of my time."

Georgianna laughed and leaned closer to him, resting her arm across his waist and tangling her fingers in his shirt. She felt silly, being upset that he wasn't taking it seriously. They'd both been perfectly clear about what they wanted, and serious didn't come into it.

"I'm sure you'd find someone to keep you busy soon enough."

"You're right, I would, but that doesn't mean I'd like it."

Giggling, Georgianna rolled herself onto her front and rested her head on her arms. She didn't exactly know what to say to that. He was clearly still under the belief that if she made this delivery, she would be making a mistake. Truthfully, Georgianna thought making the delivery was a mistake too, but she also didn't want her friend getting himself into trouble.

Georgianna tried to wriggle herself further into the mattress, one of the luxuries of staying so long in one place to live out the mid-heat. When the thought came to her, however, Georgianna suddenly pushed herself up. She'd only known Keiran for a month or so; they'd never talked about what they would do for the freeze.

"Will you be travelling?" she asked, looking down at him.

Their traditions, their survival from the days before had become unreliable of late. Some wanted to escape the Adveni and the freeze and move south, but others believed that their work in Adlai was too important. Not to mention that the Adveni were rather particular about the Veniche to whom they gave travel permits.

"Nah," he answered. "I'll stay here. No use in travelling anymore."

Georgianna raised an eyebrow.

"I'll tell that to the snow when it's covered every entrance to the tunnels."

Keiran, chuckling a little, reached out and slid one arm under Georgianna's waist, tugging her towards him until she laid against his chest. Georgianna squeaked in amusement, but didn't try to fight him off.

"Which means I get to hibernate in here," he said.

Georgianna frowned and placed her hands against Keiran's chest, pushing herself up.

She'd not made the trip in six years, and she missed it. Every year she planned to go, she thought about going to get a permit, but each year something came up. Braedon's mother had been pregnant with him, Braedon was too young to travel if they didn't have help. Something came up every year. But Georgianna didn't want to miss the journey again.

"I'm going to try travelling," she answered.

For a moment, Keiran looked up at her, his pale eyes narrowed thoughtfully as he watched her face, perhaps waiting for a smirk to part her lips or a laugh to echo through the shack. In the light, his eyes were a cool blue, but here, with nothing but the lamp, they looked more grey than anything. When no answer came from Georgianna, he licked across his bottom lip.

"They won't let you go," he answered plainly. "Not many medics are willing to go into Lyndbury. Plus, it isn't as if any Belsa can go. It's not like we can go and request passes from the Adveni. You imagine Casey going up there?"

Any hope left in Georgianna's face slipped away. She'd thought she would go because people would need help on the trail. They always got injured one way or another, but what about in Adlai? With the Adveni around they weren't going to let every Veniche just waltz on off down south. The people left behind would need care too, perhaps more so than those on the trail because they'd be suffering out the freeze.

"Yeah, I guess you're right," she said finally, lowering herself back down onto his chest.

"Wow, George, don't sound so happy about it!" Keiran scoffed.

Georgianna shook her head and glanced up at him.

"I didn't mean…"

Keiran pulled his hands back from her body and wedged them underneath his head as he stared up at the ceiling. Even if it hadn't been his plan to convince Georgianna to stay, he seemed a little angry that she wasn't more enthusiastic about it.

DEAD AND BURYD

Georgianna frowned and rested her cheek against his shoulder, staring blankly down his chest. Her fingers, caught in his shirt, pushed the material up just enough that her thumb could slide effortlessly back and forth across his skin.

"I was only thinking about it," Georgianna murmured.

Keiran's chest rose and fell with slow, deep breaths, but Georgianna didn't dare move. She didn't want to get them into an even more awkward conversation than they were already in. His hand came out from underneath his head and wound into her hair, tugging her head gently back until she could look up at him. Shifting his body a little further down the bed, Keiran smiled.

"Well, I suppose I should make the most of now, just in case," he answered.

Then, without another awkward word between then, his lips were on hers, and all thoughts of travelling south were forgotten.

6 The Kahle in the West

Leaving the tunnels, the morning sun was already high, radiating constant, sticky heat. Despite the fact that Georgianna knew she would be more comfortable in a short-sleeved shirt, one which allowed her skin to breathe, she had pulled on a thin smock that covered her from neck to wrists to protect her from the sun's rays. The walk from the last tunnel exit over to the camps was long, and she couldn't risk too much exposure, not in the mid-heat sun.

On either side of the beaten path leading out of the city and into the camps, buildings were being erected under Adveni supervision. Veniche of every race and tribe queued for hours in the early morning to get a place on one of the construction crews. Construction was high-paying work and places were limited and heavily controlled. Anyone with even the slightest mark against their registration was turned away, regardless of their skill.

Crossing her arms over her chest, Georgianna continued down the beaten path to the camps. They built up slowly: first the odd, outlying building, before these became more frequent until you were in the middle of a sea of houses and other small buildings.

While they were officially called "The Veniche Camps", they were actually split into a number of smaller encampments that bled into each other as space became sparse. The Kahle, one of the largest tribes that used Adlai as a settling ground, were in the north and spread out towards the west, furthest from the city.

The Nerrin had taken over the south-west, and while the east held relatively neutral grounds to allow safe passage between the camps for all, there were a number of smaller tribes and nomad settlers who had taken up their own private space.

Near the main road through the camps, a woman was hanging out laundry while five children played in front of the house. From the fact that the children were all the same age yet looked absolutely nothing alike, Georgianna could only assume that this woman had been asked to look after children by other families while they went to work.

Further in, back from the path, a man was skinning a kill, the thick hairs of the pelt still dirty from the hunt. Beside him, a large dog lay chewing on one of the deer's leg bones, paying no attention to the large amount of meat only a few feet away. Georgianna chewed on her bottom lip, watching out of the corner of her eye and taking note of the surrounding buildings. Having not been home in a few days, she didn't want to take a large amount of meat if her family were stocked already, but it was useful to know who had meat in, just in case. Most people probably wouldn't trade such a large kill so easily, but her medical supplies could prove a worthy trade if they didn't know someone within their own tribe. Unfortunately, medics had been one of the hardest hit during the invasion, going in to help those injured and then being killed or captured by the Adveni. Luckily for Georgianna, she had been young and inexperienced, mostly kept back to treat the smaller wounds of those who managed to return from the fighting.

Georgianna walked though the neutral safety area and, passing between the buildings, into the Kahle encampments. With every home she passed, and every person outside who greeted her as if she were their own child or sibling, Georgianna felt the familiarity of home. Even before the Adveni had arrived and pushed the Veniche further out of the city by raising prices for land, the Kahle had camped in these spots. Their homes had been destroyed in the first attacks, but that sense of place could not be broken. So when the Kahle moved north to Adlai to resettle during the heat, they returned to the same area they always had. Georgianna was sure that her bed at home was still in the same place it had been when she was a child.

"Gianna!" a voice called, little feet rushing forward until a small body collided with her legs, wrapping its thin arms tight around them.

Georgianna almost lost her balance from the impact. Looking down, she smiled broadly at the ruffled brown mop of hair and the thin, smiling face hidden beneath it. She bent down and wrapped both arms around Braedon's waist to lift him up against her body.

The young boy immediately wrapped his arms around her neck. Curling his short legs as far around her body as he could reach.

"You're not meant to be learning, are you?" Georgianna asked, glancing at the boy suspiciously through the corner of her eye.

Braedon lifted his head and shook it vehemently.

"No, Grandda' was tradin', Miss Kadey lookin' after me!"

"Well, alright," Georgianna answered, glancing off to see Kadey Lane standing in her doorway.

Lifting a hand and waving to Kadey, Georgianna began walking back towards their home, Braedon in her arms.

"Where's your da'?" Georgianna asked.

Braedon shrugged, which only meant one thing: her brother had a job from an Adveni. The only reason Halden wouldn't share something with his son was because it involved things Halden thought Braedon was too young to know.

It was a short walk from where Braedon had collided with her to their house. On the front doorstep, Georgianna's father sat with a hide across his lap, a thin knife in his hand which he was using to cut away the extra patches of fat and muscle.

Braedon, having grown up around such things, showed no disgust or queasiness at the sight, but instead began wriggling in Georgianna's grasp until she finally put him down and the young boy could go running a little lopsidedly back towards his grandfather.

"Aren't you meant to be with Kadey?" her father asked as the young boy ran into his eye line.

"Gianna got me!" Braedon exclaimed, pointing back at her.

Georgianna's father lifted his head, smiling brightly at the sight of his youngest. Putting the hide aside, he got to his feet. Quickening her step, Georgianna moved over towards her father who placed his hands on either side of her face and kissed her forehead gently.

"My girl," he murmured, smiling down at her for a moment before the hand from one cheek was gone and quickly came back with a light smack upside the head.

"Ow!" Georgianna complained, stepping back and reaching up to rub her head. "What was that..."

"You come home far too little!" he claimed, pointing at her. "Anyone would think I have no daughter, just sons!"

"Son, Da', you only have one!"

"Sons run off and sleep in odd places, not daughters!" he claimed, narrowing his eyes at her.

Georgianna had received this talk many times before, and even though she was twenty-six years old, more than capable of looking after herself, she still frowned and chewed her lip at her father's disapproval.

"You sorry?" he asked.

"Yes, Da'," Georgianna mumbled.

Her father nodded slowly.

"Good!" he answered. "Now, help with the stew, will you?"

Georgianna rolled her eyes as soon as her father wasn't looking, a motion that made Braedon giggle and cover his mouth. Georgianna smirked and winked at him, ruffling his hair as she dumped her bag on the ground and climbed past her father, who was taking his seat in the doorway again.

The house was cooler than it was outside. All the windows and doors were flung open to let what little breeze could be found circulate through the small rooms. In the back of the house, two large doors stood open, leading out onto a small patch of dried grass. Just past the doors, vapour swirling up into the air, a large pot stood above a small fire holding the stew her father had been talking about. Georgianna watched the boiling bubbles for a moment and moved over to the trunk in the corner of the kitchen. She lifted the lid and took one of the spoons from its place in the trunk. The lid dropped with a snap, and Georgianna dipped the spoon into the stew and sucked the juice from the back of the metal. It was decent enough, but the quality of the Lennox family cooking had definitely dropped off since her mother's death.

Lifting the lid and removing the tray that lay across the top of the trunk, she placed it on the rough-hewn wooden table that took up most of the simple kitchen. The kitchen wasn't used much anymore, the different pots and utensils that her mother had made such good use of during her life, abandoned. Her father preferred to make simple meals in large quantity so that they would last for a number of days.

She dug through the contents of the trunk, finally finding what she was looking for. Down near the bottom, clearly not used all that often by her father and brother, a small cloth satchel held a number of paper packets filled with spices. Her mother had been obsessed with collecting spices. Whenever the Kahle camped near another tribe, she would insist on going over with some trade in the hopes of finding something the Kahle couldn't find on their trail.

Georgianna took each packet out in turn, carefully opening each one and sniffing it tentatively. She had never had the flare for cooking her mother had, no matter how much her mother had tried teaching her. Georgianna wasn't good at automatically knowing which kind of spice a dish needed to really bring out the flavour, nor did she know how to counteract things when they went wrong. While Georgianna was a good medic, she was not good at reviving injured food.

She tested a number of spices and herbs, sprinkling them over the stew in turn. She closed each packet just as carefully as she'd opened it and placed them back in the satchel, going to the stew and stirring it carefully. Lifting the spoon, she sucked on the back thoughtfully, wondering what it was her mother would have done. There was something wrong with it: it was full and tasted of the meat, but there was something missing, some flavour that, as a child, would have had Georgianna initially wrinkling her nose.

Blinking for a moment, she wondered if it could really be

that easy? She reached into the trunk and pulled out a dark green cantina. Opening it, she sniffed and immediately wrinkled her nose. Dark berry wine. That was it. She liked the taste of the wine, and she had certainly become more accustomed to it as she got older, but there was still that slightly acidic smell that she had never fully gotten used to.

She stood over the stew for a moment, wondering how much she was supposed to put in: too much and it would overpower everything; too little and what was the point? Grimacing as she tipped the cantina, she waited for three healthy glugs to spill from the mouth before she brought it away, replacing the cap and returning it to the trunk.

Her third tasting yielded better results. While it still didn't taste like her mother's—she was pretty sure nothing ever would—at least it tasted of more than meat and root vegetables. She stirred the concoction once more before placing the spoon to the side and returning to the front porch, leaning over her father's shoulders and kissing his cheek.

"You smell like your mother," her father commented with a fond smile.

"Of dark berry wine?" Georgianna asked.

For a moment, her father pondered the idea, before he slowly nodded.

"I think that may have been part of it."

Georgianna climbed past her father and slumped down onto the dry earth near his feet. Braedon, who had been playing with a couple of carved wooden horses from Halden's childhood, picked up his toys and rushed over, wriggling himself into Georgianna's lap so that she could wrap her arms around his waist and rest her chin on top of his head.

"How've you been Da'?" she asked.

Her father shrugged. He looked older than he used to, far older than he should have looked. Georgianna could remember her father scooping both her and Halden up under his arms, carrying them through camp when they misbehaved. He wasn't a giant, but he had seemed that way, the way he held command. His dark hair, the same as her brother's, was now heavily sprinkled with grey, his beard going the same way. Yet his bright green eyes still sparkled with the energy of a much younger man. Despite his strength and skill with a weapon, Lyle Lennox had become a carver, taking wood and whittling it away to create useful objects. For his joining present to Georgianna's mother, he'd made an entire cooking set, large enough for a family of six.

Taking one of the small wooden horses from Braedon, Georgianna galloped it across the boy's knees and up his arm until she nuzzled it into his neck, neighing playfully. Braedon giggled and tried to wriggle away until Georgianna handed him back the toy.

Georgianna turned back to her father and frowned.

"Beck says hi," she told him with a careful smile.

It was odd to think that her father had been friends with Beck, knowing the man now as the marshall of the Belsa. But apparently, when they were young, Beck Casey and Lyle Lennox had been thick as thieves. Beck had trained as a hunter and scout, Lyle as a carver and carpenter, but the two remained close whenever they were in camps. Now, however, the two barely saw each other.

"Of course he does, lazy bastard can't get over here himself," her father chuckled. "How's that girl of his doing?"

"Lacie is great," Georgianna nodded enthusiastically. "She's a really fast learner."

"Good. It's about time you had an apprentice," he claimed, pointing the knife he was using to clean the hide at her. "No good letting those talents go to waste."

Nodding, Georgianna reached out and pulled her bag towards her. While her father hadn't originally been happy to know she was visiting the Belsa to help out, knowing how badly the Adveni wanted them eradicated, he had slowly come around to the idea as long as Beck was looking after her. When Georgianna had brought back news that Beck had a young girl living with him, a girl the marshall was treating like his own daughter, Lyle Lennox had been over the moon. He wouldn't tell Georgianna why, of course. He said it was none of her business unless Beck decided to tell her on his own, and that she was not to ask him about it.

"I still need to meet that girl," her father announced thoughtfully, scratching the edge of his knife against his jaw. "Beck's a good man, a loyal Kahle, but those tunnels are no place for a young girl."

He looked pointedly at Georgianna and nodded very suddenly:

"You'll bring her here! Lots of people to help out this way, you could call it work!"

"She's wanted, Da'," she lamented. "A drysta runaway."

DEAD AND BURYD

Her father tilted his head to the side and dug the knife a little further into the hide as he tried to think up a reasonable solution. After a minute, he finally huffed, which Georgianna knew to take that he'd not been able to think of one. No doubt it was annoying him. He wanted to meet his friend's daughter.

"You know, you could always come down to the tunnels with me," she suggested. Glancing beneath her eyelashes at her father, Georgianna quickly occupied herself with opening her bag, like her suggestion had been perfectly innocent.

"And risk being hauled off as a Belsa?" he asked. "Who will look after your nephew when I'm buryd, huh?"

Georgianna opened her mouth to argue but quickly closed it again, knowing it wouldn't do any good. It wasn't the first time she'd tried to convince her father to visit the tunnels and Beck. Scooping Braedon off her lap and onto the dried grass, she carefully got to her feet.

"I'm going to check on the stew."

7 Love and Loss

Braedon was spawled on Georgianna's lap asleep by the time his father returned home from work. Splattered with paint, Halden flopped straight onto the floor next to his sister and son. He rolled to the side, kissed Georgianna's cheek in greeting, and immediately slumped onto his back again. Georgianna didn't blame him. While she had spent a relatively relaxed afternoon with Braedon and her father, Halden had been working for the Adveni, probably ordered to work faster and harder every step of the way.

Georgianna carefully prised herself out from underneath Braedon, adjusting the boy to sleep on his father before she slipped out to the kitchen and ladled Halden a generous portion of stew. It was a little cold, her father having put out the fire beneath it an hour or so before, but Halden was grateful when Georgianna handed it to him and he took his first mouthful. As Georgianna curled up at her father's side, Halden told them that he'd been working on one of the new buildings.

The older Lennox continued to whittle, refusing to tell them what he was making.

"Wood is a living thing, my little Gianna," he used to tell her. "And like all living things, you can't tell them what they should be. You can only help them find what suits them best."

She had never really known what he had meant when she was a child, but it sounded very profound, so she'd never questioned him. Now, she thought she understood a little better. Just as she had decided for herself that she wanted to be a medic, and her parents had used their skills to help her along, Halden had decided that he wanted to work with horses. It had also been their parents' acceptance of not forcing other living beings into what they might want that had stopped them from questioning the news that their eldest son would not join with a woman. Instead, at the age of nineteen, Halden Lennox had claimed that he was in love. Nobody had even known he had dated before.

His name was Nequiel. He was a nomad who had come to the Kahle to sell a foal. As Halden was working with the tribe's horses, it had been Halden who had to look over the foal to see whether it was bred well enough to bring into the Kahle stock.

It had been Georgianna who first knew of Halden's infatuation with the nomad, who had stuck around longer than had probably been considered necessary after the foal had been given the clearance to be bought. Halden told his younger sister while travelling south towards Nyvalau. Georgianna, admittedly, didn't understand. She knew there were men who joined with other men, but at the age of thirteen, she wasn't entirely sure why. Watching her brother with Nequiel, however, she quickly learned that it wasn't about finding someone suitable to join with, someone you could live with. It was about joining with the person you couldn't live without.

Watching Halden with Braedon now, Georgianna knew that this was why she hadn't joined, why she couldn't see herself joining any time soon, because she had not found that person she could not bear to be parted from. There was a sadness every time Halden looked at his son because, by blood, Braedon wasn't actually his, and looked far more like his biological father. The boy's mop of brown hair was blacker than Halden's, the olive hue of his skin darker than her brother's, and his eyes were the bright reddish brown that had been so distinctive in his father. The boy, almost five years old, was actually Nequiel's son by blood. Nequiel had been asked to father a child when he officially joined the Kahle. The Adveni had wiped out a lot of the Kahle, and the elders wanted to ensure that their blood continued.

A woman named Heather, widowed by the war, begged the elders to let her be the one chosen. Her husband had always wanted children, and they'd simply never had the good fortune to conceive a child. It had been decided that, should the coupling be successful, the child would remain predominantly with their mother, but both Nequiel, and Halden, who by this time was joined with Nequiel for all under the sun and moon, would also be parents to the child.

The baby boy was brought into the world in the middle of the freeze. While Georgianna did everything she could, Heather succumbed to cold and, having lost so much blood, did not survive the birth.

Braedon, named for the wild flowers that grew within the heather, came into the Lennox home, and was immediately accepted as family despite not being any blood relation. As a gesture to his place with them, he was given the name Lennox instead of Yinah, Nequiel's family name.

It had been almost three years since Nequiel was captured by the Adveni, a trade with an Adveni that went wrong. When Nequiel could not deliver the items promised, the Adveni claimed he was a criminal and a traitor, and he was executed in the square for all to see. Halden had stood among the crowd, held back by three Kahle men who kept tight hold on him the entire time.

As the last of the sun disappeared behind the horizon, the lengthening shadows melted into the night's darkness, held at bay only by the oil lamp's flickering glow. Halden finally peeled himself from the thick woollen blanket on the floor and lifted Braedon into his arms.

"I'm going to put him to bed," he explained, carrying Braedon from the small family space.

Her father lifted his head and gave a brief nod before returning to his whittling. A low, melodic hum slipped past his lips into the air. Georgianna leaned against him, her cheek against his shoulder as she watched the knife's progression over the surface of the wood.

Her father's humming was threatening to send Georgianna off to sleep herself, so she sat up straight, shaking out the cloudy tendrils of sleep, and clambered up. Placing her hand on his shoulder, she gave it a brief squeeze before following her brother.

The house was built of thick beams of wood that held the structure while a sandstone mix made up the walls. The family space stood at the front of the house on the right-hand side, her father's room on the left. Behind those were two rooms once occupied by Georgianna and Halden, and now by Braedon as well. Mostly, Halden shared a room with Braedon, though Georgianna had often told her brother that she would share with the young boy, seeing as she wasn't home every night. Whether it was through convenience, or because he didn't want to be separated from his son, Halden had refused her offer, meaning that mostly, the last room stood empty, waiting for her return.

Even after all the work gone into making the house, the sandstone was still rough in places, and tickled her fingers when she ran them across the surface. The thin corridor out towards the kitchen was dark except for the light flickering through the doorway to the family room. Through the open front door, the continued bustle of activity from nearby houses filtered in. A little way away, she could hear a group of men playing musical instruments, singing an old song she had heard as a child. Despite the fire having been put out, the breeze from the back doors out of the kitchen wafted the smell of stew through the thin corridor, making Georgianna's stomach rumble appreciatively. Wrapping her arms around her stomach, as if the sound would be enough to rouse her young nephew, she rested her shoulder against the doorframe, watching in fond silence as Halden tucked Braedon into his bed.

"I should take advantage of you being here," Halden teased as he came back to the doorway and slipped past her into the corridor. "Make you do it."

Georgianna's whisper of a giggle still sounded far too loud so close to the slumbering child, and so she reached in, hooking her finger around the door and pulling it towards the frame.

"I entertained him all afternoon, thank you very much," Georgianna defended. "Including stopping him from putting a whole host of new spices into the stew, namely dirt."

Halden snorted, his green eyes lit like gemstones pressed in his tanned skin. Instead of returning to sit with their father, he pushed open the door to Georgianna's room, ducking his head to get through the low doorway. Slumping heavily down onto the bed, he rested against the wall, patting the mattress next to him. It was a thin bed, just wide enough for one person to sleep comfortably, but Georgianna made her way around to the other side and perched on the edge next to him, shoulder to shoulder. She rested back against the wall.

"You've been alright?" he asked.

She glanced at him. His eyes were closed. Even knowing that he wouldn't see it, she nodded.

"I'm okay."

"Doesn't sound it."

Turning her head, Georgianna was surprised to find Halden's eyes narrowed at her, a curious suspicion etched into his face. Lifting her feet from the floor, she laid her legs down the mattress next to his.

"It's nothing," she answered.

Halden reached out, taking Georgianna's hand and turning it palm up to face him. Pressing his index finger into the centre of her palm, he moved swiftly on to each of her fingers in turn, pressing them down with his own. He moved idly back and forth between her fingers, quick patterns that made little sense. Georgianna narrowed her eyes, but before she could pull her hand away, or even protest, he pushed her little finger back until a spasm of pain shot up her arm.

Georgianna squeaked, tugging on her arm to free it from his grasp, but Halden kept a tight hold, returning to his pattern of gentle taps. He used to do this as a child. Older than Georgianna, and much stronger, when she wouldn't tell him something, he would play the game. She never knew when a strong push was coming, and waiting for it with each gentle tap only made the pain worse when it came.

"Alright, alright!"

Halden glanced at her, a devilish smirk across his lips as his finger hovered above her own. He raised an eyebrow, waiting.

"Let go then," Georgianna said.

"Not until you tell me."

"Vtensu."

Halden beamed at her despite the Adveni insult.

"A friend wants a favour," Georgianna admitted. "Taye, he wants something delivered to Nyah."

"I thought Nyah was…"

"Buryd, yeah."

Halden's smirk promptly vanished to be replaced with a worried frown. He knew Taye and Nyah. While Taye was closer to Georgianna's age, and Nyah a good few years younger than them both, it was impossible not to know them within the tribe, especially when Taye and Georgianna had been close friends as children.

"What's he expecting?" Halden asked.

Georgianna paused, her gaze set on her hand, still clasped within her brother's. She sighed and shrugged.

"I don't think it's much, just a note, but… but it's still risky."

"I doubt risk is factoring much to him right now, is it?"

She shook her head. She didn't want to upset Halden by bringing up Nequiel, but having never been in their position, she couldn't imagine how it felt to be separated from someone you felt so completely bound to.

"Did you ever try?" she asked. "To get messages to Nequiel?"

Georgianna could see the tightening in her brother's jaw immediately, the way his face hardened into a mask she saw so rarely.

"Once," Halden answered. "A few days before he was brought to the square."

Shifting her position, Georgianna sat up a little

straighter, watching Halden.

"You never asked me to…"

"And risk you being caught?" he asked. "No, I couldn't put you in that position."

"Then how?"

"A cook. He promised to pass it to one of the men who collected the food each day."

"Did he get it?"

"I don't know. The cook passed it on, but whether it got to Nequiel, I'll never know."

"You don't think I should try?"

Halden sat up straight, turning to look properly at her. Keeping hold of her hand, he enclosed it in both of his own, resting them in his lap.

"I'm not saying that, Gianna," he murmured. "To hear from Nyah, for Taye, would be worth more than anything else in the world. I would have given anything to hear from Quiel in those last few days. But remember that it is your risk. I didn't understand just how much I had asked, and Taye does not realise either. We become blinded by a connection like that. This must be your decision. You are a smart girl; you will make the correct choice."

Georgianna turned towards him and rested her temple against her brother's chest. Keeping a tight hold on her hand with one of his own, the other came up to rest on the back of her neck, holding her against him as he dipped his head and kissed her scalp.

"No matter what you decide, little sister," he whispered. "You must do one thing for me."

Georgianna didn't move, her breath whispering across the hairs on her arm.

"What's that?" she asked.

Halden grinned against her hair.

"Don't tell Da'."

8 THE FRIEND IN THE SOUTH

Despite the lack of windows in Georgianna's bedroom, the morning light streamed through the open door. She rolled onto her front, burying her face into her pillow in the hopes of blocking out the offensive rays, but movement throughout the house and even outside chased her dreams further and further away. From the kitchen, she could hear Braedon asking Halden what he would be doing while her brother tried to get ready to leave.

In the tunnels, when she stayed below, it was easier to keep consciousness at bay despite the bustle of movement and everyday business. While the murk of the constant shadows remained, it was easier to push distractions aside, but not here. Sure enough, Georgianna had only just set her feet on the floor when Braedon ran past her bedroom with a racket disproportionate to his small size.

"Grandda', grandda'!" he called. "Da' says you take me tradin'!"

Her father's low rumbling laugh echoed through the small home as Georgianna pushed herself from her bed and padding over to the trunk that held the majority of her belongings.

"Did he really?" her father's voice echoed. "Well, I guess if your da' says so, it must be so."

Lifting the trunk lid, Georgianna rummaged through her clothes, pulling out a dress. Tugging her shirt from her body and over her head, she tossed it onto the mattress and swung the dress around her, slipping her arms into the long sleeves and wrapping the material around her body, buttoning the inside together before pulling the leather belt around her waist to tie at the side.

By the time she emerged from her room with a change of clothes already tucked under her arm, her brother was almost out the door, turning back to give her a quick pat on the cheek and a thoughtful gaze. Georgianna returned a weak smile, clapping her hand on top of Halden's for a moment before he left.

"Gianna, you coming tradin' with us?" Braedon asked, already dressed in clothes that were a little too big for him.

Georgianna pouted back at him, crouching down in the light of the open doorway.

"Afraid not, Brae. I have to go do my own work."

"Med'cines," Braedon nodded knowledgeably.

"That's it," she said.

Glancing up from Braedon's shining face, Georgianna smiled sadly at her father. He smiled back, though it wasn't a true smile. His green eyes remained distant, and there was a forced look to his expression.

"You'll return soon, my Gianna?" he asked.

Georgianna leaned closer and kissed her father on the cheek.

"Soon as I can."

He held her face in his hands.

"Soon as the sun allows," he told her before the moment was over and he lightly swatted the back of her arm to get her moving.

Georgianna collected her bag from the front room, stuffing in the change of clothes, and stepped out into the glaring morning sun. Heading south through the camps, she wove a winding path through the houses. Even though the camps of the different tribes bled into each other in an uneven pattern, Georgianna had walked the path so many times that she knew immediately when she had stepped into Nerrin territory. She didn't feel fear at the different tribe, not like she used to, but her father had always told her that it was best to tread with caution when dealing outside your own. These days, Georgianna supposed that related more to the Adveni than it did to the other tribes, but unlike the Kahle, the Nerrin had no reason to protect her should anything happen while she was on their ground.

Still, despite the difference, people were cheerful and friendly when they recognised her. A decade of treating their wounds and helping when none of their own medics were available had given her a good reputation. Her father also had a good reputation. Since before the Adveni arrival, her father had been known as an expert craftsman, and trading in Adlai amongst the other tribes had been good for as long as Georgianna could remember.

"Georgianna!"

Georgianna glanced around to see her friend, Liliah, seated against the wall of her home, a leather hide across her lap. Across the hide, balanced precariously on her legs, a number of small paper packets lay open, each one holding a small mound of coloured powder. Careful not to knock any of them, Georgianna approached Liliah and sat down beside her.

"Hi," she said. "How are you?"

"Can't complain," Liliah chimed. "I missed you yesterday."

Georgianna frowned. For a moment, the worry that perhaps she had missed a shift at the bar fluttered through her stomach. She'd been sure she was free, otherwise she would have chosen another day to come home.

"Yesterday?" Georgianna repeated. "I wasn't working."

Liliah laughed; a bright, cheerful laugh that suited her face perfectly. The girl was one of the prettiest women Georgianna had ever known. With a beautiful figure, dark ringlets fell over her shoulders as naturally as water slipped from a cliff. Bright blue eyes sparkled with mischief in her olive skin.

"Yes, I know," she answered. "Doesn't mean I didn't miss you."

DEAD AND BURYD

Patting Georgianna's knee affectionately, Liliah collected up one of the packets in her lap. She shook the paper gently to smooth out the mound of lilac powder, and began folding the paper around it in quick, intricate motions.

"You worried me for a second there," Georgianna scolded.

"You? Worry? Like that's even possible."

Georgianna let out a breath of laughter as she reached out and carefully picked up one of the papers. Copying Liliah's motion, she shook the paper, grimacing when a small sprinkling slipped over the edge and dusted her dress. She quickly tipped it the other way a little, gathering the powder in the centre of the paper and began folding it carefully, without any of the skill or speed at which Liliah's hands worked.

"I was with my family."

"Oh, so you weren't with…"

Georgianna narrowed her eyes as she looked back at Liliah. The brunette had a keen ear for gossip. Georgianna often had no idea where she'd heard it.

"Was I with who?" Georgianna asked suspiciously.

Liliah bent the last fold in the paper, tucking the pointed corner under one of the other edges. She leaned forward a little, glancing both ways past Georgianna. Georgianna followed her gaze, wondering why she was being so secretive about it. Possibly her family didn't approve of the Belsa. It wouldn't be surprising. There were those who felt that things would go a lot more smoothly with the Adveni if people stopped fighting them.

"Keiran!"

"How do you kno…" Georgianna cut herself off a moment too late. She'd given herself away, and Liliah squeaked in happiness and wriggled where she sat, her corkscrew curls bouncing on her slim shoulders.

"I knew it," she trilled triumphantly, settling back against the wall again and collecting up another powder-covered paper.

Georgianna frowned and turned her own paper, making another fold.

"How do you know about that?"

Liliah quickly waved her hand dismissively, turning the paper around and around in her fingers.

"Oh, no matter about that, I just can't believe you didn't tell me!" Liliah lamented. "Nerrin and a Belsa, you are doing well, George!"

Georgianna glared at her as soon as the word Belsa slipped from the other girl's lips. They were safer out here than they would have been at the bar they worked in together in the Rion district, an area almost exclusively Adveni. Though that still didn't mean they were safe discussing the Belsa so openly, not when the Adveni paid good money for information. Some people were desperate enough to sell over lifelong friends.

"It's not serious," Georgianna assured her. "We're just…"

"Joining!" Liliah interrupted with a laugh. "In the way your parents don't approve of!"

Georgianna tried to look indignant at the suggestion,

but failed miserably.

"Yes, alright!"

Liliah looked like her head was going to explode from giddiness. Or maybe her smile would simply get too wide for her face and the top half of her head would fall off with a wet slap onto the warm ground.

"We're having fun, okay? It's not... It's not anything. He's still seeing other girls."

The chances of Liliah's head splitting into two promptly disappeared as her smile faltered and she looked at Georgianna in surprise and suspicion. Georgianna had known Liliah for a few years. The girl was about as traditional as they came. She had been with her partner Qiyan for almost five years and the only reason they hadn't joined was because... well, Georgianna wasn't sure of the reason, but she knew it was the plan, as Liliah had told her many times.

"Why do you let him?" Liliah asked finally.

Georgianna shrugged.

"Because, well, he's great and all, but... I dunno. I'm not ready to be all serious about it. I'd rather enjoy spending time with him when I can, than not see him at all because he chooses someone else."

"That is the most stupid thing I've ever heard!" Liliah exclaimed. "If I was you, I'd tell him to choose and choose fast! He can't be so selfish! Life's too short, George, you know that better than anyone!"

Georgianna stared as Liliah went back to her packets as if that was the end of the conversation, folding papers with rapid precision. She knew Liliah was traditional, but those were her own beliefs, not Georgianna's, and certainly not Keiran's. It actually hadn't really occurred to Georgianna until now that Liliah would know Keiran. They were both Nerrin, and Georgianna wondered whether perhaps she should have asked Liliah about him earlier. No. There was no point in asking because there was nothing she needed to know. She didn't need to know about Keiran's past because they were just having fun.

Having seen the effect that losing Nyah was having on Taye, and what losing Nequiel had done to her brother, Georgianna was more certain than ever that she wasn't ready to settle into a relationship. The pain Taye was feeling seemed unbearable, his desolation at being able to do nothing sending him into a frenzy. Georgianna hadn't stopped worrying about what Taye would do if something didn't change soon, and right now it wasn't something she wanted to open herself up to by trying to make things more serious with Keiran.

"Anyway," Georgianna breathed after a minute of awkward silence. "I was hoping to get some herbs from you. I used up my last batch."

Liliah's accommodating smile slid onto her lips as if the conversation had never happened. She placed the newly folded packet in amongst the open papers and grasped the edges of the hide, holding it taut and lifting it carefully from her lap. She got to her feet.

"What do you need?" she asked.

Georgianna held the half-folded packet in her lap,

chewing on her bottom lip and staring blankly at the dry earth.

"Same as last time, if you have it."

"Lijiam, Gwetua, and Goas, right?"

Thinking about it for a moment, Georgianna finally nodded.

"Yeah, I think that was it," she agreed. "Though, if you have more of the Gwetua, I use it quite a lot."

Liliah nodded and pushed open the door into the house, already taking a step inside before Georgianna looked up.

"Oh, if you have any unground, could you grab me some hyliha?"

Liliah looked at her curiously. Hyliha wasn't all that useful, not when you had better remedies.

"Lacie is practising."

She nodded and disappeared into the house. Georgianna watched two children at the house across from them playing, drawing symbols in the earth with sticks. Folding the paper absently, trapping the powder within the folds, Georgianna smiled. She supposed it might be nice, being settled. Not until she was older, and not while things were so dangerous, but maybe someday.

"I don't have much Goas," Liliah said, appearing at her side. "But Qiyan is out hunting today and he usually brings me back things, so can I bring some in a few days?"

Dropping the packet she'd been folding down with the rest, Georgianna nodded gratefully as she opened her bag and tugged out a small leather purse. Pulling open the strings, she tipped out the coins and counted them out, swapping them with Liliah for the packets of herbs, one much larger than the rest, the hyliha.

"Whenever is fine," she agreed.

Settling down into her position against the wall, Liliah lifted the hide and draped it across her legs again, careful not to spill any of the loose powder. Georgianna stashed the packets into a pocket in her bag so that they wouldn't pierce and spill herbs through her supplies.

"I'll catch up with you later," she said. "Got to see if anyone needs anything before I head back into the city."

"Stay safe, George," Liliah said.

Georgianna nodded. Liliah waved Georgianna off before returning to her packets of herb powders, leaving Georgianna to wander through the camps, checking to see if anyone needed any treatment as she made her way back into the city.

9   Deal on Delivery

The overnight shift in Medics' Way had been quiet, which Georgianna had been grateful for. After spending the day out in the camps, and the evening serving drinks at Crisco, Georgianna had been exhausted. Being a medic had been her dream since she was a child, but after the arrival of the Adveni, it had not been enough to live on. While the Veniche often dealt in trade, the Adveni system revolved around money, and not many Veniche had enough money to afford medical treatment when they most needed it.

    She had taken the bar job during the freeze a few years before. After a large number of Veniche had moved south to escape the worst of the blizzards, there had not been enough people for Georgianna to make her way in trade. Greunn, the owner of the bar, had been sceptical at first, but settled on giving her a shot, believing that her pretty face (for a Veniche, anyway) would help sell his drinks. She hadn't been sure how she felt about being looked on in that way by Adveni, but had decided that as long as they kept their hands to themselves, she could deal with their eyes and lewd comments well enough.

Georgianna took over from Keinah in the early morning hours. Keinah was huge, her stomach swollen with the coming birth of her second child. She didn't take many shifts on the Way anymore because the child could arrive any day, but she'd explained that Jaid had been getting increasingly frantic as, after three days' missing, they had still been unable to locate her husband, Si. While Georgianna had wanted to ask more, it was clear that Keinah was desperate for some sleep, so she'd let her go.

Jaid showed up mid-morning, looking like she had not slept a wink in days. Georgianna asked her about Si, but with no news on her missing husband, the older woman didn't seem up to talking about it. While packing her things into her bag, Georgianna offered to stay, though Jaid would hear none of it. There were a couple of Belsa out looking for Si, and Jaid wanted to ensure that she was in a place where people knew how to find her if he showed up.

Unfortunately, Georgianna partly knew how Jaid felt. While she'd never had a husband go missing, the days before they discovered her mother's fate had been much the same. There was nothing to do but to keep looking and hoping. Her father had been unwilling to accept that anything had happened to his beloved wife, and so it had been

DEAD AND BURYD

Georgianna, eighteen years old at the time, who went to the Adveni registration buildings after the fifth day.

She'd been killed in a fight in the Oprust district, among Veniche fighting to keep their trade lands. She'd not been involved. Georgianna knew her mother didn't have a fighting bone in her body, but she'd been killed none the less, caught by an Adveni Agrah's stray bullet. Her body had been disposed of before Georgianna made the trip to the registration buildings, so nothing was left but the possessions she'd had on her. There were a few dresses, finished for trade, a bag filled with cloth for new designs, and her joining ring, slipped from her cold finger. Georgianna still had that ring, buried in the trunk at their family home, but she didn't dare put it on for fear of losing it.

However, a mother lost almost a decade before would hold no comfort for Jaid, so Georgianna slipped away, heading out of the Way and south through the tunnels to the Carae. From the things her brother had told her about Nequiel's last days, to Jaid's current desolation over her lost husband, Georgianna knew that she had to tell Taye her decision sooner rather than later.

Taye had managed to secure himself a spot deep in the Carae tunnels, furthest away from the main lines. There weren't many of the old tunnel cars down this way since most of the tunnels were far too narrow to have held them. Instead, members of the Carae used whatever they could salvage and scavenge to create their homes, much like Keiran had done for his shack in Belsa territory.

Taye had built a place for himself and Nyah at the end of

a narrow tunnel, using the walls of the tunnel and attaching heavy sacking across the front. Georgianna let out a whistle as she neared the entrance to Taye's home, covering her eyes in mock worry as she pulled the canvas to the side, making a show of groping along the wall. Taye groaned out a laugh, and Georgianna could hear him moving on a mattress. Peeking through her fingers, she let out a sigh of relief to see that he was, thankfully, fully dressed.

"Nothing you haven't seen before, Gianna," Taye said, shifting the lamp from its precarious stance on the mattress and onto the floor.

"We were nine!" Georgianna exclaimed, shaking her head.

Stepping further in and letting the canvas fall back into place behind her, Georgianna stood in the centre of the makeshift room, ignoring Taye's laughter as she clutched her bag in front of her, her fingers absently tracing the medic symbol stitched into the front.

Taye looked up at her, his smile faltering. He let out a sigh and looked away from her.

"You won't do it, will you?" he asked.

"I will."

It took a moment for the words to sink in, and Georgianna wondered if Taye had been preparing himself for the worst since he'd asked her about it. He stared at her, but once he grasped her answer properly, he leapt up, gathering Georgianna in a tight hug that lifted her off her feet.

"Alright, alright," Georgianna complained, batting her hands against his shoulders.

Taye set her back down. He had one of the biggest smiles Georgianna had seen on her friend in a long time.

"Really?"

Georgianna nodded. She couldn't deny him this, not when she knew how much it would mean.

"I can't promise when it will be, Taye. I go as often as I can, but with the Way, and Crisco, it's mainly when they send me an alert."

Taye waved his hand. It was clear he wasn't worried about when the packet would be delivered, just that it would be.

"It is small, right?" Georgianna asked.

"Yes, I promise, you'll have no problems, I'm sure of it," Taye said, grasping her shoulders.

As he released her and turned away, a small shudder of happiness ran visibly through him. Kneeling on the edge of the mattress, he leaned over and dug his hand in behind it, finally tugging out a cloth bag, seemingly from inside the stuffing. Opening the bag in his lap, he searched through it, pulling out a paper packet.

He was right: it was small, no bigger than one of the packets of herbs Liliah had given her. Should she want to, she could keep it in her bag with the herb packets. From the look of it, there would be no difference to the Adveni. It would only be if they chose to open each packet to check the contents that she would have a problem.

Taye held it up, letting Georgianna take it and tuck it away while he pulled some coins out and closed up the cloth bag, stuffing it back into the hiding space.

Pushing himself to his feet, he picked up the oil lamp and snuffed it out, plunging them into darkness.

"Come on," he said cheerfully, tugging back the canvas. "I'm going to buy you lunch."

* * *

Nothing had been able to put Taye out of his good mood, not even when a customer had cornered him at the Trade Inn and accused him of cutting his smoking leaves with something else. Taye remained resolutely calm, explaining that he would exchange the foinah leaves for another batch if the man wanted. Georgianna had traded with Taye on many occasions, but it wasn't often that she saw other deals. Taye was very careful about this, which was probably why he'd stayed under the Adveni radar for so long. His father hadn't been happy about Taye's decision to join the Carae. Taye had two younger brothers who he didn't want being dragged into it, but despite his father's refusal to see him, Georgianna knew that Taye passed money to them through his uncle whenever he could.

Having slipped back into the tunnels as the sun set, the two parted ways, Taye returning to the Carae to collect supplies, Georgianna to Medic's Way. It wasn't her turn for a shift, but with Jaid so worried about Si, she decided that if she could take a shift, she would. Jaid was grateful, and immediately set off to continue her search for her husband.

Things in the Way were quiet. Jacob, the escaped drysta, had been given a book by Lacie, and while he barely spoke when Lacie wasn't around, he was surprisingly comforting company on a long shift.

Georgianna had been dozing when Keinah showed up. Apparently her baby had been kicking so ferociously that sleep was not an option. Georgianna had squeaked in excitement when Keinah let her feel the spot where tiny feet pressed through the skin, and had finally agreed to leave Keinah on the Way.

The shack was quiet and dark when Georgianna got there, pulling the tarpaulin aside. It took a moment for her eyes to adjust to the dark, but seeing that Keiran was alone, she stepped further in, sitting on the edge of the bed and leaning over him.

Placing a gentle kiss against his bare shoulder, Georgianna smiled as Keiran rolled onto his back, cracking one eye open to look up at her.

"Hey," he murmured, reaching up and rubbing the heel of his hand into his eyes.

"Hi," Georgianna whispered. "Mind if I stay with you?"

Keiran smiled sleepily and shook his head, groping out until he found the edge of the blanket, flinging it back. Georgianna undressed quickly, clambering over him and settling down on the mattress.

"Good day?" he asked.

"Kind of. I saw Taye."

Tugging the blanket over her, Georgianna wriggled her body into Keiran's warm skin. He slid his arm underneath her body, tugging her in against him.

"Did you make a decision?"

Georgianna nodded against his shoulder, her fingers skating absently across his stomach.

"I'm going to take the delivery to Nyah."

A burst of low laughter rumbled through him, tensing Keiran's stomach beneath her fingers before he rolled towards her, wrapping his other arm around her waist.

"Of course you are," he answered. "I'm just surprised it took you this long."

Georgianna frowned at his mockery, but it was nice that he'd known which decision she would make. Yes, he teased her for being so predictable, but half the time, she didn't think he was actually listening to her, seeming more interested in getting her clothes off. To know that he did sometimes pay attention and care about what she was saying felt reassuring.

She would have said something about it, but before she had even opened her mouth, he let out deep snore. Too late.

* * *

A hand thumped on the side of the metal shack, rousing Georgianna from sleep. With a moan of protest, she stretched her body out, toes just peeking from underneath the blankets draped across her legs, flung away from her body in the stuffy heat. Even through her shifting dreams, she didn't feel like she'd been asleep long.

Sleep claimed her once again as she relaxed back into the mattress, nuzzling her cheek against Keiran's neck and the warmth of his skin. She was just slipping back off when two more blows sounded.

"Hey, come on, get up. Keiran, I know you're in there!"

Georgianna answered the man outside with an unintelligible grumble and a smack of her hand against Keiran's stomach. It was his shack.

Opening one eye as Keiran let out a pained breath at her attack and swore quietly, Georgianna glanced through the shadows, trying to gauge the time. It was impossible. This far away from the main encampment, they didn't always have the lights lit, plunging them into a perpetual gloom.

"What is it?" Keiran grumbled, not even lifting his head from the pillow.

There was a static rustle of the tarpaulin being pulled back and Wrench stepped in. It wasn't unusual at this time of year for blankets and sheets to be abandoned in the middle of the night, kicked and flung away from the skin as sleeping inhabitants tried desperately to find a little relief from the overbearing heat. As Georgianna's gaze met Wrench's, she shifted to shield the most intimate parts of her body from view while she reached out, groping around her hips for a handful of blanket, tugging it further up her body.

Wrench glanced down to the blanket before he had the decency to turn his head and stare at the wall. His manners, however, did not stretch far enough to conceal the grin that told Georgianna exactly how much he had seen. A blush burned through her cheeks though she couldn't hide an embarrassed smile as she buried her face into Keiran's neck.

"Good night?" Wrench asked.

"Wrench, stop standing there like a horny virgin,"

Unlike Georgianna, he made no effort to cover himself up. Wrench and Keiran had known each other for long enough to have seen it all before.

"What do you want?"

Wrench glanced towards them before averting his gaze again, nodding his head sideways in Georgianna's direction.

"Came to get you, Med," Wrench said.

"Me?"

"Got a situation down the Way."

While it wasn't the first time someone had burst in on them early in the morning, it was certainly the first time the person coming in had not been looking for Keiran. Generally, people didn't know that she stayed there, so anyone coming to the shack was looking for the Belsa sergeant. Yet Wrench was aware of her fondness for the man lying next to her, so he would have known where to look. The other medics knew about her home in the camps with her family, but that was a two-hour walk—too far to travel in an emergency. It was much easier to find Jaid or Keinah who lived with their partners in the nearby tunnels.

"What's going on?" she asked.

She sat up, holding the blankets against her chest as she carefully manoeuvred herself over Keiran, who groaned as her elbow hit his stomach.

"Found Si," Wrench explained, giving her a hard look.

Georgianna pursed her lips into a frown.

"And?" she urged, glancing up at Wrench.

"Not entirely sure, he's rambling something bad," Wrench explained. "But from what Jaid says, he's been gone more than three days, and from the looks o' the burns, he's been out in the sun for most of it."

"Shit," Keiran groaned, pushing himself up onto his elbows.

Georgianna echoed Keiran's moan as she waved her hand towards Wrench. He was shifting his weight anxiously back and forth, but quickly turned his back as Georgianna began reaching for her clothes.

Someone who had been out in the sun more than a few hours without proper protection would most likely be suffering in some way or another, but three days was sure to have caused lasting damage.

"Who's down there?" she asked.

"Just Jaid at the moment. I was on guard down the black line and she was bringing him past, asked me to get you and meet her there."

"I thought Keinah was…"

"Jaid sent her off," Wrench interrupted. "Didn't want her close if he gets upset."

"If Si's been out there that long, we might need to restrain him," she agreed.

Behind her, Keiran was moving about, wrestling his way into his trousers. Georgianna threw his shirt over her shoulder.

"What was he doing out there for three days?" he asked.

"Don't really know," Wrench answered. "Most of the stuff coming out of him as she took him down there was nonsense. Jaid said he'd gone over the Adveni quarters on a regular job, but never came back. Figuring something happened over that way."

"Why would he be in the Adveni quarters? What kind of job takes a Belsa over there?" Georgianna asked. "Seems a bit of a dangerous place to send one of you guys."

"You'd have to ask whoever gave him the job," Keiran said quickly, getting to his feet and stepping past her, reaching for the tyllenich rifle. "Lots of jobs go down without the rest of us knowing, best way to stay safe if someone's caught."

Georgianna nodded. That made a good deal of sense. She got to her feet and grabbed up her bag, slinging the strap over her shoulder.

"Come on then, let's go," Keiran nodded.

Wrench pushed back the tarpaulin, waiting somewhat impatiently until Georgianna had slipped out of the shack. The two Belsa followed in her wake.

10 Taking Them Down

They hadn't even made the turning onto the Way when the first scream came echoing down the tunnel. Glancing at Keiran and Wrench, Georgianna broke into a run, holding her bag tight against her hip. Behind her, Wrench and Keiran's boots pounded into the tunnel floor. Another female cry was followed by an angry shout.

Skidding to a stop outside the first car, Georgianna launched herself inside, falling forward in her haste. But the sight that met her stopped her in her tracks.

Jaid sat on one of the makeshift beds, her back braced against the wall as her husband Si leaned over her. Her arms were stretched out, hands pressed against her husband Si's chest, but this wasn't enough to stop the knife that was being pressed against her throat. She was shaking her head, words streaming so fast from her lips that they were almost unintelligible. Si, however, obviously understood what she had been trying to say as he shook his head, his long, ratted hair slapping against his reddened, raw skin.

"You're lying!" Si growled.

"I'm not, I'm not!" Jaid cried, tears streaming down her face. "You're my husband, Si. I love you. I would never sell you out to them!"

Wrench pushed past to grab Si. Turning his head, Si's eyes widened in fury as he pointed the knife at Wrench for a moment before returning it to his wife's throat.

"Stay back!" he screamed. "I'll do it, I will!"

Georgianna grabbed Wrench's muscled arm with both hands, yanking him backwards with all her might. Wrench stumbled back into Keiran who braced him, both hands on his shoulders.

"George," he murmured, glancing between Georgianna and Si.

Georgianna could guess what Keiran was thinking. It wouldn't be too difficult for the two of them to restrain the Belsa. The risk was whether they could do it before Si slashed at Jaid's throat, one Georgianna wasn't willing to take. Even if Si didn't do any lasting damage, he would never forgive himself for hurting Jaid in a moment of madness.

Georgianna shook her head. She slowly reached up, lifting her bag over her head and lowering it to the floor. She kept her gaze locked on Si's panicked, bloodshot eyes.

"Si," she whispered.

Jaid gasped at the pressure of the knife against her skin. A drop of red blood slipped smoothly down the metal blade and dripped into her lap.

"Si, look at me!" Georgianna said, a little louder this time. "Si, you don't want to hurt Jaid."

"Sold me out! Told them I'd be there," Si rattled, his gaze flicking around the car too fast for Georgianna to spot what he was focussing on.

Lifting her hands and keeping them open towards Si, Georgianna watched him as calmly as she could, trying to keep the panic and fear out of her face. She could feel her blood pulsing through her ears, but she shook her head.

"Why would she do that, Si?" she asked.

Glancing to the side, Georgianna waved Keiran and Wrench back again. The two men had been inching forward. Reassured that they were staying put, Georgianna turned back to Si.

"Why, Si?" she asked again. "Jaid loves you, you know that. She wouldn't have done anything to harm you."

"You're lying! Someone told!" he cried desperately. "It was safe. We were safe and then..."

"And then what, Si? What happened?" Wrench asked, his voice gentler than Georgianna had ever heard it. "Tell us. Maybe we can help."

Si looked to Wrench, and for a moment the knife came away from Jaid's throat allowing her to gulp in large breaths until sobs overtook her, choking. He hesitated, the knife hovering an inch away from Jaid's neck as he watched Wrench suspiciously.

"No help," he muttered, shaking his head. "No help. No one to know."

"Si, you're hurt," Georgianna urged. "Let me help you. You'll feel so much better. Please, just… just give me the knife so I can help you."

Si's reaction was instant. He leapt back away from them, swiping the knife fruitlessly.

Keiran and Wrench didn't wait any longer. They surged forward past Georgianna, past Jaid, towards Si and the knife. As soon as they were past Jaid, Georgianna reached forward and tugged Jaid from the bed. Jaid let out a choking sob and buried her face against Georgianna's shoulder, holding herself tightly against her.

Si let out an angry scream, slashing the knife as Keiran and Wrench closed in. Keiran swore loudly, his hand coming to his arm as blood sprayed across the floor of the car. Georgianna choked back a cry and hugged Jaid all the tighter. Wrench and Keiran wrestled Si to the ground with a heavy thump, the knife clattering away underneath one of the beds.

It took another few minutes for Wrench and Keiran to secure Si, Wrench kneeling across Si's shins and Keiran pinning his arms above his head. Keiran was still bleeding, blood dribbling down his arm and soaking through his shirt from a slice near his elbow.

Georgianna let go of Jaid, handing her a cloth to wipe off her face as she placed a small dressing against the cut underneath her jaw. Jaid gave a weak smile and held the dressing in place for a moment before pulling it away to check how bad the injury was. From the look of it, it had stopped bleeding already; it would probably just sting for a day or so.

They didn't use the restraints often as there was rarely a need for them. Georgianna couldn't remember the last time she'd used them, though she knew exactly which box to open to find the long ropes. Jaid took one of them, helping Wrench to attach the cuffs around Si's ankles, tears sliding down her cheeks throughout. Keiran held Si's hands in place as Georgianna attached the cuffs around his wrists. Keiran let out a huff and rubbed the slash in his arm once he'd secured the ropes to the bed.

Grabbing up a larger dressing from one of the crates, Georgianna moved to Keiran, slipping the dressing through his cut shirt onto the wound and holding it in place with a bandage wrapped tightly around his arm. He might need a stitch or two, but she'd be able to look at it more closely once they'd calmed Si down and treated his burns.

"No!" Si screeched, tugging against his bonds. "No, Alec! Got to get Alec!"

Georgianna froze. Her fingers remained tangled in the bandage around Keiran's arm where she'd been trying to tuck the end underneath. Her gaze shot to meet Jaid's. Jaid looked back at her, confused. Georgianna looked away.

"What?"

"Get off me!"

Si pulled at the bonds, rocking his hips one way to the other in an attempt to throw Wrench off him. It was no use, the bonds holding him down were strong enough as it was without the fact Si had been out in the sun for three days, probably without much to eat or drink.

"Get Alec! He'll tell you! He'll tell you they sold me out!"

A pain tightened in her chest as she held back a dry sob. She'd fought so hard to forget, and now here Si was, bringing him up like he would walk through the door any minute.

Georgianna didn't know what to do. She knew that there was no chance of giving Si what he wanted. She returned to her bag, opening it up and taking out a couple of small cloth bags, opening each until she found the ones she needed. She took out a pale yellow pill and dropped the rest of the packets. Moving to stand next to Keiran, she looked down at Si.

"Si, I need to give you a pill. It's medicine, it'll help," she told him softly. "We'll sort your burns and I'll send these guys to get Alec for you, alright?"

Her voice cracked around his name.

Si looked at the pill in her hand and shook his head violently, his cheeks slapping against his arms. Keiran frowned at her for a moment, questions in his gaze that he didn't put voice to. He shook his head, moving forward and grasping Si's chin, prising his mouth open. Si's protests slipped into an unintelligible gurgle of sounds as he struggled against Keiran's hold.

Georgianna dropped the pill into Si's mouth and pinched his nose hard as Keiran let Si close his mouth, holding his hand over it until he saw the motion of swallowing move down Si's throat. Si began coughing, shaking his head again.

Grabbing up a cantina of water, Georgianna returned to Si, placing the spout near the man's lips.

"Water, Si," she said.

Si reluctantly accepted the water, gulping down a half-dozen mouthfuls before he began spluttering and Georgianna pulled the cantina back, screwing the lid in place. There was nothing to do but wait and sure enough, within minutes Si had begun to relax.

"You'll get Alec," he murmured. "Get Alec, he'll tell you."

Leaning over Si, Georgianna nodded.

"We will, Si. We'll get Alec. He'll be here."

She felt horrible lying to him, but she could see no other way out. Whatever had happened to Si, the sun had made him delusional. Maybe, for the moment, it was better to play on his delusions and keep him calm than to tell him the truth and risk his anger.

Georgianna checked that Jaid was okay before they set to work. She was definitely shaken, and Georgianna couldn't imagine the pain the other woman felt knowing that her husband believed her to have sold him out in some way, but Jaid was a hard worker, and quickly assured Georgianna that she was fine before setting about treating the burns on Si's arms.

"Jaid, do you know what happened?" Wrench asked, taking a seat on the bed opposite.

Jaid shook her head, glancing over towards Wrench for a moment before turning her attention back to her husband. She collected up some dressings and placed them next to her before grabbing a jar of pale blue powder and pouring a large amount into a clay bowl.

"Every ten days or so, Si goes off on some job the marshall gives him," she explained. "He won't tell me where it is or what he's doing, just that it's really important. The last time he came back, he said he had some great news and he had to tell the marshall straight away."

"What was it?" Keiran asked, looking up from where he'd been peeking underneath the dressing around his arm.

"He wouldn't say," Jaid answered. "He said it could change things, but he needed more time and information before he would know for sure."

"So, what changed?" Georgianna asked.

"I don't know. He went off that evening and everything seemed fine. When he wasn't back, I just assumed he had other jobs. Wrench and I went around to check for him when I got off shift in the morning when you showed up, George, but we couldn't find him. And then... that night Marshall Casey came down asking if I'd seen him, saying he hadn't shown up for his duties nor checked in with him."

Georgianna glanced at Wrench. He'd told Beck about Si not showing up. Had Beck known where Si was all along? Surely he would have known where to send people looking for him?

"When nobody had seen him, I began to panic. I found him in one of the northern tunnels, rambling to himself."

Jaid took the cantina Georgianna had used to give Si water and poured a small amount into the powder. Returning the cantina, she began stirring the mixture into a thick paste which would be used to take the heat from Si's burns.

"Saying?"

Georgianna glanced at Keiran. He was watching Jaid curiously but his gaze kept flickering to Si's face. Si wasn't one of the Belsa under Keiran's command, but Georgianna could only assume he was curious as to this special job and why he hadn't been told about it.

"Something about taking them down," Jaid answered, brushing the back of her hand across her eyes. "That taking them down would give us an opening."

"Take what down? The Adveni?" Wrench asked.

"I don't know, I don't think so, or at least it didn't sound like it. It sounded, the way he was muttering about it, like something that would help against the Adveni, a target to destroy."

"He didn't say anything else?"

Jaid frowned and shook her head.

"That was when he started claiming I sold him out. He was so angry I barely got him back to the Way."

"And Alec?" Wrench asked.

"Belsa," Keiran explained. "Alec Cartwright."

Wrench rubbed the back of his thick neck, glancing at Si.

Georgianna shook her head and stepped over to Jaid.

"It'll be okay. He'll be calmer when he wakes up," Georgianna assured her.

Jaid glanced at Georgianna, a sadness in her eyes that showed she already knew how much damage had been done. There were no medicines they knew of to reverse completely the effects that being left out in the mid-heat sun could have on a person.

"I know," Jaid whispered, putting down the bowl. Leaning down, she kissed her husband's forehead, her lips lingering against his raw skin.

"But he'll never be my Si again."

11 A Twisting of Wills

Georgianna had been right to some extent. After waking up from the sedative, with his burns treated and having got some relief, Si was much calmer than he had been before. However, he was still muttering to himself when Beck came down to the Way to check on how things were going.

"You mind giving me a moment?" he asked, glancing around at the different faces in the small car.

They trooped from the car, all except Keiran moving a dozen steps or so away from the opening. Keiran stayed next to the metal shell, his expression twisted in curiosity. Jaid shifted her weight anxiously back and forth between her feet, and when the marshall appeared at the opening, she was the first to leap forward toward the car. She didn't pause to speak to Beck as she pulled herself past him, vanishing inside.

"Anything?" Keiran asked.

Beck shook his head and jumped down.

"Nothing helpful," he answered. "Maybe after a couple of days, once he's settled, he'll be more forthcoming."

"So he stays here?"

Glancing into the car again, Beck nodded.

"I'll station someone at the end of the Way. With the other end blocked, there won't be anywhere for him to go."

Georgianna clambered into the car whilst Beck ushered Keiran and Wrench a little further down the tunnel.

Si kept on muttering about Alec, asking where his friend was, and Georgianna could only continue with the lie, telling Si that Alec was out on orders from Beck, but he'd be back soon.

She felt awful about it. Si was her colleague's husband, she didn't want to lie to him any more than she would have her own friends. While she knew that it was better to tell the truth, the truth would only hurt him. Georgianna had asked Jaid about it, but she'd agreed: until Si was better, they wouldn't tell him anything.

Georgianna had stitched the gash on Keiran's arm before bandaging it again. It hadn't been long before he and Wrench both had to get back on duty, leaving Jaid and Georgianna to watch over Si for the rest of the day. Georgianna knew she could have left, that Si would be more than safe in Jaid's capable and loving hands, but she didn't want to leave the woman alone, not when she knew there was a chance Jaid might need someone to talk to.

It was only when Lacie came down to the Way that Georgianna finally excused herself to head out. Lacie could keep Jaid company while the woman was unwilling to leave her husband, and Jaid would help Lacie if any emergencies came in.

Wandering through the Belsa territory, Georgianna made her way to the guard's sight, coming up slowly to find Keiran sitting against the wall, his Tyllenich rifle resting across his lap. He glanced up, giving her a tired grin.

"How's he doing?" he asked, shifting the rifle off to the side and patting the space next to him. Georgianna stepped over and pressed her back against the wall, sliding down to sit beside him.

"He's..."

Georgianna sighed. Bringing her knees up towards her chest, she turned to look at him, resting her temple on her arms. Si had been agitated after the marshall had spoken to him, not to mention that Jaid had been rather indignant at being asked to leave.

"He's still muttering, still thinks Alec will be down to see him any minute."

"You didn't tell him?"

"Couldn't," Georgianna explained. "The moment I even tried he got all freaked out, saying we'd sold him out. I had to change mid-sentence, telling him that Alec was on duty."

"Didn't know he even knew Cartwright," Keiran admitted.

"All Kahle. Alec and my brother were good friends,

back before all this."

"Shit."

Georgianna nodded.

Alec Cartwright had been another of those difficult disappearances. From what Georgianna knew, which was little, he'd been out on orders from Beck with another Belsa, Ashoke. The two of them had been scouting a building out and next thing anyone knew, Ashoke was dead and nobody saw Alec again. With a pass to get into the compound, Georgianna had kept an eye out for him, but with each trip, her heart sank and her guilt rose a little more. It looked more unlikely that any of them would see Alec Cartwright again. After a few weeks people stopped looking, his friends stopped expecting him to come back. Even his brother Landon gave up. Georgianna gave up on ever hearing his voice or seeing that look in his eyes when he believed she was being reckless. Alec Cartwright was dead. Now they just had to find a way to tell Si.

"Did you know him?"

Keiran's tongue swept out, wetting his bottom lip before he shook his head.

"Not really," he answered. "I mean, suns, it was two years ago. We may have had duties a couple times, but we weren't friends or anything."

Keiran was blunt, but Georgianna didn't blame him: deaths were common, especially among the Belsa. If Keiran let every one of them get to him, he'd probably never pull himself out of bed. Better to care about the people he was actually close to, she supposed.

"Look, I've been thinking."

Georgianna lifted her head and looked back at Keiran. He was staring at the wall opposite, his gaze occasionally flickering down the tunnel.

"What?"

He placed the rifle down next to him on the ground. Leaning forward, he rested his elbows against his knees, clasping his hands together.

"After Si and all," he said slowly, "are you sure you should be taking that delivery?"

Georgianna stared past him down the tunnel, not sure what she was supposed to say. She'd agreed to take the packet into the compound for Taye and when she'd told Keiran, he hadn't said it was a bad idea. If anything, he'd been amused that it had taken her so long to say yes, as if it was clear that this was the only option she would choose.

"I don't…"

"Si was almost caught doing something, George," Keiran interrupted. "He had to hide out for three days. If you get caught, you'll already be in the compound. It'll be a short trip."

"I promised, Keiran."

"I know, but he'd have to understand. Things change."

"Not for him."

Keiran let out a frustrated huff, wringing his hands tighter together. Georgianna was at a loss, she'd never seen Keiran worried, not about something personal. He had always been so carefree and charming, almost cocky even.

"It's only small," Georgianna assured him. "I can hide it

under my clothes, it'll be nothing."

She let out a breath, leaning towards him. Resting her elbow on his shoulder, she gave him a bright smile.

"It's adorable that you worry," she murmured.

Keiran glanced at her and rolled his eyes.

"Yeah, tell me that when we're sneaking stuff in to you."

"Better make it alcohol when it's me," Georgianna teased. "This thing is tiny. No way there is actually more than a note inside telling Nyah that he loves her."

Keiran's eyes narrowed as he looked back at her. He sat up straight, and Georgianna's arm slipped from his shoulder as he turned to face her a little better.

"Why don't you just open it and memorise the note?"

"I can't do that."

"Why not? It'd be safer."

Crossing her arms over her chest, Georgianna frowned back at him. The Adveni couldn't read minds, she didn't think even they had a machine for that. Still, the idea of reading a personal message from Taye made her feel dirty.

"It's not mine. I can't open and read Taye's private words to her. It wouldn't be the same."

"Seriously?"

Georgianna shook her head, her nose wrinkled in disgust.

"Fine," she argued. "What if it's dirty?"

Keiran's grin slid easily across his lips. In a single moment, all the worry and argument had melted away, replaced with a dirty smirk and a suggestive glance.

"Well, then you bring it to me and I'll read it," he answered, waggling his eyebrows.

Georgianna reached out and smacked him. If he thought she was letting him read Taye's dirty messages to Nyah, he was going to be sadly mistaken. At her attack, Keiran laughed, grasping her wrist before she could pull away.

"Then again, I'm sure I could come up with much filthier things," he wagered.

Pulling back in an attempt to free her wrist from his grasp, Georgianna rolled her eyes. Keiran's grip tightened a little and he tugged her closer. Shifting her weight against the hard ground sent a spasm of pain through her leg, but as he grinned as her, she couldn't bring herself to pull away.

"I'm sure you could."

"Come over tonight, I'll prove it."

Georgianna frowned.

"I have work."

"After?"

"Will you still be awake? You passed out pretty quick last night."

Keiran nodded as he leaned in, settling a soft kiss against her lips.

"Promise," he mumbled.

"Alright," Georgianna agreed. "But if you're sleeping, I'm throwing cold water on you."

His laughter washed over her skin, sending an excited tremble through her. Giving him one last, lingering kiss, she pushed herself to her feet, freeing herself from Keiran's grasp.

The way Keiran could turn the tables on her so quickly was unsettling. She was sure that he knew how quickly he could twist her around to his way of thinking, especially when it meant being close to him. She enjoyed his company and never found herself getting bored, even when they disagreed.

As she stepped over his legs, Keiran reached up and caught her wrist.

"Think about it, alright, George?" he asked. "The note?"

Her mind was already made up. Georgianna knew that she couldn't back down from her promise now, especially not after Taye had been so happy that she'd said yes. Though, the way Keiran's gaze searched her face so earnestly, all trace of the dirty humour and the promise of pleasure gone from his eyes, she found her resolve faltering. Gulping back the rising lump in her throat, she nodded, and walked away before he could twist her further to his will.

12 A Promise Sold

It was a week before Georgianna was scheduled to visit the compound again, and no new emergencies came through to her tsentyl. Each day leading up to the regular visit, she could feel her stomach fall a little further, her heart rise a little higher in her chest. She didn't tell anyone that she was getting worried that this would go wrong, that maybe this time she'd be caught. Each time she'd passed things into the compound before it had been messages, lines she could remember by heart from loved ones of those who had been buryd. She didn't want to admit that maybe Keiran had been right, that she was risking too much for Taye. Though each time she thought about leaving the package behind, Taye's face appeared behind her closed eyelids with the knowledge that his fear for Nyah would lead him to do something far more stupid than try to slip an innocent package into the compound.

Georgianna hadn't opened the packet Taye had given her over a week before. Even as she walked the tunnel to the east, the slim, flat packet stuck to the underside of her breast, she didn't dare look to see what was inside. She couldn't betray Taye by looking at something that was obviously so personal and important that he could no longer keep it in his possession. Georgianna wanted to convince herself that the packet was nothing but a message of love, a promise of continued devotion, but there was something that fell from side to side when she tipped it that stopped her from believing this.

Despite the object being slim and light enough to conceal beneath her shirt, with each step Georgianna became more aware of its presence against her skin. The closer she came to leaving the eastern tunnel, the heavier and more obvious it felt. She stopped twice within the tunnel, and once again on the steps leading out onto the path, slipping her hand up beneath her shirt to ensure that the glue paste was holding it securely to her skin. There could be no leaving it behind so close to the compound. Even if she could have peeled it from her skin, she had nowhere to put the packet that the Adveni guards would not find.

As she was admitted through the gates of the compound, Georgianna's heart fixed itself in her throat, making it hard to speak even as the guard asked her simple questions. It was Edtroka again, his deep eyes continually suspicious under his dark cropped hair. Georgianna followed him inside and emptied her bag like every other trip, trying to make easy conversation with the man though she had to think carefully about every word.

When his hands found her body, smoothing his palms over her skin through her clothes, checking for hidden weapons or items, Georgianna could barely breathe, sure that Edtroka would feel her heart pounding through her chest or one of the sharp corners of the paper packet. It was only once he deemed that she was safe to go in that Georgianna finally let out a relieved breath.

The walk through the corridor to the block seemed to take forever, and when the door of the block finally slid closed behind her, Georgianna's eyes instantly began scanning through the masses for that familiar face she needed to see.

Men came up to her for help, an infection here, a cut that needed stitches there, and with each patient, Georgianna wished that Nyah would come to her. She'd not seen the blonde, and like the trip over to the compound, each passing minute was making her anxiety to find Nyah that much worse.

She only had a couple of hours. Two hours to see whoever she could get to before she was expected to leave again. Time was ticking away and Georgianna's hands were slowly becoming unsteady as she searched desperately for her friend's girl.

Still, Nyah did not show her face.

Her tsentyl beeped, a warning that she only had a few minutes before she was expected to be by the door.

Grabbing a slim, tall man by the arm as he passed, Georgianna looked at him desperately.

"Where's Nyah?" she asked.

The man stared back at her blankly.

"Nyah!" Georgianna repeated quickly. "She's short, maybe twenty-two? Blonde hair, pretty, in here for an attack on an Adveni!"

"Oh," the man replied, lifting his head in acknowledgement. "She was taken, maybe two days ago."

Georgianna stared at the man, her eyes wide as her frantic mind tried to figure out if Taye had been right that her punishment would not be permanent, if Nyah had really been freed for her crime.

"She was freed?" she demanded, she still holding his elbow.

The man let out a rough laugh and shook his head. He stuffed one grimy hand into his pocket, seemingly uncaring that Georgianna still had a hold of his arm. He dragged the other hand through a mess of long, matted hair.

"Nope," he answered. "Sold. Fetched a hefty price too from what I hear."

Georgianna's mouth dropped open and for a moment, there was nothing she could do but stare at the man in shock. She couldn't see how Nyah would have been sold. She had been in the compound for months, there was no reason they would have sold her so suddenly.

"Oi! Medic!"

The authoritative voice rang clearly across the block and all around, men and women alike hurried back towards their cells, away from Georgianna. Even the man she'd been holding on to wrenched his arm from her grasp and rushed back to a barred cell.

Georgianna, still stunned, turned her head to see the guard, Edtroka, standing in the block doorway, looking annoyed. Running with small, uncertain steps, Georgianna glanced desperately around the block, hoping for some proof that what the man had said wasn't true. Hoping she would see Nyah up on one of the balconies, or peeking her head out of a cell.

There was nothing, only a sea of curious faces who watched as Georgianna gathered up her bag and returned to the block door.

"I'm sorry," she mumbled to Edtroka, slipping past him and out into the corridor.

"You should be more careful with your time, Med!" Edtroka warned her as he returned her to the table.

As Edtroka rechecked her bag and felt his way across her body to ensure that she wasn't sneaking items out of the compound, Georgianna's heart once again rose into her throat. She didn't breathe in, though her body screamed for oxygen, terrified that a single breath would give away the packet beneath her shirt. Edtroka found nothing. She followed him mutely as she was escorted out of the compound and down to the gates, and was left to return to the city in the burning sun. So distracted was Georgianna that she almost walked straight past the tunnel entrance before she remembered to turn and go inside.

Once in the tunnel's dark shade, she took a seat on the

bottom step, leaning forward and resting her head in her hands. She let out a wracked sob, pushing all the air from her body, letting relief flood in and fill the spaces left behind. Blood thudded through her ears, pulsing past her temples under trembling fingers.

She had said that it would be alright. She had promised herself that there would be little risk. It was only as she'd been standing there, watching Edtroka search her bag, feeling his sweeping check over her hips and down the small of her back, that she realised just how close she had come. One wrong rustle of material, and she would have been walking back into the block. One sharp edge of the packet, and she would never see her family again. One wrong word, and she would be sold as a drysta... Just like Nyah.

There was no way she couldn't tell Taye what she knew, that Nyah was out of the compound, but sold as a drysta to an Adveni. There was no way she would be able to lie and tell him that Nyah loved the packet and sent back promises of continuing love. If she told him those things, Taye would still believe that Nyah would one day be released. He would ask Georgianna to keep checking on Nyah and her growing guilt would stop her ever wanting to see her friend.

Georgianna blinked. In the shock, she'd completely forgotten about the packet glued to her body. Reaching under her shirt, Georgianna tugged the packet from the underside of her breast, hissing as the paste pulled painfully on her skin.

With the packet in her fingers, Georgianna wondered if she should return it to Taye untouched. Whether she should leave it closed so that he could keep his privacy with Nyah. However, curiosity got the better of her, and sadness at Nyah's situation made her unwilling to fight the urge. She carefully opened up the packet and tipped the contents gently out into her hand.

It was less than she thought had been inside, but the single item unfortunately meant that much more. In her hand, a perfectly woven grass joining ring lay against her palm. Yellow from the sun and being disconnected from the earth, the grass had grown delicate and brittle. Georgianna could only wonder how long Taye had kept the ring in his possession, hoping for Nyah's return to him. The grass ring was only symbolic, used for the ceremony. Afterward it would be replaced with one made of silver. The grass was used to show that everything, all natural elements from the grass to the sky, would know of their joining. It was an old tradition, one that had mostly gone out of fashion since the Adveni had arrived, but the meaning was clear just the same.

As Georgianna turned the ring over in her fingers, she looked at the other item that had been in the packet. On a small, torn piece of paper, in Taye's almost illegible handwriting, he'd scrawled a Kahle promise.

I love you above all others.
Under sun and moon, you will be the only one.
My ship to carry my heart
I join myself to you for now and ever more.

Georgianna remembered the promise word for word, even before she'd finished reading the first line. It had been used in every ceremony she had ever attended, including that of her brother to Nequiel. In the darkness of the tunnel, alone and holding a joining ring that did not belong to her, a ring that might never be placed on the finger of the person it was intended for, and thinking of all the rings that now lay cold on lost partners' hands, Georgianna wanted to cry.

* * *

She was unsure how long she sat on the steps leading down into the east tunnel, but when a group of five Adveni came down the steps behind her, Georgianna leapt to her feet to get out of their way, keeping the grass ring and the paper slip concealed tight in her fist.

Marching amongst the Adveni men, Edtroka looked at her with an odd expression. Cold and calculating, in the moment his gaze met hers through the shadows, Georgianna feared that he knew exactly why she had been sitting on the steps. Stepping a little further away, but unable to break the guard's gaze, Georgianna watched him until he finally turned away, making a crack in Advtenis that had the other men laughing.

They barely looked back as they disappeared down the tunnel, and though Georgianna knew most of them would barely think to check for her presence behind them, she waited a full ten minutes before she made her own way back into the city.

When she came to the place where the eastern tunnel intersected with the main line, Georgianna paused. She wasn't sure what to do, whether to head south and find Taye to tell him what she knew about Nyah, or to go north and seek council from Beck or one of the other Belsa. In her heart, she knew that Taye deserved to know the truth as soon as possible, but the fear that he would try to do something was now stronger than ever. She knew that if Taye decided to try to free Nyah, there would be no words that could put him off finding out who had bought her.

Georgianna wondered if it might have been easier if Nyah was gone, if they'd never known what had happened to her. There wouldn't be a chance of freeing her and Taye would have been able to move through his grief, like her father had done, like her brother had. Georgianna knew that the chance of merely seeing Nyah again was enough to fuel him, and there would be nothing she could do to stop it.

Unable to stand at the intersection all day deciding what to do, Georgianna made her turning and began a slow progression through the throngs of people.

The man standing guard was nobody Georgianna knew, and she was submitted to a search and a call-in before she was allowed passage. In the Belsa tunnels, her footsteps slowed the closer she came. Having lost friends, lost her mother; she knew the pain of not knowing what had happened to them and the devastation when the truth was revealed. It was torture, one that Taye would now feel sooner than Georgianna would ever have wanted for him.

13 Guilt in Hiding

Georgianna walked through the Belsa encampment, merely nodding to those who greeted her. She paused at the tunnel turning that led to Beck's car, but while she knew the marshall would know what to do, Georgianna continued on without making the turn. She didn't know what she would say to Taye, let alone explaining the situation to the head of the Belsa, a man who hadn't known Taye or Nyah since their childhood within the Kahle. From the turning, her feet moved automatically through the tunnels, leading her onward until she reached the familiar canvas opening of Keiran's shack.

She smacked her hand on the metal a few times and waited for a reply, but when none came, she frowned. She'd not thought about the chance that Keiran might not be available, that he may have had Belsa duty, or errands of his own. Tugging the canvas back, Georgianna lowered her head to look through. The lamp wasn't lit, the shadows broken only by the low light that filtered through the gap she had opened up.

Slipping through the opening, Georgianna placed her bag down in the corner. Taking the grass joining ring and paper from her pocket, Georgianna looked down at them for a few moments before sighing. She tucked the ring and slip of paper back into the paper packet, carefully closing it and slipping it into one of the small pockets on the side of her bag. She stood for a moment, staring at the bag and the hole the ring was trying to burn through it into her mind.

Georgianna sighed and slipped off her boots, before climbing onto the bed and burying her face into the pillow. It smelled like Keiran, the soft clean smell of his hair, what little he hadn't cut off. Curling her arms around the pillow, Georgianna stared at the darkness until she fell asleep.

The soft pressure of a hand in the small of her back, the gentle caress of lips against her cheek weren't quite enough to rouse her from sleep. In her dreams, a butterfly found in the midst of the wash beat its wings against her cheek as it fluttered around her head. Georgianna turned to look for it, but was surprised with the sight of a southern coyote making its way towards her on all fours.

"George," it whispered, its lips bared just enough for the sound to hiss past bared teeth.

It sounded too soft for the yote, and the curious way it looked at her was puzzling. In fact, as the yote held her gaze, Georgianna had to glance behind her to make sure there wasn't something far more tempting that the animal was looking for.

"George, come on."

Georgianna turned away from the yote, about to start running when the voice slipped through her dream again, rousing her a little more. The butterfly was back, its wings against her temple now, and as Georgianna's eyes fluttered at the feeling, the butterfly was gone, replaced with the soft flickering of lamplight on an upturned crate in the shack.

Keiran sat on the side of the bed, his body bent low over her, lips right where the butterfly had beaten its wings. Georgianna reached up and rubbed the heel of her hand into her eyes.

"Hi," she murmured, rolling a little further onto her side and looking sleepily up at him.

"Hi yourself."

"Sorry," Georgianna muttered. "I must've..."

"Hey, don't apologise to me. Not every day I come back from orders to find a beautiful girl in my bed."

Leaning closer to her, Keiran's lips travelled in a series of kisses across her skin, finally pressing with soft pressure against the corner of Georgianna's lips. She turned her head, capturing him in a gentle kiss as he used his thumb to push a lock of tangled hair from her cheek. Opening her eyes, Georgianna fixed her brown-eyed gaze onto Keiran's blue and reached up, trailing a single finger along his jaw and grinning a soft smile up at him.

"Really? You should tell those other girls to step up their

game then, they're making it far too difficult for you."

"Damn right." Keiran chuckled and sat up. "You could give them lessons."

Georgianna rolled onto her back and slowly pushed herself up from the mattress, drawing her knees up towards her and leaning over them, rubbing her hands across her eyes again.

"What time is it?" she asked.

"Late," he answered. "Wrench was late showing up, said he had errands."

She nodded slowly, the memory of why she'd come here in the first place coming back to her like the first streams of the wash.

"Not that I mind, but why are you camped out in my bed?" Keiran asked.

"I…"

Frowning, she covered her face with her hands and flopped backwards onto the mattress again. "I went to the compound," she admitted through the gap between her hands.

He remained silent for a minute, and though she could feel him moving around, she didn't move her hands from her face. As the pressure from the spot next to her on the bed disappeared, Georgianna finally spread her fingers and glanced at him.

Tugging his shirt over his head, Keiran threw it down into the corner and kicked off his boots before returning.

"If you tell me the sight of mangy inmates made you think of me, I might kick you out."

He slipped down onto the bed, turning onto his side and lying so close that her arm pressed against his bare chest. Georgianna glanced down, quickly looking away and staring up at the ceiling through her fingers. By this point, she didn't know why she was covering her face, it wasn't shielding her from anything, but she kept them there just the same.

"I'm hiding," she admitted.

Keiran chuckled and reached up to her face, poking the back of her hands.

"I can see that, and a good job you're doing too. But why?"

She looked at him and rolled her eyes.

"I'm hiding from Taye," she answered.

"Ah! Yes, of course! Taye!" Keiran murmured as if the answer was obvious to nobody but Georgianna, which most likely it wasn't. He watched her curiously for a moment, but when Georgianna didn't respond, his trademark smirk slipped back into place. "His girlfriend not like the present?"

"She wasn't there."

Keiran's tongue darted out and swiped across his bottom lip before he spoke.

"Freed?" he asked carefully.

"Sold."

Keiran's frown was a little too measured for Georgianna. She knew he didn't really care about Taye or Nyah. He didn't know either of them that well and Georgianna was sure that he was only trying to look worried for her sake. In some ways, she wished he'd not even tried, seeing as the result didn't look sincere this close up.

"That sucks," he answered finally.

"It's a nightmare," she almost cried, closing her fingers to cover her eyes. "I have to tell Taye, and he'll... He'll want to go after her. He'll get himself killed!"

Silence settled like the first snowflakes of the freeze, slowly blanketing them. Neither moved, perhaps worried of what they would find beneath the beautifully perfect, glittering silence. So, for a while, they simply lay that way.

It was just as Georgianna was wondering if they would speak again before falling asleep in this position that the tips of Keiran's fingers prised in between her hands, gently pulling back one and then the other.

"George," he murmured. "If he wants to go after her, you can't stop him. You shouldn't try."

"I shouldn't try?"

"Try to stop him and he'll hate you."

"Maybe he should! Maybe he needs someone to hate for this, and if it's me..."

"One more selfless act and I'm officially signing you up for martyrdom." Keiran murmured mockingly.

"Ha ha!" she mumbled, moving to roll away from him.

He placed his hand on her shoulder and forced her to remain on her back. Looking down at her, he quirked an eyebrow, fixing her with an even stare.

"Seriously, George, you did the guy a favour. You tried delivering the thing."

"Ring."

"What?"

"It was a ring," she said slowly. "Inside the packet he

wanted me to give her. A joining ring."

"Okay, but that doesn't change the fact that she wasn't there. Tell him. Then you can come hide in my bed when you're not all guilt-ridden over something you had no hand in."

"You know you're an ass, right?"

Keiran nodded as his gaze left hers, watching his own fingers leading a winding trail over her collarbone and along her arm. He reached around her waist, the tips of his fingers just slipping in between her flesh and the mattress.

"I'm sure I am, but you wouldn't be saying that if I wasn't right."

"Maybe."

Leaning over her, he smiled just before he settled his lips against hers. For a moment, Georgianna considered not responding. She was still mad that he suggested she do nothing. However, his soft insistence overcame her and she found herself lifting her head to return the pressure.

"Are you ready to admit that I'm right?" he asked against her flesh, lips curving into a broad smirk.

Georgianna shook her head.

"I should try harder then."

"Yes, you should," she murmured.

His hand tightened on her waist, tugging her body up towards his, bringing a sigh from Georgianna. No doubt she would feel bad that she'd distracted herself from Taye and Nyah's problems, but for now there was probably little she could do anyway. Her palms slid across his stomach, fingertips slipping under the waistband of his trousers, pushing them further down his hips. Keiran smiled a knowing, almost predatory grin as he grasped the edge of her shirt, leading it up her body, watching it reveal expanses of bare flesh.

As Keiran had suggested, she would tell Taye and try to push back the guilt. Now wasn't a time to feel guilty. She couldn't go looking for Taye at this time of night. So instead she lifted her shoulders, letting Keiran pull her shirt over her head before his lips returned to her body, following the same path as his fingertips. She arched her body up to meet him as his hands, then lips, soothed her flesh in smooth strokes followed by fluttering kisses, across her breasts and down her stomach. She reached between their bodies to undo his trousers, then slid her hands to the small of his back, using her foot to urge the material down his legs.

It wasn't her fault that Nyah had been sold. She had not had a hand in Nyah's capture. She had done nothing but try to help a friend make a delivery. She couldn't be blamed for it.

Keiran slid her trousers from her hips, taking her underwear with them in a single, fluid motion. Slipping her hands over his shoulders, she pulled him against her, drawing in a desperate breath as his hand slipped between their bodies. Her body followed his fingers like a magnet drawn up to the softest touch, begging for more. He smiled down at her, his amusement painfully obvious when her hips rocked up to meet him, physical urge forgoing rational thought.

She hooked one leg around his hips, heel pressed into the

back of his thigh as she pulled him more forcibly against her. Forgetting whether Taye would be angry or upset, she decided that, for now, she could do something that she would not feel bad about, and leave the guilt for tomorrow.

14 THE SIDE YOU'RE ON

Georgianna woke before Keiran the next morning. She didn't have any pressing business except for telling Taye what she had found out in the compound, which she didn't want to do, but she still clambered carefully out of the bed without waking Keiran and dressed herself. No doubt, if she woke Keiran, he would try to convince her to stay longer and, with the knowledge of the pain she was about to bring down on Taye, she knew it wouldn't take much convincing before she was back under the covers.

Tripping as she pulled on her boots, Georgianna turned and stared at Keiran for a moment, making sure he wasn't stirring from the noise. It was easier to leave when Keiran was asleep, even when she wasn't worried about him tempting her back to bed. There was an awkward moment in the mornings, whenever she was getting ready to leave, Keiran talking to her, when she realised that she would rather stay and spend time with him. So, whenever possible, she preferred to skip out while he was still asleep. She could tell herself that it was better this way.

She slipped through the canvas opening. After a quick check in at Medics' Way to ensure that there were no emergencies, Georgianna left Belsa territory and walked slowly through the main tunnels.

Every time she saw a blonde head of hair, she glanced to make sure that she wasn't wrong, that maybe Nyah had been let go. Each look held only disappointment, and before Georgianna had managed to come up with a reason why she shouldn't tell Taye, she was inside the Carae tunnels, making her way carefully across the uneven tunnel ground.

"Stop there!"

The man walking towards her was not Taye. In fact, Georgianna didn't think she'd ever met this particular Carae before. He didn't look particularly happy about the fact he actually had to talk to someone either, looking her up and down with a scowl evident even through the gloom.

"Who're you?" he asked.

"I'm looking for Taye," Georgianna answered, trying for a polite smile, but the result a worried grimace.

"That's who you're looking for, not who you are."

Georgianna blinked and shook her head quickly.

"Sorry, yeah, I'm George," she answered. "Lennox."

"Well, George Lennox, Taye ain't here."

Crossing her arms over her chest, Georgianna frowned

and looked sceptically back at the man. He didn't seem particularly believable at the moment, too quick to turn her away. She didn't want to call him a liar, but she also didn't want to walk away without proof that she wouldn't be able to see Taye.

"Do you know where he is?" she asked.

"Where a man goes is his own business."

"Okay, can you tell me who will know where he is?"

"I know," the guard answered with a smirk. "It's just none of my business."

Georgianna was getting annoyed. She knew he was only doing his job, but she was already having trouble working out how she would tell Taye about Nyah, let alone having to argue with a guard to get the chance to try to actually do it.

"Will you stop with the fucking mind games?" Georgianna snapped. "It's my business, alright?"

"What makes you think it's your business?"

He pressed his fists against his hips, his elbows jutting out across the tunnel. Through the small gap, there would be no way for Georgianna to get past without knocking him. Though, chances were, the man was in a bad enough mood that he might try to shoot her just for trying it.

"Will you stop being a Vtensu and just tell me?" Georgianna demanded, glaring back at him. "It's important I find him as soon as possible. It's about Nyah."

The guard's smirk vanished and after a moment thinking about it, he nodded. Georgianna hadn't wanted to use Nyah's name that way, but she'd been a member of the Carae, and from what Georgianna knew, she'd been a relatively friendly face amongst them. From the guard's instant drop in attitude, it seemed like Taye wasn't the only one missing her presence around their section of the tunnels.

"He's down Oprust," the guard answered. "Had a deal with some guy."

"Oppression City is a big place. Can you narrow it down?"

She tried to keep the annoyance at being jerked around out of her voice now that he was actually helping her.

"The Trade Inn, I think."

"Thanks!"

She returned quickly to the main tunnel, taking the first exit she came to, out into the Oprust district.

* * *

The Oprust district in the south-west of the city had always been neutral, used as a trade centre between the different tribes, who would set up stalls of meat and skins from hunting kills they didn't need themselves. Different herbs and plants people had gathered from the different areas of the trails were dried and crushed down into powders with different purposes. Blankets, clothes and household objects made with the people's various skills were traded for necessities.

In the very south of the district, families brought livestock to trade. A single sheep wrangled for a flock of chickens saved from coyotes, or a horse foal for a couple of dog pups. Different tribes were known for their different skills and specialities, and while every tribe could get by on its own, Oprust trading was always an excitement because people knew that they could get the best.

When the Adveni arrived, they'd set up buildings, large metal monstrosities that held the different elements of their science. The buildings, or factories as they called them, created food and drinks on a mass scale as was rumoured to have been common practice centuries before, weaponry and special clothing that protected the body from firearms injuries.

In one factory, the Adveni had begun instructing the Veniche on electricity, an invisible force that powered the lights down below in the tunnels and the buildings in the Adveni-controlled areas. In another, they harvested water from the local rivers, purifying it before sending it through large constructed pipes that separated off into each Adveni-made building.

It wasn't long before the district was renamed by the Veniche. While formally still called the Oprust district, amongst themselves, the Veniche named it Oppression City, a place where, when driven to desperation, A Ven might get work from the Adveni. The work was horrendous manual labour. Workers were forced into cramped areas amongst loud machines, and the money it paid was hardly worth what you had to go through to get it. Yet when a family was starving, Oppression City was often its only hope without resorting to illegal or compromising measures.

The market was still set up each day, but cramped into a single street. It was flooded with people trying to get to the stalls and attempt a decent trade. As such, it had become a haven for thieves and other criminals, who took advantage of those trying to get by. As the thieves moved in and business was forced to be done faster within the market, up popped those who wanted to trick and scam. Dried, crushed lemongrass replaced the rarer quinati, which cured aches and gave off the same smell as the lemongrass. Other such substitutions made trading for good products difficult.

Georgianna used to shop in the Oprust for supplies. It was easy and she liked giving the business to those who needed it, but the more dangerous trading became, the more she relied on the Carae and people she knew for her medical needs. Sure, the Carae may have charged her more, and they also took advantage by selling the mind-altering substances that people became so dependent on over time, but at least she knew what she was getting, especially by dealing with Taye, who she knew would never knock her over for a scammed sale.

The Trade Inn was one of the few remaining bright spots in Oppression City. Before the Adveni it had been used as a place to get specially made delicacies, sweets that most couldn't make. Yet, as time wore on, and less people had the ease to spend money on such luxuries, they slowly began selling other food. It became a place for workers in the district to stop in and get a meal on their short breaks.

One of Georgianna's reasons for liking the Trade Inn was that Oz, the owner, had worked in one of the Adveni alcohol factories for a time and now brewed the stuff in the back room, selling it at a much cheaper price. Many complained that the alcohol Oz brewed was akin to the oil used to clean the machines in the factories, but from how much business the place received, it seemed no one cared enough about that to turn it down.

Taye was sat at one of the back tables when Georgianna walked in. A watered-down wheat beer sat in front of him despite the time not really being appropriate for drinking. Before him, a man was hunched close, his hand jangling with coins whenever he moved. Taye leaned in too, obviously arguing with the man, but as the man got up to leave, Taye made no effort to stop him.

Georgianna quickly busied herself at the counter as the man passed, giving Taye enough time to pocket something that had been placed on the table, before she went over and slipped in opposite him.

"Georgianna!" He seemed surprised at her arrival. "What are you doing here?"

"Looking for you."

He didn't answer, but drank a mouthful of his beer and placed the glass back on the table. She shifted her bag onto the chair next to her and rested her elbows on the wooden table top.

"I went to the compound."

Taye's interest was piqued. He leaned across the table, almost knocking over his beer in his hurry to wrap his fingers around her wrist, pulling her hand towards him.

"Did you get it to her?" he asked. "What did she say?"

Georgianna gulped. This was the moment she'd been afraid of. She didn't know how to say it. She didn't know whether she should be blunt and simply tell him, or if she should calm him down and explain slowly. Carefully, Georgianna reached into the side pocket of her bag with the hand Taye wasn't clutching between his own, and pulled out the small packet.

Taye's gaze shot to it and his excited expression faded instantly to one of confusion.

"Gianna..."

"Taye, I..."

"But we had a..."

"She wasn't there."

Staring at her in shock and confusion, he released her hand.

"Nyah was..."

Georgianna paused. Taye's face was so readable, always had been. She wondered how in the world he got through sales with a face as clear as a sign post. Yet, there it was, staring at her, waiting for her to admit what she knew.

"She was sold. Three days ago."

He was on his feet almost before she realised what was going on. Leaping up, she grabbed him by the arm, forcing him back towards his seat. Perched on the edge of his chair, looking ready to jump up again at any moment, he glanced between Georgianna and the packet still lying on the table.

"To who?"

She shook her head and released his arm, letting him slide farther back.

"I don't know. I was told by an inmate."

"They could be lying!"

"Why would someone lie about that?"

Taye frowned at the table.

"I don't know."

She watched as he slipped into silence, head bowed, one finger slowly tracing the rim of his glass. For the first time in a long time, she couldn't tell what he was thinking. His mouth curved into a determined frown, and she pursed her own lips together, wondering what to say. She couldn't tell him that the idea of finding Nyah and freeing her was ridiculous. It would be catastrophic if he wasn't already thinking it. On the other hand, he would be angry if she suggested he was doing the right thing in leaving it be if he were already planning an attack. So Georgianna stayed quiet.

"Who would know where she is?" Taye asked, not looking up.

Georgianna furrowed her brow and shrugged.

"The guards at the compound, I guess. Apart from that…"

"You're allowed in there, maybe they'd…"

Her mouth dropped open as she realised what Taye was suggesting. She could still see the look Edtroka had given her, as if he was suspicious of something. There was no way he would not realise something more was going on if she started asking questions.

"Taye! Do you know what you're asking of me?" Georgianna replied, glancing over her shoulder to make sure nobody was around them.

"To be a friend, Georgianna!" Taye snapped back under his breath.

Georgianna's nose wrinkled as a snarl threatened to hiss through her teeth.

"Friend?" she repeated. "And when you have this information, you're not going to go straight after Nyah? If anything happens to her, they'll suspect me immediately!"

"So?"

"So I don't want to be buryd, Taye!"

Taye pushed his chair back sharply, stood up, and leaned over the table.

"You have it so sweet. You're allowed into the compound, a decent living in that bar. You need to remember whose side you're on!"

Georgianna could do nothing by stare open mouthed as Taye got up from his chair. She thought about how she helped the Belsa, that she was a good daughter to her father and a good sister to Halden. She helped her friends and did what she needed to in order to live. How was she on the Adveni side? She detested what they were doing in that compound, how they pulled families apart with their drysta yard.

No, she had to believe that Taye was just angry, that he was upset about Nyah and he was looking for the easiest outlet. That had to be it. Georgianna was positive that she wasn't helping the Adveni any more than Taye was.

Taye stepped around the table, snatching up the packet and pocketing it. For a moment, Georgianna thought he was going to leave her there without another word, leaving them both angry with each other, but as she stared stubbornly at the other wall, Taye leaned over her.

"I'm getting Nyah out! You can either help me or not, but I'm getting her out."

Georgianna didn't have a chance to reply before he was gone from the Inn. She sat at the table with Taye's abandoned beer, staring through the grimy window long after the door had slammed closed behind him.

15   Blood and Choice

"That self-indulgent, selfish Vtensu!"

Keiran had worn a shallow rut in the dry earth as he paced continually back and forth, boot prints merging into one another. Dust clouds puffed out as each foot landed, but Georgianna had grown tired of watching them settle amongst the dry grass since Keiran had begun ranting. A rolled cigarette was hanging from his fingers, ash gathering on the end as he forgot to flick it away while he paced. Georgianna watched him silently from her position on the wall, her heels knocking against the brick as she swung her legs. She'd tried telling him not to be angry, tried slipping her arms around his waist and telling him to forget it, but she was as good at calming Keiran down as she was with Taye. The more she tried to change the subject, the more it came back to Taye and his—in Keiran's opinion—ridiculous demands.

Georgianna had been closing down the bar for the night, sweeping the floor while Liliah and Penn put the glasses away and restocked the bottles behind the bar. As she reached the front of the building, she'd been caught by surprise to see Keiran leaning against the building opposite, a bottle of wheat beer hanging from one hand, a cigarette from the other. Glancing back towards Penn and Liliah, Georgianna had signalled to Keiran that she just needed a few more minutes before she locked the door behind her, carrying the broom back out towards the back of the bar. Seeing as Georgianna had offered to finish up many times for Liliah in the past so that she could get home to her partner Qiyan, Liliah had grinned broadly and quickly ushered Georgianna out of the side door towards the Belsa.

He hadn't planned much, but he'd brought a couple of bottles of wheat beer, and with the promise that he didn't have to be on duty until later the next day, they'd decided to spend a little of their time together outside the tunnels. They headed to the park that the Adveni had cornered off next to the Rion district.

The park was nice enough, with plants organised in straight lines and low walls cutting it off from the road. Once they'd hopped over the wall, Keiran had brought out the bottles, opening both and handing one to Georgianna before asking about her day.

She had started explaining about Taye's reaction, and almost immediately Keiran had been up off the wall, his beer abandoned as he began pacing, throwing out questions that Georgianna was sure he already knew the answer to, making comments she was already painfully aware of. However, now he'd started, she wasn't sure how to stop him. Every time she tried, he would find a way back to his annoyance with the younger Carae man.

"What does he think you'll do? Walk up to the first Adveni and start demanding to know the location of his little girlfriend?"

"I don't know. And he didn't demand anything, he just..."

"He insinuated you were fucking grutt if you didn't help him break half a dozen laws," Keiran cut her off matter of factly.

Georgianna raised an eyebrow, watching him with a small smile. She was grateful that he was standing up for her, even if it was only the two of them listening, but his lecturing her on law-breaking was, admittedly, a little funny.

"Because you're such a good, upstanding Veniche," she commented sarcastically. "Shall we check that one with the Adveni? Maybe there has been a mistake over that pesky law of being a Belsa meaning an instant death sentence."

Keiran rolled his eyes as he glanced at her and brought his cigarette up to his lips, inhaling a large breath of the sweet-smelling smoke. He finally flicked the gathering ash off the end, and Georgianna watched as it flittered through the air into the dry grass.

"That's not the same," Keiran dismissed her before pointing his cigarette at her. "And it's not like you can claim complete innocence either."

Laughing, Georgianna brought her knees up to her chest and perched her heels on the edge of the wall, wrapping her arms around her legs. Resting her chin on her knees, she nodded her head in determination.

"I certainly can, thank you very much!" she claimed happily. "I am just a medic. A nice, wants-to-help-others medic who always follows the rules."

Keiran paused in his pacing, watching her for a moment before turning and stepping up to stand before her. With the cigarette still perched loosely between his fingers, he leaned over, placing his hands against the brick on either side of her body, smirking at her.

"You, Miss George, are anything but innocent." His hand moved closer to her, his thumb stroking gently back and forth against her hip.

"That's not a very nice thing to say." Georgianna tried to look moody, but failed. She grinned instead.

"Nice, no," he replied, cocking his head to the side as he considered it. "But true, yes. I don't think there is a person alive who'd think you were innocent if they knew the truth about you."

"Oh?"

"If the Adveni found out that you help the Belsa, you're not an innocent young medic anymore. If your boss at the bar finds out you swipe a bottle or two practically every shift you work, you're not the sweet, cheerful barmaid."

Georgianna opened her mouth to argue. She didn't swipe alcohol nearly as often as he was making out, but just because she didn't do it every night, it didn't mean she didn't do it at all. Seeing as his point was relatively valid, she pouted at him, nodding for him to continue.

He leaned in closer towards her, his lips just shy of brushing her skin as he spoke. Georgianna shivered, his breath flowing over her lips and past her cheek.

"And let's not forget your da' and how innocent he'd see you if I were to tell him just how much you like it when I…"

"Alright!" she yielded, placing her hands on his shoulders and pushing him sharply away from her body. "Let's just agree right now that you are never meeting my father!"

Keiran laughed as he grinned triumphantly and took another drag of his cigarette.

"Agreed."

She nodded.

"So, I know you're already uninnocent," Keiran said slowly, the amusement from his voice gone in an instant as he took a seat next to her. "But that doesn't mean you have to be stupid. He's asking too much, George."

The smile faded and she let out a huff. She should have known better than to think they were off that conversation. Staring out across the grass of the park, she couldn't think what to do. She didn't want to hurt Taye by saying no, but the risk of getting caught had been weighing on her long before Keiran had put it so bluntly.

"I just hate seeing him miss her like this."

"Yeah? How much is your family going to miss you? I mean, forget the things you do for the Belsa, and how much time I'd have on my hands if you weren't turning up in my bed when you're bored, what would your da' be like if you were caught? Or your brother..."

Keiran paused and she glanced at him. His brow was furrowed, his tongue darting out to wet his lips.

"Halden," she confirmed.

His expression immediately loosened and he nodded.

"That's it! What are they going to do if you get locked up?"

Georgianna frowned. She hadn't really thought about how it would affect her family. She worried about things happening to them, but it was never the other way around. They'd already lost her mother to the Adveni and Halden had lost Nequiel. Neither her father nor brother would be happy if anything happened to her. She would be inconsolable if anything happened to Halden, Braedon, or her father. She would go to the ends of the world for them, put herself in the line of five bears if it even gave one of them a slim chance of getting away unharmed. The way she saw it, she had been selfish to even consider leaving them to such sorrow.

The more she thought about it, staring out across the dry, yellowed grass, the words her father had constantly driven into her began replaying in her head. The same words her mother had told her as a child. The Kahle were family. It didn't matter that they were not all connected by blood; they were family because they chose to be. They looked after each other. They cared like family and so that made them one. She couldn't leave Taye to his sorrow and heartache any more than she could abandon Halden. Nyah was her sister, and Taye her brother, both by choice. If it were Halden in the compound or sold on, Georgianna knew she would not stop until he was safe, until he was free, so how could she expect Taye to leave Nyah to her fate?

"You're right," she exclaimed, nodding her head.

Keiran leaned back and let out a sigh, a thin stream of sweet smoke billowing up into the warm air. She pursed her lips, watching as he stared up at the sky. From the look of relief on his face, he obviously thought he'd convinced her, and he had.

"I have to help him."

He sat up much faster than he leaned back and turned his head, glaring down at her.

"What?"

"I have to help," she repeated. "If it were Halden, I would want help getting him out. So how can I not expect the same of Taye?"

"George, that wasn't what I…"

She cut him off, reaching out and placing her hand over his, resting it in his lap.

"I know it isn't what you meant, but it's what I have to do. You won't change my mind on this."

Keiran groaned and untangled his hand from hers, reaching up and rubbing his fingers over his face. For a moment, he frowned up at the stars, his gaze darting amongst them before he finally looked at her, giving her a resolute glare.

"You're going to be the death of me."

16 Games of Escape

The next few days after her discussions with Taye and Keiran, Georgianna hardly had any time to think about what she might be able to do to help Nyah. There had been a fight between some Belsa and a number of Adveni trying to push their control further into the Camps, which ended up with three dead and two injured men who needed almost constant care on the Way.

She hardly found the time to go back home, let alone go down to the Carae grounds to look for Taye. She could, in the end, only hope that Taye hadn't rushed off to do anything stupid without waiting for her.

The tunnels were sweltering, a constant mist of sweat dampening the dry heat that emanated from the earth. Georgianna had finally convinced Jaid to take some time off from watching over Si. Getting Jaid to leave the Way was a good sign, but it also meant Georgianna had to stay in case anybody came in for help, and to keep a general eye on the patients they already had in, Si included.

In the furthest car from the entrance to Medics' Way, Georgianna sat cross-legged on one of the makeshift beds, a pile of freshly washed dressings next to her, one wound tightly around her hand. Across the car, Jacob was sitting up in bed. Lacie perched on the end of the mattress, a leather bag in her lap and a selection of small wooden tiles in her hand. It was nice, watching the two of them. While they never really spoke about anything very serious, the two kept up an almost constant stream of cheerful chatter.

"How can you say you prefer the wash?" Jacob asked in disbelief. "Everything is so... wet."

Lacie let out a laugh, a high giggle that chimed like the metal bells that hung from caravans on the trail. Georgianna smiled down at her knees. Lacie was much more cheerful than when she first came to the Belsa, a tiny, thin, battered girl in Beck's arms. Georgianna had hardly ever heard the girl laugh. There was usually a sadness to her that she had barely asked about, past needing to know her injuries.

Jacob, too, was much happier in Lacie's presence. When others were around, even Georgianna, the young man was quiet and withdrawn, pulling himself back into the corner any time anyone came near him. Yet with Lacie he seemed like any other man of his age, almost rambunctious while talking with the younger girl.

"But freeze is so cold!" Lacie complained, a wide grin

across her lips making her complaint almost impossible to take seriously.

"Snow!" Jacob answered quickly. "Snow is so much more fun than water."

Lacie shook her head quickly and crossed her arms over her chest in determination. Jacob, seemingly ignoring the girl's silent defiance, placed one of the wooden tiles onto the pile.

"Only three to go," he teased, reaching out to take the small leather bag from her and selecting a new tile.

Georgianna looked up just in time to see Lacie pout in frustration as she turned her attention back to her own tiles, moving them one at a time from one hand to the other.

"Well, I only have two to go," Lacie quipped.

Jacob looked at her, a competitive glint in his eye, and chuckled.

"I never liked snow," Lacie admitted, flicking through the rest of her tiles. "Maybe it would have been different if I had brothers and sisters."

Jacob, holding his tiles up in front of his face to shield them from being looked at by his opponent, furrowed his brow.

"I guess my sisters made it more fun," he said slowly. "Dessie loved the snow, even as a tiny girl. She liked caking it onto me like a coat so I was a walking snowman."

Georgianna smiled as another bell-filled giggle spilled from Lacie's lips.

Shifting her position on the bed as she placed the tightly

wound dressing into the linen pack, she glanced over at the couple, smiling for a moment. It was nice that the two of them had each other. Even while the young man was unconscious, Lacie had taken it upon herself to tend to his every wound and to make sure that he was always comfortable. She was sure that even if she hadn't been in Medics' Way all the time, Lacie would have found reasons to come check on him.

She wondered whether it had been curiosity on the young girl's part, knowing that this man had been through the same things she had, felt the same pains and in some cases, worse. She wondered if he was a little slice of salvation for the redhead. If he could get past his injuries, maybe Lacie could as well? Up until now, Georgianna hadn't dared ask the young man anything too stressful, but as she watched, she realised that here was her perfect opportunity.

"Jake," Georgianna opened cautiously, placing the dressings aside and leaning forward.

Jacob looked up from his tiles in surprise, glancing over towards Georgianna with wide brown eyes. Beneath his mop of curly, dark hair, he looked so childlike, so innocent, that Georgianna wanted to scoop him into a tight hug and never let him go. On the other hand, it made asking her question so much more difficult.

"Yeah?" he asked.

Lacie was watching from beneath a fan of fair eyelashes, keeping her head down towards her lap though her gaze darted between Jacob and Georgianna. Georgianna shifted her legs out, placing her feet on the ground.

"I was wondering," she continued, "How did you escape?"

For a moment, Jacob simply stared at her. There was no shock on his face, no anger, just a quiet sort of expectation, like he'd known the question would come and it was only a matter of when, and from whom. Georgianna blinked, wondering if he'd already been asked by others and he was checking off each person and how long it would take them. If that was the case, Georgianna could only hope she'd lasted longer than others.

"George," Lacie complained quietly. "That's... That's not... He's still healing."

Georgianna frowned and pushed herself back, opening her mouth to apologise. Lacie was right. Jacob was still healing from his wounds, was still sent into fevers from the continued pain of the Nsiloq mark branded into his skin. However, before Georgianna could spill a single word of apology, Jacob reached out, sliding his hand cautiously over Lacie's and squeezing her slim fingers in his own.

"It's alright," he whispered.

Georgianna and Lacie both stared at the hand in Lacie's lap, grasping the girl's pale flesh. Yes, Jacob had been friendly and cheerful towards the girl, but he was still incredibly skittish about being touched by anyone, including Lacie. It was why they changed his dressings while he slept, because everyone on the Way knew how much anxiety it gave him to have people close. Lacie's mouth dropped open, her expression doing nothing to hide the fact that the gesture was as shocking to her as it was to Georgianna.

It only took a second, a single second of them both staring at his hand, for Jacob to quickly tug his arm back, breaking the connection. He buried both his hands into his lap, staring at his knees for a moment.

"What do you want to know?" he asked quietly.

"Jake, you don't have to," Lacie urged.

"No, it's okay."

Georgianna gazed apologetically at Lacie for a moment before turning her attention back to Jacob. She wanted to move closer to him to hear better but she didn't dare for fear of making him retreat further into himself. Instead, she grasped the edge of the bed, holding herself in place.

"I have a friend who has been sold," Georgianna explained. "I want to know how it happens, where you go. I know this is hard, Jacob, and I don't want you suffering, but… any information you can give me might be useful."

"Are you planning something?" he asked, not meeting her gaze.

Georgianna tucked a lock of hair behind her ear. She couldn't tell them that yes, she was planning on helping to break a drysta away from her owner. However, she also didn't feel right lying about it, especially when Jacob was offering her more than he probably wanted to give.

"For the moment it's just information."

That much was the truth at least. She couldn't plan anything if she didn't have the information. Maybe Jacob's story would prove that it was practically impossible, that his escape had been a rare fluke that relied on luck and nothing more. Maybe she would find out that planning was useless.

Jacob rocked himself forward for a moment, staring intently at his knees before he finally pushed himself up straight, moving himself into the corner of his bed. He pushed his body back, bracing his feet against the bed until the walls pressed so hard against his skin that his flesh flattened to the metal. Georgianna frowned. This was too painful for him. She should stop it. She opened her mouth.

"When I was caught I was sent to the compound," Jacob said in a fast murmur. "I was there for a week when a guard came into the block. Even back then we knew it was strange. They didn't come in unless..."

"Unless for count," Georgianna nodded.

Jacob nodded.

"I'd been hiding in a cell with a couple of others. We were young so we were trying to protect ourselves from... others," he continued. "With a guard on the block, we all had to come out. He selected five of us from a list and we were taken to the Yard."

"Jake..." Lacie moaned.

This time, Jacob didn't reach for the redhead, even as she buried her face into her hands, the tiles spilling from her fingers onto the bed.

Guilt flooded through her. She had known this would be difficult for Jacob but she hadn't fully known how difficult it would be for Lacie. Their stories were so similar. Hearing his struggle had to be the same for the girl. Pushing herself quickly off the bed, Georgianna moved over to Jacob's. Jacob, without even looking up, curled his legs tighter to his chest, but relaxed a little as she, instead of coming towards him, looped an arm around Lacie's shoulders and murmured apologies into her ear.

"I wasn't sold the first day, so I was kept in the other block, where they keep the people who will be sold," Jacob explained. "The next day, a man bid on me."

"How old were you?" Georgianna asked, brushing her hand gently over Lacie's hair.

"Fourteen."

"And when he bought you, what happened?"

"You're taken to be registered," Lacie answered. "There's a room. They take you in and an Adveni takes a sample of blood."

Almost at the exact same time, Lacie and Jacob raised their left thumb and held it there for a moment. Georgianna hugged Lacie a little tighter to her.

"They take information on you," Jacob explained. "Name, age, tribe, everything. It all gets put into a… a…"

He held his hands a little way out in front of him, one hand flat, facing up, the other drawing like a pencil on paper.

"On a tsentyl?" Georgianna asked.

Jacob nodded.

"The information goes to their… their… main thing, and it's kept."

"Same as if you register yourself," Georgianna explained. "I had to go in and register with my family."

Jacob did nothing but nod again.

"So what happened, you know, after that?"

Jacob shrugged, his gaze not shifting from his knees.

Wrapping his arms around his legs, he looked like a small child, not a young man. Georgianna wondered if he'd always looked young, curled back into the corner, trying to save himself from his owner's rage.

"Whatever they want," he answered. "After they've registered you, you're theirs, they can do anything."

Lacie untangled herself from Georgianna's arm and set about methodically putting all the tiles into a neat stack in her hands. Each tile facing the same direction and the right way up.

"The cinystalq?" Georgianna asked.

Cinystalq collars were an Adveni design used on dreta. Clamped around the neck, the collar could not only track a person's movements, but also issue punishment in the form of painful shocks travelling through the body. From what Georgianna knew, they were difficult to remove. Doing it wrong could end up killing the wearer as the energy inside escaped into the body when the connection was broken.

A couple of years before, it had been thought impossible. It was only when a Belsa turned up, collar in hand, that they realised that the impossible was actually doable with a little training and care.

Jacob shook his head, his lips pursed. It looked like he was thinking about it, but when he answered, it was clear he'd already known what to say, just that it was harder to say it.

"Personal choice. They are expensive, so most Adveni don't bother unless they are having… problems."

Georgianna pressed her lips into a thin line as she

considered his answer. It was good news in a way. Knowing that most Adveni who purchased a Veniche as a drysta wouldn't bother with a cinystalq.

As she thought about it, Georgianna hadn't even realised that Jacob was rubbing his hand back and forth over the side of his neck where a long burn had healed not long before. Now, against his skin, a thin white line curved from just beneath his ear and disappeared under the neck of his shirt.

"How did you get away?" Georgianna asked.

His fingers paused halfway down his neck, and Jacob glanced off to the side, a curl of dark brown hair falling in front of his eyes before he impatiently pushed it away.

"My owner didn't pay a lot of attention to me."

Georgianna's gaze crept to the scars she could see on Jacob's arms, long faded marks mixed with newer, angrier reds. From the look of him, Jacob's owner had paid a lot of attention to the young man, and none of it in the way anyone would like. However, looking at him, Georgianna didn't dare disagree.

"It was only when he was bored that I became worthy of notice." His voice was barely more than a whisper. "It was… it was almost okay at first, but then… After the last time, I knew I'd not last and so I ran when he was asleep. I figured I'd get far enough and the collar would kill me, but someone found me and they got the collar off."

"Are they so open with security? Why doesn't everyone run?"

"Some are."

Georgianna looked down in surprise as Lacie spoke

instead of Jacob. She was looking at the tiles, flipping through them, though it had been unmistakably her voice.

"At first they keep you locked away, all doors and windows shut. After a while, you stop thinking about running except when it gets really bad," she continued. "But then, you're scared of what will happen and…"

"And you stay put," Jacob finished when it seemed Lacie had lost her will to continue.

Georgianna nodded slowly. From the sounds of it, Nyah would still be the type of drysta locked away, kept on a tight leash while she became accustomed to her new position. Unfortunately, that also meant that, most likely, she would be kept close to the Adveni who had bought her. It would be difficult for her to get away for any length of time.

"Jacob, when you were sold… do you remember who did it?"

Jacob frowned, and for the first time since he'd began speaking about what had happened to him, his gaze met Georgianna's. His eyes were narrowed, but Georgianna was sure it wasn't in anger, it was confusion.

"Who bought me?"

"No, who sold you from the compound? Are there specific guards, or do they all do it?" she asked.

"Oh." He looked back down at the bed. "There are a few who deal, but the one who sold me? His name was Edtroka."

Georgianna's mouth dropped open as she stared at Jacob, and though he looked like he wanted to find out what was so surprising about that name, he didn't ask. Edtroka couldn't have been his favourite person. She didn't want to have to explain to him that she knew the man who had sold him to an Adveni who would torment and beat him for almost six years.

"Thank you, Jake, for telling me."

Jacob nodded gently but didn't speak again. When she stood up, Jacob shifted and lay on his side, curled into a ball at the far end of the mattress. He held his pillow squashed in his arms. Georgianna considered suggesting to Lacie that they should give him some time alone, but Lacie had already moved, stretching out her arm, entwining her fingers with Jacob's.

No words passed between them as Georgianna collected her things and left the two alone. She felt horrible for asking Jacob and Lacie to relive what had obviously been the most horrific of times for them, but as she took a final glance back at the pair curled on the bed, she couldn't help but feel that maybe talking about it had actually been the best thing she could have done for them. Maybe talking about things they had kept to themselves for so long had given them the chance to begin to move on.

17 Question of Delicacy

Georgianna's conversation with Jacob and Lacie remained in her head for two days. In some ways, getting Nyah out seemed more possible than it had before, as the story that cinystalq collars were placed on every drysta at the moment of purchase had been proved a myth. However, knowing that a drysta would be more heavily controlled while they became accustomed to their new situation made the idea of breaking her out any time soon look virtually impossible.

Still, even though it had been days since her argument with Taye, Georgianna had yet to approach him about helping out. She knew that the longer she left it, the more likely it was that Taye would do something reckless, but Georgianna also didn't want to go to him with a half-baked idea that would wash away at the lightest touch. She needed something positive, something they could work with, like who it was who had bought Nyah in the first place.

She had meant to go to the compound the next day, feigning that she had her days mixed up, but as things usually went, she'd been caught up with other responsibilities, one of which included looking after Braedon while her father went down to the Oprust district and Halden worked. Her nephew had been more than happy to spend the morning with her, especially as it meant going to various sections of the camps to make small trades. Georgianna had been a little worried about taking her nephew with her, but Braedon had been fascinated with the different places and people. He was thrilled when his aunt, someone who was usually seen as someone to entertain him, had been asked to stitch up a rather ugly-looking wound on an equally ugly-looking man, something Georgianna was grateful Braedon had not commented on.

Having left the family home early that morning to get back into the centre of the city before sun up, Georgianna made her way through the tunnels towards the east of the city, taking the familiar lines until she could come up out of the entrance a few hundred metres from the entrance to the compound.

Getting through the gates was a rather regular affair, though with Edtroka not standing guard, it had been up to Georgianna to ask whether he was on duty.

"Dreta," the guard had grumbled at her, handing back her bag, now checked for contraband, for Georgianna to take inside.

Georgianna gave a small, polite nod and instead of taking the first door into the compound, walked down a bricked path that led along the side of the high walls.

Between the wall and the fenced cage surrounding the compound, the thin path felt more like a tunnel than anything else. Georgianna could only guess at the reason they'd made it so narrow, but as she saw the crowd of people gathered in the yard at the end, she wondered whether it was to prevent a quick getaway should anything happen. Only so many people could get through the fenced corridor at a time, not to mention that at the other end they would face guards with heavy copaq weapons. Her father had once told her that, should you wish to fight off a large number with only a few men, leaving them no entrance or retreat but a small corridor meant only so many could attack at any one time. Looking at the swarm of Adveni and the number of Veniche lined up to be sold, she decided that was a useful thing to keep in mind here.

It took a while to locate Edtroka. She'd first made her way respectfully through the crowd to the other end of the yard, letting Adveni bump and push her around and apologising to them each time they did. When she could not see Edtroka standing guard near the dreta waiting to be sold, she instead stood near the high wall of the compound, looking out through the sea of people. She finally spotted Edtroka. He was talking to a man with a pompous, self-important expression on his face. Edtroka was nodding politely, but even through the stiff, polite smile, Georgianna could see that he was not enjoying the conversation.

Georgianna slipped through the crowd, once again apologising to anyone who barged into her, until she reached Edtroka's side. She held her distance a few yards away, giving the two men the space to continue their conversation. It only took a minute or two before Edtroka held the side of his fist to the middle of his chest in the Adveni mark of respect, and the other man turned to walk swiftly away.

"Guard Edtroka?" Georgianna asked cautiously, stepping forward.

Edtroka turned, the forced smile on his lips fading for a moment, to be replaced by a look of amusement. Georgianna looked at him, surprised that his expression would not be one of annoyance, especially seeing as he'd seemed almost incapable of fully hiding his contempt from someone who was clearly his superior. Edtroka stepped forward and nodded to her.

"Med," he answered, his head cocked to the side. "Don't see you here often. You do know I'm not allowed to sell to you, right?"

Georgianna gazed back at him in surprise. The only time she'd seen Edtroka for long enough to hold an actual conversation, he'd been stiff and surly. Today he seemed practically happy to see her.

Not entirely sure how to respond, she faltered, glancing up towards the area where Veniche were waiting to be sold as dreta. There was such a stark contrast among them, young and old, male and female, defiant to downright terrified. She couldn't look at Edtroka, his gaze was too piercing for her liking, as if he could see what she was thinking, what she was planning.

"I was hoping you'd be able to give me some information," she said. "On a sale."

His gaze flickered over to the soon-to-be dreta and the Adveni guarding them. Georgianna suspected that he was about to tell her that he wasn't allowed, that giving over information like that was considered dangerous. However, when he looked back at her, he nodded for her to go on, holding one hand out and curling his fingers over his palm to ask for the details.

Georgianna was stunned. She'd expected to be drilled with questions about why she wanted such information, but instead she was being treated like an equal to this man. At least, for the moment. With no idea how long the pleasure would last, she quickly adjusted the strap across her shoulder and glanced around them to see if anyone was listening.

"Her name is Nyah Wolfe, she was Kahle," she continued. "Twenty-three, blonde."

Edtroka nodded, his lips curved into a momentary frown before he shrugged.

"Gone eight days," he answered. "Maybe nine, this heat makes it hard to remember."

She nodded enthusiastically.

"That's right. She was in the block for an assault."

Edtroka let out a laugh, a gruff sound that didn't suit his face. Georgianna looked at him properly. His eyes, the mottled brown of yapoque leaves after they had been dried for smoking, held more warmth than she'd noticed before, and his features were almost delicate. High, curved cheekbones on a slim face above a pointed jaw and a straight nose led the gaze directly down to the bow of his lips. She blinked and glanced down, forgetting about his face as she realised he had about five methods of killing her strapped to his uniform that didn't include his bare hands. Her gaze settled on his slim fingers, capable of killing a person with ease.

"She wa..."

"E'troke!"

The voice came out of the crowd and despite the difference in the pronunciation of his name, Edtroka turned his head towards the sound. As Georgianna fell back a step, not wanting to get caught in the middle of a conversation between two Adveni, she wondered whether the difference in pronunciation was because she'd been saying it wrong. Yes, Edtroka had introduced himself as such, but Georgianna knew that there were certain pronunciations Veuric tongues never got right when it came to Adtvenis words. Maybe Edtroka's name was one of them, so he'd just given up trying.

"Tzanlomne," Edtroka greeted the newcomer with another fixed, polite smile.

The man was short compared to most Adveni, almost a head shorter than Edtroka, but with dark features to rival the taller man and a wider stance, he seemed to demand as much respect as the guard. Georgianna averted her gaze, but unfortunately not fast enough.

"That one, how much?"

Edtroka looked over his shoulder at Georgianna and shook his head.

"She's a medic, not drysta."

The man, Tzanlomne, snorted in derision and rolled his eyes. Edtroka's word meant little as he reached out, grasping Georgianna's chin in a grip so tight that she thought his fingers might crush straight through her jaw. She jerked backward away from him, but his grip was too tight, holding her still with one hand while he waved the other dismissively.

"I don't care what she was, E'troke," he answered. "I care what you will sell her for. She'd make a nice addition."

Tzanlomne barely looked at Edtroka. He turned her head this way and that, his gaze travelling over every inch of her face. He reached out and tugged the ribbon from her hair, watching as it fell in a tumble of messy blonde waves over her shoulders.

"I won't, and she wouldn't," Edtroka snarled through gritted teeth.

She struggled against him. Grasping his wrist, she tried to pull his grasp away from her face. Tzanlomne's grin of approval slid into a sneer. He grasped her hair in a tight fist, yanking her head back.

Georgianna yelped and her ribbon sailed silently to the ground.

"Now, E'troke, I have my ways, you might as well be part of the..."

Edtroka cut him off by snapping something in such rapid

Advtenis that even if Georgianna had known more than a few names and swearwords, she still wouldn't have understood. It was no more than a few sentences, but the snarl on Edtroka's lips, or perhaps the words that hissed forth, were enough to make Tzanlomne narrow his eyes and turn his attention away from his new potential toy.

She could barely see Edtroka from the way she was held, but she felt the extra fingers in her hair as Edtroka pried Tzanlomne's hand from her. Tzanlomne released her and Georgianna hurried back a few steps. She rubbed her fingers over her skin, glancing to Edtroka to find his face twisted into a murderous mask. Tzanlomne took a step back, and when Edtroka's expression didn't soften, he turned, stalking away through the crowd.

Georgianna watched with cautious curiosity as Edtroka glared after Tzanlomne. She didn't dare ask him what had been said in Advtenis though she was dying to know what had transpired between the two Adveni men. Once Tzanlomne had disappeared into the crowd, Edtroka turned back to her, the frown still present on his pursed lips.

"Everything alright?"

Edtroka gave a dismissive wave of his hand.

"Vtensu varsonnir!" Edtroka answered without any more explanation.

It was an insult, one Georgianna had learned a few years before. Vtensu could be used in a number of ways, but as an expletive, it was very similar to the insult 'bastard'. Varsonnir, however, was specific. You had to listen carefully, as a Veniche anyway, to hear the difference from

Volsonnar, the name for the Adveni leader much like the Elder of a tribe. Varsonnir, on the other hand, was reserved for someone who thought they were more important than they were.

From Edtroka's insult, Tzanlomne was a self-important bastard, and Georgianna found herself grinning.

"Well, thank you," she muttered.

"For?" Edtroka asked, looking at her in surprise.

"For not selling me."

He laughed again, the same gruff burst that in Georgianna's opinion didn't suit him.

Glancing over his shoulder in the direction Tzanlomne had disappeared, Edtroka reached out and took hold of her elbow.

Georgianna tugged her elbow back away from him. She didn't feel as safe as she had before. The man had cared little whether she was legally for sale, and if other Adveni were the same, what would it take for Edtroka to turn a blind eye and accept the payment? She was in the compound already, it wouldn't be difficult for him to create some charge that stripped her of her legal registration as a free Veniche.

Edtroka's grasp, while not as tight or restricting as Tzanlomne's, was just as unbreakable. He kept hold of her arm and began leading her through the crowd towards the compound doors.

"Even if you were up for sale, he would not have you," Edtroka told her with a wicked grin. "I would be in front of *him* in the queue."

"Is... Is that a compliment?"

"Perhaps."

Georgianna couldn't help but notice the glances she received as she was half-tugged towards the walls of the prison. Maybe it was because she wasn't out here often, or because she was being held onto by a guard of the compound, but she received more than a couple of curious looks before they slipped through the door and into the cool relief of the compound corridor.

The shadows that flung themselves through the corridor stunned her into blindness once the door swung closed with a bang. She blinked rapidly as she was tugged along. Edtroka seemingly had no problem with the sudden shade, or knew the corridors too well to need sight to navigate them. Surging forward, he turned them down a slimmer corridor that ended in an open door. With her sight slowly returning, she glanced over her shoulder, any exit now out of sight.

Fear surged through her as she wondered whether Edtroka's protection of her in the yard had more to do with his own desires. Had she asked about a drysta's whereabouts to an Adveni who'd been looking for a reason to keep her in the compound? Was that where he was taking her now?

As they proceeded through the open door, Edtroka made no effort to close it behind them. Instead he released Georgianna's elbow and marched across the small room, collecting up a jacket. Georgianna stood just inside the doorway watching him, her hands clenched before her. She wondered whether he was retrieving the device that opened the block door, or perhaps a pair of binding cuffs before he took her back to the yard. He dug into one of the pockets of the jacket, and pulled out a tsentyl, swiping his thumb casually across it.

She didn't feel any more reassured, wondering if he was registering her capture. Glancing over her shoulder through the open door, Georgianna wondered how far she could run before the guard would catch her.

She'd never reach the gates, and even if she did, Edtroka could easily send a message to make sure the other guards knew not to let her pass.

"The girl, she related?" he asked, barely glancing up from the device as it opened onto his palm.

"Who?" Georgianna asked in surprise, looking at him again.

Edtroka glanced up, raising an eyebrow.

"You wanted information on a sale, right?"

She blinked, staring at him for a moment before she realised what he was talking about. The run in with Tzanlomne had driven Nyah from her mind. Now the memory was back, she nodded.

"Nyah."

Edtroka nodded, but didn't look up as he moved his thumb over the tsentyl again.

"Not by blood," Georgianna answered. "I grew up with her and a friend, though. I just…"

Lifting his head, Edtroka fixed Georgianna with a hard glare, one that immediately told her that she was not to argue with him.

"You just want to make sure she is safe."

Georgianna paused, taking a slow deep breath before she nodded.

"That's right."

"Maarqyn," he answered. "She was bought by Maarqyn Guinnyr."

"Maarqyn," Georgianna repeated. "Who is he?"

Edtroka shook his head as he slid the tsentyl closed and stuffed it back into the pocket of his jacket. Slinging the item over the back of a chair, Edtroka perched himself on the edge of the table, watching her like a hawk hunting for prey.

"No one you should be pressing for information, Med," he said. "My advice: find out your friend is okay from a distance and then leave be. Your pretty neck will be the better for it."

Georgianna's eyes widened as she looked back at Edtroka. She didn't want to think that Maarqyn was really that dangerous, or that he would hurt Nyah. She knew better than most that only a small number of dreta got through unscathed. Even if they weren't physical wounds like Jacob's, they were always there.

"Thank... Thank you for telling me."

A shudder moved down her spine when Edtroka's gaze didn't falter from her face. She took a step back and his lips flickered into a momentary grin.

"No need to thank me."

She didn't like the sound of that. Taking another small step back, she was again wondering how far she could run when Edtroka shrugged, almost chuckling.

"Dreta owners are public record. I could have sent you into the city to find out from them, but they ask more questions and... well... not a problem."

Georgianna froze. Had she really just worked herself up over nothing? Every look, every motion, she'd thought meant something else. She almost didn't know what to do now. She'd worked this whole thing up in her head as such a problem when, as it turned out, it was almost as if it were a common occurrence.

Edtroka pushed himself quickly up from the edge of the table. Georgianna didn't think anything of it until a hand clapped onto her shoulder, making her jump. She turned her head, looking up at one of the other guards.

"What you doing here?" he asked. "E'troke?"

"I'm guessing she's looking to be let onto the block," he suggested. "Got turned around, right, Med?"

Looking between the two guards in surprise, Georgianna hesitated for a moment.

"Yes, Volsonne," she answered, glancing at Edtroka with a cautious smile.

"I'm going that way anyway," Edtroka said, patting the guard on the front of his shoulder as he passed through the doorway into the corridor. "I'll take her."

The guard shrugged and removed his hand from Georgianna's shoulder.

"Thought you'd have known better, Medic," he warned.

Georgianna nodded.

"Yeah, me too," Georgianna replied.

She followed Edtroka down the corridor, wondering why, if it was all public record, Edtroka had lied to the other guard. However, the guard was right about one thing. When it came to the compound and asking about things that went on within it, she really should have known better.

18 Into the Northern Quarters

"Are you sure we're going the right way?" Georgianna asked, looking over her shoulder for what felt like the hundredth time.

Taye nodded, though she didn't think he seemed all that sure about it, the way he kept looking around. She frowned, chewing on her lip as she stared down the street, the houses melting into each other.

"It was the eighteenth?"

"Yes, Gianna, will you give it a rest already?" Taye hissed irritably. "I know where I'm going."

Frowning and gritting her teeth, Georgianna resisted the urge to roll her eyes. It was fine him telling her not to worry, but he wasn't the one who had asked the questions about

Nyah, and to an Adveni no less. If something happened, who did Taye think they would suspect? She had done her part, she was doing it. She'd found out who Nyah had been sold to, Taye couldn't ask more of her than that.

She remained silent, even though she itched to get a straight answer from him. Crossing her arms over her chest, her fingers drummed against her skin. Silence stretched between them like rubber, threatening to snap.

Who knew how long they would have before an Adveni spotted them and asked them what they were even doing in this district? Taye had brought some 'product' with him, an insurance plan so that, should they be asked, he could say he was delivering a purchase. He'd even memorised the street name of a client so that he could lie convincingly. However, the best option was that they were able to come, see the house, and then move away without being seen.

"Who did you say gave you this?"

Taye turned his head to glare at her in disbelief, a huff of indignation whistling through his teeth.

"Suns girl, you don't give up, do you?"

She shook her head.

"I think I have a right to be worried," she grumbled, stuffing her hands into her pockets. "We're in Adveni territory, Taye. Or had you forgotten with all these nice buildings?"

The buildings were nice, almost annoyingly so. It was just that little bit harder to hate the Adveni when you were surrounded by their technology. Georgianna didn't venture into the Adveni sections of the city very often apart from the

Rion, but even there the bright lights bouncing off smooth, polished surfaces were hard to ignore. Everything was sleek and well made, smooth lines and sharp corners. It all looked very... technical.

Out in their housing quarter things were a little simpler. The buildings were less focused, but beautiful just the same. Two- and three-storey buildings sprawled across larger areas of land in the wealthy areas, tall blocks that housed dozens of dwellings for those who were not as high on the pay scale.

The biggest building they had seen so far, a little way in past the beginning of the dwellings, had been a two-storey complex that spread like a lake, sprawling further than Georgianna could see. The pale yellow stone shining in the sunlight made it almost blinding. Outside there had been no signs in Veuric as to what it was. Unfortunately, Taye didn't know.

"It was just a guy I do a deal with," Taye sighed finally. "I promised him a couple extra doses if he found out where this Vtensu lived."

"Doses?" she shrieked. Taye glanced fearfully at her, so she lowered her voice. "Please tell me the guy was at least not taking while he agreed."

Taye waved his hand, a smug grin on his face.

"You want to take issue with my sources, Gianna, you might want to return the Adveni stuff I get you."

Georgianna clutched her bag against her hip and pressed her lips together as Taye laughed.

"Yeah, that's what I thought."

Georgianna had dosed a couple of times, though not for a while. It was a slippery slope. The euphoric sensation the powder gave when smeared onto the temples was thrilling, and she could understand why some chose to do it more often. However, she'd also seen the effects of dosing over a long period, so she made sure to keep her own use to a minimum.

"Remember Taye, we're just looking!" Georgianna reminded him forcefully.

Taye glanced at her, turning his head and glaring for a moment, his steps slowing as he seemed to consider whether to answer her or not. Not, it turned out, won the argument and he quickened his steps along the road, crossing his arms defensively over his chest. Georgianna immediately lengthened her stride to catch up with him.

"Taye! We're just looking... right?"

"Yes!" Taye snapped, not looking back this time. "Just looking. So stop, alright?"

"You're just... you're not filling me with a lot of confidence here."

Taye stopped, turning on his heel to move in front of her. Georgianna wavered for a moment mid-step, quickly righting herself and coming to a stop in front of him.

"What do you expect?" he demanded.

Georgianna frowned and shrugged. She didn't know what she expected from Taye. He'd been so anxious since the moment she had told him that she knew who had bought Nyah. No, that was wrong, he had been this way since Nyah was taken. There were times when he was cheerful, but mostly, he wasn't the same guy that she had known before. Even after the Adveni arrived, Taye had always been happy and confident, yet these days Georgianna hardly recognised him.

"I know you're worried about her, but…"

"Yes, I am, but, can we just talk about something else?"

Georgianna sighed and nodded. Maybe it was best.

"Like?"

Taye turned away from her, starting off down the road again, though Georgianna couldn't work out how Taye could keep his head straight in this maze. The roads twisted and turned and she had no idea how many turnings they'd taken onto different streets. Taye, apparently, was keeping track, because he was walking with the determination of someone who knew exactly where they were going.

Georgianna hurried to keep up, a few long strides before she fell into step with him. Taye was naturally tall and long legged, so it meant Georgianna had to push every step to stay close. Luckily, however, she was used to walking next to her father and brother, both a good head taller than her.

"I dunno, how's your da'?" he asked.

Smiling and giving him a careless shrug, Georgianna glanced sideways up at Taye.

"He's alright," she answered. "I think he likes having Braedon around to keep him company when he's at home."

"Yeah, he's what, four now?"

"Almost five," she answered. "And exactly like Halden."

Taye glanced at her and raised an eyebrow. Taye knew

Braedon was not theirs by blood, but he didn't comment on it.

"Well, out of the people to be like, Halden's a good one," he said. "How is Halden doing, anyway?"

Georgianna's grin faded and she looked down at the floor, watching the smooth path pass beneath her feet.

"He's... surviving."

"Aren't we all?"

"Some better than others."

Taye rocked his head from side to side.

Georgianna brought her hands from her pockets and clasped them in front of her, idly picking at a notch in her thumb nail.

"I dunno, he seems fine, work and all, but I don't think he's even trying to move on."

"Should he?" Taye asked. "He was joined, that's not an easy thing to get past."

Georgianna nodded. She knew she couldn't expect Halden to move on from Nequiel, not when his death had been so horrific. Yet like Taye, her brother was no longer the same person she had grown up with. He was quieter, more reserved, and less willing to talk about anything important. As selfish and as stupid as it was with everything Halden had been through, Georgianna missed her brother.

"It's not like Nyah," she said slowly. "Nequiel is gone."

"You say that like my missing Nyah is worse," Taye answered. "I still have hope that I can see her, maybe even get her back one day. Halden doesn't."

Taye looked sideways at her, raising an eyebrow as

Georgianna glanced up at him.

"We don't all flit easily onto someone new."

Georgianna opened her mouth in indignation. She'd never been in Taye's situation, or Halden's. She'd never even considered joining with someone, not past a silly teenage fantasy.

"I don't..."

"Oh yes you do," Taye cut her off. "You think your brother likes that Keiran?"

"He doesn't..."

"Yeah, he knows," Taye confirmed. "You're not half as secretive as you think you are. They know you're seeing someone, someone who doesn't treat you the way you deserve."

Georgianna harrumphed at his suggestion and shook her head.

"He's nice to me!" Georgianna argued. "And it's not like I've been begging him to join and he's saying no. I'm not ready for that either."

"That doesn't mean your family like it. They want you settled with a decent guy."

"Settled is..."

"Safe?"

"Boring."

Taye laughed and rolled his eyes. Georgianna looked away.

"Well, boring or not, Keiran is not who I would suggest doing it with."

"Oh, and I suppose you have a host of guys for me to

choose from?" she asked. "There is nothing wrong with Keiran. He's Nerrin, he's a Belsa!"

"He's a Vtensu!"

Georgianna reached out and smacked Taye. He stepped away, rubbing his arm.

"I'll tell your uncle what you said if you don't shut your mouth."

"Tell him. He'll agree with me," Taye argued.

"He's…"

"Oh, admit it Gianna, you like him because he's handsome, not because he's a good guy."

"He *is* a good guy!" Georgianna exclaimed.

"No, he's not. If he was, he wouldn't be running round with other girls."

"How do you…?"

"Everyone in the tunnels knows he has a different girl most nights," Taye answered with a hard look. "You're more often than most, but there are others."

"You think I don't know that?"

"Then why put up with it?"

Georgianna stopped, glaring at Taye in annoyance. Though, it did occur to her for a moment that maybe she was more annoyed that so many people apparently knew the ins and outs of her private life. Liliah, Wrench, Taye, and apparently her family. Now, Taye was making out that everyone in the tunnels knew as well. The Belsa, the Carae, her sex life was apparently common knowledge.

She was probably worrying about it too much. Taye was over-exaggerating. He had to be.

"The last one was better," he said suddenly.

"The last what?"

"Boyfriend."

"What boyfriend? I wasn't..."

Taye uncrossed his arms from over his chest, clicking his fingers together as he waved his hand around, as if that would help him remember.

"Al... Al... Alec?"

Georgianna looked at Taye in surprise. As surprised as she was that Taye knew about Keiran, it was even more of a shock that he knew about Alec.

"Alec was never my boyfriend," Georgianna said.

Taye opened his mouth, ready to reply, but Georgianna held up her hand, cutting him off.

"Plus, you can like him all you want," she muttered. "He's dead, so there's no point talking about it."

Taye looked away quickly. Whether he'd not known about Alec's death, or he'd simply not thought about it before bringing it up, a slight colour rose on his cheeks and he stuffed his hands into his pockets. Georgianna felt a little bad. She hadn't meant to bring it up quite so bluntly, but it was the truth, Alec was dead and there was nothing that could be done. Like Nequiel, people simply had to find a way to move on.

Alec had been fun to hang out with, and they certainly found each other attractive and enjoyable enough to keep going back, but they had both known what it was. She wasn't looking for a relationship, and Alec was trying to forget the loss of one. She had asked him about her once, his wife, but he simply said that she was gone and that was that, conversation over.

That was the thing about Alec: everyone knew he was a great guy, that he was a skilled fighter and had impeccable morals, but he was hard to actually know on any intimate level. His unwavering belief in his hatred of the Adveni, which admittedly he had good cause for, made it difficult to talk to him about anything regarding them, including her work at the compound. Alec had made his opinions on her working there abundantly clear: it was a bad idea and she shouldn't go back because one day she would get caught up in it.

When Georgianna refused, the argument had not been pretty. It was, unfortunately, one of the most honest conversations they ever had, yet it had turned into a shouting match which ended in her storming out. She didn't need some guy she fooled around with telling her who she should and shouldn't help.

She'd been stubborn, refusing to go back and apologise, even though she really did think Alec was a decent guy. However, before the stubbornness had even begun to fade, she'd learned that he was missing. She'd looked for him, she'd checked the compound and she'd listened in on conversations between the Belsa, but in the end, they'd agreed that death was the only logical explanation for his disappearance.

For a while, Taye and Georgianna walked in silence, Taye watching the buildings pass around them, Georgianna watching her feet. She tried not to think of Alec too often, even though she knew that his death had not been her fault. He was a Belsa: short life expectancy was almost a given. Despite her difficulty in getting to know him, he had been a decent friend if nothing more.

Georgianna still hadn't told Si about Alec, though she suspected that Jaid might have explained it to him. She hated pretending that Alec was alive, as if he would walk in at any moment, having come off guard duty to visit his friend. Hearing Si speak about Alec as if he were still around had been much harder than she'd thought. It had been two years, but it still caught her breath when he was brought up so casually by Si, by Keiran, and now by Taye.

"I think that's it," Taye suddenly announced, lifting his hand to point at a house coming up on their right.

Georgianna slowed her steps, trying not to stare. She glanced around at the other houses, scanning across them until she came to the one Taye had pointed at. For a moment she paused, her gaze washing over everything she could take in before she quickly looked away to the other side of the street.

"You're sure?" she asked.

Taye looked around too, but his gaze locked back onto the house pretty quickly. It looked much the same as the others, a little bigger than those next to it, but the same style and general appearance. Slowing their steps even more, Georgianna scuffed her foot idly against the pavement, looking this way and that but always landing on the same spot.

"Yeah, this is the eighteenth," he answered after a moment. "I'm sure of it."

She looked away, not wanting to be seen staring, but when she looked back, Taye was already two steps ahead of her, moving across the road towards the house. Squeaking in horror, Georgianna lurched forward and grabbed Taye's arm, tugging him back.

"Taye!" she hissed under her breath, looking up at him furiously.

Taye, however, wasn't listening. His gaze never wavered from the window at the front of the house, which was flung open. Georgianna followed his gaze and gasped as she saw a blonde figure there, looking out of the house.

Her face was partially masked by her long blonde hair, the clothes not her own but those given to her, but it was Nyah. Georgianna paused, unable to tug Taye along any more as he stared at the woman he would have been joined to. His mouth opened, his chest heaved, and a groan issued from his mouth.

Georgianna kept a tight hold on his arm, especially when a deep voice echoed out of the house.

"Nyah!"

Nyah flinched, her hair flying back as she turned towards the voice and disappeared back into the house. This time, Georgianna moaned as well: for the briefest moment before she disappeared, clamped securely around Nyah's throat, a cinystalq collar had glinted back at them in the mid-heat sun.

19   STILL NOT GROWN

The house dripped in shadows, the flickering light from the oil lamp dancing in dappled spots across the corridor through the open doorway. Georgianna sat on the floor, her back against the corner of the doorframe, watching the specks and flames of light across the sandstone. It had been a long time since she'd heard one of her father's stories, but the moment he'd begun telling it, Georgianna could remember it in its entirety.

Halden was out, working long hours again, so the task of putting Braedon to bed had fallen to her own father, as did storytelling. As Georgianna was home so infrequently compared to her brother and father, Braedon had quickly demanded that Georgianna be the one to tell him a story, but she had managed to talk him out of it. Her tales were far too dull, and didn't always have happy endings. It was better to have a tale from his Grandda', who was experienced in such things. Her father had scowled and smacked the back of her arm for passing the job onto him, but she'd noticed the small smile as he tucked Braedon in, and the look of fond surprise when he moved to sit down and noticed her perched outside the door to listen too.

It was the one about the coyote who found himself trapped in a deep hole. He needed to learn to be nice to those who were different if they were to help him find a way out. Braedon had complained and whined when he couldn't have the ship story, which was apparently his favourite, but Georgianna knew all too well that the coyote story was the best. It was the longest, which meant you got to stay up longer. For twenty-six years, she had neglected to tell her father that particular reason for requesting it as a child.

She'd considered going back to the tunnels with Taye after their trip into the Adveni quarters, but after seeing Nyah, with the collar fastened around her neck, Georgianna felt the longing for the familiarity of home. Taye was so separated from everyone he considered family, and so she found herself making the long trek through the camps, looking forward to the safe and protected feeling when her father gathered her into his arms.

"Holding on to the head of the snake, they began lowering his long body into the hole."

Georgianna giggled, quickly covering her mouth so as not to disturb the story. She'd never considered as a child, just how odd it would look for a bear to lower a snake into a hole so that a coyote could climb up the animal like a rope. Her father's stories, except for the ships, had always been a little strange, and it hadn't been until she got older that she realised the life lessons in them all.

Resting her head back against the frame, Georgianna closed her eyes, listening to the low rumble of her father's voice. In fact, she had almost drifted off herself when he stepped over her legs, nudging her shoulder so that he could pull the door closed. Georgianna got to her feet, following him back into the front room where she slumped down onto the thick rug. It was bare in places, and there were some stains that just wouldn't come out, but it was still more comfortable than the bare floor.

Her father took a seat on his whittling stool, collecting up his knife and a half-finished piece, glancing over at his daughter lying flat on her back staring up at the ceiling.

"You will need your own stories soon, my Gianna," he said.

Georgianna let out an amused breath, shaking her head.

"Hardly."

"No, you will. When you are ready to tell them."

She turned her head, her cheek pressed against the coarse fibres of the wool. Her father didn't look up, his knife making smooth strokes against the wood, slivers coming off against the blade, floating down onto the floor.

"I don't think that will be for a while, Da'," she replied. "I don't even know if that's what I want."

Her father gave a low hum of laughter, and though he

didn't look up, she could see the amusement sparkling in his eyes through the lamplight.

"You're still a sapling."

"I'm twenty-six."

"And still a sapling," he said. "Your mother was the same."

Rolling onto her side, Georgianna curled her arm underneath her head, using it as a pillow. Brushing a curl of hair away from her face, she grinned at him.

"She was, what, twenty-one when you had Halden?"

He thought about it for a moment, nodding his head.

"Yes, I suppose she would have been."

"That's hardly the same."

Her father lifted his head, his gaze locking onto her. Leaning to the side, he placed the block down on the floor, resting the knife on top of it, and rested his elbows onto his knees.

"I always knew what I wanted," he explained. "I wanted a family and a steady life. Your mother, she didn't know. She was free and adventurous."

Without warning, her father let out a sad laugh. What had seemed so happy in his eyes only moments before filled with a desolate longing.

"She called me her tether."

Georgianna blinked as unexpected moisture began collecting in the corners of her eyes. She wasn't sure whether it was the memory of her mother, who she had missed for such a long time, or the sight of her father missing her so deeply, but even blinking couldn't keep the tears at bay. Reaching up, she swiped the heel of her hand across her eyes.

"You may not know what you want now, my girl, but one day you will find your tether and it will all fall into place."

She shook her head, the tears gathering faster than she could brush them away. Blurring her vision, she felt the first drop slip along her lashes and drip down onto her cheek, rolling towards her ear. She pushed herself up, crossing her legs and leaning forward into her lap.

"I don't want that." She looked down at her feet. "Not when I can see how much it hurts when it's gone."

She heard a slow sigh. Without looking up, she could imagine his look of puzzled concern, brow furrowed, adding even more lines to his worn, tanned skin.

"Nyah was sold."

"The Wolfe girl? She used to follow you kids around like a pup."

Georgianna nodded, staring at her fingers while she dug at a crack in her thumbnail. She'd not remembered that, the way Nyah had always followed them around. It probably looked different to her father, the eight-year-old children being trailed by this five-year-old little blonde girl. Taye had adored her, even then, though it had been different that long ago.

"She was arrested a few months ago, and we found out that she was sold as a drysta. Taye's devastated."

"Yes, I can imagine he would be. His mother wagered their joining by the time you were, oh, fifteen?"

Georgianna breathed a breath of bittersweet laughter. If anyone had had the traditional plan of joining, it had been Taye and Nyah. They'd been friends longer than any of them could remember, and that bond had grown into something unbreakable as naturally as the grass grew after the wash.

"I've never felt that way."

"Who says you should have? You're still a sa...."

"Please stop calling me a sapling, Da'!" Georgianna pleaded. "I'm not a sapling."

Her father frowned back at her, clasping his hands in his lap. He hunched further over his knees, considering her for a moment before he spoke.

"When you were young, I told you that you couldn't force wood to be a certain way."

Georgianna nodded.

"Well, wood also cannot tell you what it wants to be when it doesn't know itself," he explained. "You are still becoming who you want to be; you cannot be what someone else needs as well."

It was Georgianna's turn to frown. She wasn't entirely sure that she knew what he was talking about. She thought she had it, but she didn't feel any better about herself, or about what was happening to Taye and Nyah. For an inspirational talk, she wasn't feeling all that inspired. She felt more depressed than ever.

"You are still growing, Gianna," he smiled. "Emotionally, at least. I don't think you're ever going to be tall."

She couldn't help herself, a laugh slipped forth, and she smiled a wet grin back at her father.

"Mum was the same?"

"She grew so unexpectedly," he beamed. "Maybe that will be how it is for you, that you will meet the man and... it is a man, right?"

Georgianna's eyes widened in surprise.

"Yes, Da'."

"Okay then," he nodded. "Well, maybe you'll meet him and you'll... feel grown."

She remembered her father's stories being more eloquent than this. Or, at least, easier to follow. He sounded so profound and wise when she was a child, though maybe he wasn't as sure about how to deal with a daughter who didn't dream of her joining the way other girls did. She had been running after medics, asking them to show her injuries, or climbing trees and getting lost on the trail.

"If Mum had been sold..." Georgianna cut herself off. Even the thought of that was horrifying to her.

"I would have walked off the edge of the world to get her back."

Georgianna pushed herself up onto her knees, shuffling across the floor to kneel between her father's legs. Wrapping her arms around his waist, she buried her face against his chest. He wrapped a strong arm around her shoulders, holding her against him as tightly as when he'd been able to pick her up in one arm and carry her through their camp. With Taye's desperation for a plan and Keiran's objections to carrying one out at all both vying for attention in her mind, her father's words were exactly what she needed to hear.

Georgianna sniffed, her final tears brushed away by his shirt.

"So would I."

20 Behind the Bar

The Rion district was alight with Adveni electricity by the time Georgianna trudged through their streets. While the district was controlled by Adveni, Veniche huddled on street corners, waiting for an Adveni who might give them a second glance.

On one corner were the Olcinyty, who would sell their bodies for an Adveni's pleasure at the right price. On the next, a couple of Carae who would sell the Adveni their pleasure in substances the Adveni did not know how to create from Os-Veruh's plants.

Georgianna travelled past them all, before turning down an alleyway to go in through the side door of a bar. Closing the door behind her, she moved through the back corridor to a small room assigned to the workers. She placed her bag on one of the shelves against the wall, and pulled out a ribbon to tie her hair in a knot high on her head.

Leaving the small room, she passed along the corridor that led out to the bar. Greunn, the Adveni owner of the bar looked out of his office as she passed, clucking his tongue against his teeth.

"Late."

She gave him an apologetic smile.

"I'm so sorry. I was on my way, but there was an emergency."

He didn't look convinced. He raised an eyebrow, scratching his jaw.

"Always is," he grumbled.

Georgianna's smile faltered as he turned away, grasping the door handle to his office.

"Docking wages, maybe that'll teach you."

Nodding respectfully at his back, she slipped past Greunn and headed out towards the bar. It happened to be the third time he'd told her such a thing, so she wasn't too worried.

Lifting the thick wedge of wood that closed the bar off from the customers, Georgianna slipped past. She closed the wedge behind her and turned around, straightening the front of her shirt as she went.

"You're late," a man chuckled from his seat on the other side of the counter.

Glancing at him, her eyes widened in surprise. It was Edtroka, a drink in front of him, his dark gaze fixed on her. He looked different without his guard uniform, less scary in some ways, but odd in others. She had never seen him in anything less than a perfectly kept Adveni uniform. Sitting in front of the bar, he looked almost, dare she say it, normal.

"Has someone been telling tales on me?" she asked, glancing down the bar at Liliah, who had clearly been listening in on the exchange. She looked at Georgianna and swiped her finger swiftly across her lips. Penn, on the other hand, washing out glasses, grinned sheepishly down into the suds.

"Glad to see you take timekeeping more seriously when you work for me."

"I, Volsonne, do not work for you," Georgianna insisted. "I work to keep those prisoners alive."

"And yet you run every time I send you a message," he sighed. "Must be my irresistible charm. I should have that looked at. You don't happen to know a medic who can give me something, do you?"

Georgianna giggled involuntarily as she shook her head. She couldn't quite believe he was talking to her this way, though their exchange when she'd asked for details on Nyah should probably have alerted her to the fact there was a side to Edtroka of which she saw little. She wondered how he was with his friends, how he behaved around Adveni women. She could imagine, what with the way he was now and the way he looked, that he would be rather popular.

"Maybe some sort of sedative," she suggested. "It would certainly keep that ego under control."

Edtroka cocked his head to the side, considering her words. After a moment, he nodded slowly.

"That would certainly work. Wouldn't be half as

entertaining as what I had in mind though."

"Well, I do try to tell my patients the downsides of any medication," she told him. "Now, would you like another drink?"

Georgianna was kept relatively busy with customers after delivering Edtroka's fresh drink, and when there weren't people at the bar waiting, there were tables to clean and glasses to collect. She didn't get much of a chance to talk to Edtroka again, especially not while there were other Adveni in close proximity, and the guard kept a steely silence.

Penn apologised to Georgianna for telling the Adveni that she was late, but Georgianna dismissed the apology and told Penn that there was nothing to be sorry about. He had only been telling the truth after all.

Liliah, however, seemed much more interested in why Georgianna had been late, not to mention her banter with the Adveni, even though he was still sat at the bar behind them. As the two of them found themselves reaching for the same bottle of dark berry wine, Liliah finally found her chance.

"There's nothing to tell," Georgianna assured her. "I was out in the camps visiting my Da' and I ran late."

"So you weren't with…"

Georgianna glanced at Liliah as she took the bottle of wine from her and began pouring some into a glass.

"With who? Keiran?"

"Unless there's another?"

Giving her friend a scandalised look, Georgianna rolled her eyes.

"What exactly do you take me for? There's no one else,

and I wasn't with Keiran. I was at home."

She turned quickly away from Liliah, delivering the glass of wine to the customer with a respectful bow of her head. Liliah gathered a brewed beer and the glass of wine she'd poured, and took them to her own customer before returning to Georgianna.

"Did something happen?" she asked, placing her hands on her hips. "Did he do something?"

"Suns, Lil', what makes you think that? He didn't do anything."

"Every time I've seen you recently, you've either been working, or you've been with him, now you're going home instead," Liliah answered as if it were the most obvious thing on the planet. "Girls get their hearts broken and they run home to their Da'."

Liliah offered her a triumphant smile, leaving Georgianna to stare dumbfounded as the brunette walked off to collect some glasses from a table left vacated by customers. Georgianna didn't like it; she didn't like that Liliah thought Keiran had done something wrong when he hadn't. It wasn't her involvement with Keiran that had meant she'd gone home. She'd wanted to talk to her father about Taye and Nyah, though that did open up questions on how she would tell Keiran that she wasn't heeding his advice about the whole situation.

"He didn't do anything, Lil'," Georgianna said quietly as she returned to the bar. "Things are fine. At least, I think they are."

"You think?" Liliah asked.

Georgianna frowned, scratching behind her ear as she tried to think of what to say. She couldn't tell Liliah about Taye. It wouldn't be fair to force that sort of secret on her.

"I don't agree with him on something," she admitted, "and I don't know if he's going to be upset about it."

"Why would he be upset? After all, aren't you two just… friends?"

"Yes, we are, but this is different."

"Why?"

Resting her elbow against the bar, in front of all the bottles positioned neatly in their rows, she thought of how to explain without actually explaining. Liliah knew Georgianna worked down the Way whenever she could, but telling her that she was involved in the escape of a drysta was too dangerous.

"It's about my sister's job," she said, making sure to pronounce every syllable correctly. "It's not the safest job."

Liliah stared back at her in blank confusion. Liliah knew that Georgianna didn't have a sister, and she opened her mouth twice before the light of understanding flickered in her eyes.

"Okay," she answered, pausing for a moment. "So why would he be upset? It's nothing to do with him, right?"

"No, it's not, but he's being… I don't know, he's… he doesn't want her to get hurt."

Liliah could not stop a small squeak of laughter. Looking at Georgianna, she offered an apologetic expression that didn't quite look sincere as the smile pressed against her lips. Georgianna looked back at her in surprise, raising an eyebrow as she tried to work out what was so amusing.

"Sounds like he's protective, if you ask me," she beamed.

"So?"

"So, it's not like a man who's 'just having fun' to be protective of his friend's sister, is it?" Liliah asked. "Sounds like he's not simply taking advantage anymore."

"Who said he was taking advantage?"

"Isn't he?"

"No, he's not, Lil'. He's not tricking me or promising me things he won't deliver. I knew what I was getting into."

"Short term, yes," Liliah answered. "But long term?"

Georgianna tucked an errant lock of hair behind her ear and crossed her arms. Seeing the look on Georgianna's face, Liliah held her hands up.

"Alright, alright, forget it," she said. "So you disagree. What's the problem?"

Liliah shrugged as she collected up a couple of glasses from the bar and handed them over to Penn. Georgianna grabbed a cloth, absently wiping the same spot on the bar.

"I don't want to fight with him."

"Well, there's your problem."

"Where?"

"You don't want to fight. You never do. You keep doing something while it feels good and then run away as soon as there's a problem. Isn't that why you stopped seeing the other guy, because you fought and you didn't like what he said?"

Georgianna's brow furrowed and she shrugged.

"You don't stick around to see if something will work. You just move on to the next thing that feels good. You think Qiyan and I never fight?"

Liliah gave a sudden bitter laugh and shook her head, using the glass in her hand and gesturing with it. She moved her hand so violently that, for a moment, Georgianna thought the glass might be flung out of Liliah's slim fingers and shatter into a thousand pieces.

"We fight all the time, but we stick at it because we love each other," Liliah said. "Suns, we fight over this place, but he knows it brings food in."

Georgianna wasn't entirely sure where Liliah was going with this. If she was trying to convince Georgianna that she should talk to Keiran, even though it might make him angry, telling her how much she fought with her fiancé wasn't the right way to go about it.

"You know what's best about the fighting?" Liliah asked suddenly.

Georgianna frowned.

"Nothing?"

"The sex," Liliah answered. "Angry-fight sex, or after-fight sex, it's brilliant."

From his place at the bar, Edtroka snorted with laughter. Both girls turned quickly to look at him, their eyes wide in surprise and embarrassment that he'd been listening to their conversation. Still chuckling, Edtroka raised one hand.

"Oh, don't mind me," he said through a smirk.

Georgianna glared at him before turning back to Liliah, lowering her voice significantly.

"So what? You're saying I should tell Keiran about... my sister's job? So I can have angry sex?" she asked.

"No," Liliah answered bluntly. "I'm saying that if you're not willing to tell him something just because it might cause a fight, if you won't stick around for the bad, how can you ever expect him to stick around and fight for you?"

Liliah was called away by a customer before Georgianna managed to think of a suitable response. Even as the night progressed she couldn't find a comeback to prove Liliah wrong. The problem was, the longer it took for her to think of an argument to the brunette's point, the more she thought that actually, Liliah might not be wrong after all.

21 Wrench in the Works

It was late by the time Georgianna finally finished at Crisco and made her way from the Rion district. It felt like stone blocks had attached themselves to her hands and feet, making the walk through the streets long and laborious. While it usually only took a short time to walk the stretch to the nearest safe tunnel entrance, Georgianna felt like she'd been walking for hours before she could finally slip down into the lit main line. Even then, down in the tunnels, in the quiet of the night, it felt like too long a time until she could make the turning unseen into the stretch of Belsa-controlled passages.

The guard recognised Georgianna before she even realised he was there, and proceeded to ramble and panic about a problem down Medics' Way. Georgianna didn't stop to find out what the problem was. The fact that a guard was still on post was enough to tell her the Belsa hadn't been discovered, and despite the aching in her legs, she set off at a run down the tunnel.

Coming into Medics' Way, Georgianna expected chaos. The way the guard had told her about it made it sound like it was a big problem. However, apart from a pained groaning echoing from one of the cars, all seemed relatively quiet. Still, Georgianna kept hurrying down towards the car, hauling herself up and dropping her bag to the side of the door.

Jaid had her back to her, her short dark hair mussed from being woken up in a rush. Georgianna moved further into the car, trying to see what was going on.

"Wrench?"

Wrench was lying on the bed before her. His dark skin was beaded with sweat, his breath, too fast for Georgianna's liking, came in quick pants that left no space for anything else. His trousers had been left intact but his shirt, always tattered at best, was torn from neck to hem, lying open across the bed to show a large, purple and red angry welt across his barrelled chest.

"George!" Jaid cried, stepping back from Wrench's side and reaching into a bucket, pulling out a cloth and wringing it, using it to clean an oozing wound. "Where have you been?"

"Work," Georgianna answered, stepping closer to Wrench and placing the back of her hand across his stomach to gauge his temperature. "What happened?"

The taught skin across Wrench's skin was searing hot, radiating out from a weeping wound of burned flesh. Georgianna didn't even need to hear Jaid's answer before she knew exactly what had happened.

"Copaq. He came in an hour ago, I've not been able to stop the sweats, and nothing will take the pain away."

Georgianna frowned and moved to her bag. Flipping it open, she dug through it until she found a small, linen bag. She tugged it out, pulling the drawstring open and taking out a shiny, lilac pill.

The copaq didn't injure like a normal gun. Instead of firing a metal bullet, a copaq, whether one of the small hand weapons or a larger rifle, projected a gel pellet which, though hard when shot, splattered across the skin upon contact. When the gel hit, it sent out a number of electrical charges as it reacted with the skin, slowly fading away as the chemical inside the gel was used up. Even after scraping the gel from the skin, the damage had been done. The Adveni used them mainly on capture missions because the electrical charges shooting through the body made it impossible to run. Unfortunately, healing the injuries was also made difficult, as the Veniche had little with which to counteract the chemical.

"What's that?" Jaid asked as she dabbed the damp cloth against the welt.

Wrench let out a pained cry.

"Drugs. They're Adveni."

"Where did you get Adveni medicine?" Jaid asked suspiciously.

"Compound," Georgianna explained, stepping past Jaid. "Here, Wrench, swallow this."

"It won't help."

Georgianna and Jaid spun around, the wet cloth slipping from Jaid's fingers to the floor with a wet slap. Jacob was leaning into the car, his curly hair dishevelled from sleep.

"Jacob, go back to…"

"No, wait." Georgianna interrupted. "Jake, what won't work?"

Jacob swung his legs up into the car with surprising agility for someone who had so many healing injuries. He came and looked down at Wrench.

"The cloth, it won't help. Neither will your drugs. They design it that way."

"Then what will?" Jaid snapped.

From Jacob's time as a drysta, Georgianna wondered whether he had more experience with the wounds the weapons created. She didn't want to think about how Jacob would know about copaq weapons.

"Something cold," he said. "Wrapped in hyliha leaves."

"What?"

"It can be anything cold, but the hyliha is what does it. And you should make him drink that water, not wash him with it."

Georgianna looked at Jaid in confusion. Hyliha leaves weren't often used for anything important, so why would they work when apparently nothing else would? Jaid didn't seem too pleased with Jacob's assessment, and Georgianna was sure that given the choice, she would tell him to go back to the car he currently called home. The man was only twenty-one. He had been fourteen when he was taken by the Adveni. At most, he had three years' training, not enough to know about different medicines, even if he'd been training as a medic. With all his injuries and the things he had suffered, Georgianna had never even thought to ask him.

"I don't have any hyliha leaves," Jaid answered after a moment, crouching to collect the cloth from the floor.

Georgianna watched as Jaid shook off the cloth and dunked it back into the water, wringing it out and moving back to Wrench's side. Frowning, she glanced back and forth between the three people in the train car, daring them to defy her. During her training, Georgianna had been taught that hyliha was only useful if you had nothing else. It could be used to sooth irritation and to cool the burning of heat, but there were other things that worked better. Hyliha was only used as a last resort until you could get your hands on something better.

Georgianna glanced down at the pill in her hand. She didn't know what to think. They'd treated men with copaq wounds before and the pill always took away some of the pain. Not all of it, but at least some. Stepping to the side, Georgianna picked up a canteen and shook it. Water sloshed inside the metal, and she moved over to Wrench's side.

"Swallow this," she urged, dropping the pill into his open mouth and carefully moving the canteen to his lips.

Wrench swallowed, small sips at first, but within seconds he was reaching for the canteen, grasping it and tipping more water down his throat. Georgianna stared in surprise before her gaze darted to Jacob. He was watching silently, his fingers wound in the material of his shirt. He said the pills wouldn't help, but here Wrench was, gulping down water like he was already feeling better. Georgianna's mouth dropped open as a realisation hit her. When she had been healing copaq wounds before, it hadn't been the pills that were helping; it was the water they used to wash it down.

She pulled the canteen away and dunked it back into the bucket.

"George, what are you..."

"He's right!" Georgianna cried, bringing the canteen back to Wrench's lips and letting him take hold like an infant at bottle. "The water! I... We need hyliha!"

"George, I already told him, we don't have any!" Even Georgianna could hear the edge of desperation in her voice.

"No," Georgianna answered, a smile on her lips. "But Lacie does!"

"What?"

"Lacie has hyliha leaves! I gave them to her for grinding practice!"

Georgianna signalled to Jacob.

"Give him as much water as he can drink." She turned to Jaid. "I'm going to get Lacie!"

Georgianna was already slipping past them, jumping down out of the train car as Jaid's desperate cry for her to come back followed, not fast enough to catch her and drag her back inside.

Sprinting down the tunnels, Georgianna turned through

the passageways, a stitch burning in her side by the time she reached Beck's car. She felt energised and awake, the weight in her legs dissipated in her desperation to help Wrench, and elated at a new method of treating his wounds. Leaping up into the car, Georgianna tripped and stumbled forward, straight into a pile of crates stacked against the wall.

The crash echoed and reverberated as Georgianna slid down the wall, landing with a thump against the floor. Before she could right herself, she glanced up to find a gun barrel had been levelled at her chest.

For a second, she stared down the barrel of the weapon before a relieved and admittedly frustrated sigh came from behind it.

"George?" Beck asked, rubbing his hand over his face and blinking to make sure he was right in his assessment. "What the hell you thinking, waking a man like that?"

"Lacie," Georgianna gasped. "I need Lacie."

"Huh? Why?"

Lacie's bleary voice slipped from behind the canvas hanging and out into the main area of the car. Georgianna glanced over her shoulder as the hanging was pulled to the side, Lacie's mussed hair falling over her face, a shirt large enough for a full grown man hanging down to her thighs.

"Lace!" Georgianna cried.

"George?"

"I need those hyliha leaves. The ones I gave you for practice."

Lacie blinked and stared back at her sleepily.

"I finished," Lacie answered, stepping out further into the car.

Georgianna let out a cry of frustration, having hoped that the leaves were still intact. She glanced up at Beck, who looked more than a little confused. The man reached up and rubbed his hand roughly across the back of his neck, surveying the scene cautiously. Georgianna felt awful for waking him up, she knew from Lacie how little sleep he managed to get, but right now it was necessary.

"Where are they?" Georgianna asked.

Lacie stepped over Georgianna's legs, moving to the other side of the car and collecting up a wooden box. Georgianna clambered to her feet and accepted the box from her, opening it to find the pale green powder, as perfect as if a skilled herber had done it.

She didn't know if it would work, whether it would be able to do anything for Wrench in this form, but she had to try. If it didn't work, she could always run and try to find some hyliha in the camps, but who knew how long that would take, especially seeing as she would have to wait until morning.

"George, what the hell is going on?" Beck asked, placing the gun back onto a blanket crumpled beside his chair.

"Wrench has been hit with a copaq," Georgianna explained. "Jaid was following normal procedure, but Jacob came in and…"

"Jacob?"

"The guy down Medics'," Lacie explained.

"Yeah, well Jacob said hyliha leaves really help!"

Georgianna finished, brandishing the box.

"Should I..."

Georgianna quickly shook her head as Lacie offered to come back. While Georgianna knew that this was a good opportunity for Lacie to learn, she highly doubted Wrench would want to be surrounded by people when he was injured. Not to mention that Beck would probably have something to say about Georgianna dragging the girl off in the middle of the night.

"Stay here, I'll tell you how it goes."

Out of the car before she even thought to thank them, Georgianna called back an apology for waking them. She was soon sprinting back through the tunnels.

The change in Wrench's condition was marked by the time Georgianna pulled herself back into the car. Despite not being gone more than thirty minutes, his breathing had improved and he was not sweating nearly as much.

"Did you get it?" Jacob asked, pausing with his hand and the canteen dunked into the bucket.

"Not exactly," Georgianna explained. "Lacie had already ground it. It's been dried and crushed, but..."

"What about a paste?" Jaid asked. "Put some in a bowl with some water? The water's not cold, but it's decent."

Georgianna and Jaid both looked at Jacob expectantly. It was his cure after all. However, he simply stared back in surprise. Then he shrugged.

"No harm in trying."

Opening the box and grabbing up a bowl, Georgianna tipped a generous amount of the powder in and went to the bucket. Taking the canteen from Jacob, she poured a small amount into a well in the centre of the mound, letting the granules of the powder float in and around the cool water. She handed the canteen back and swilled the bowl, digging her finger into the power and beginning to mix. It smelled just like hyliha trees in the rain, their large leaves working perfectly for protection from sudden downpours during the wash. After a few minutes mixing in most of the granules, Georgianna had the bowl filled with a thick green paste. She stepped to Jaid's side, nodding to the older woman. Jaid pulled the cloth away, holding it tightly in her hands as Georgianna began slathering the paste onto Wrench's side.

The man groaned loudly, startling both of them, but then a relieved hiss slipped through his teeth, and he laid his head back against the bed.

"Kid's a genius," he moaned, closing his eyes. "Tha's… tha's amazing."

He didn't stay conscious long, his breathing slowing and his body releasing the tension that had been held within it. By the time he was fully unconscious, Georgianna wasn't nearly as worried as she might have been. The hyliha seemed to be doing its job and Wrench was beginning to look much better, if that was possible so soon after being hit.

22 WHO SHE WAS

Once Wrench had passed out, his copaq wound slathered in hyliha paste, and as much water as he could safely drink in his stomach, Jaid had sighed and slumped back against the wall. The woman, stubborn as she was, having been dealing with Adveni-made wounds for a decade, refused to thank Jacob for his input.

"We'll see how he's doing in the morning," she insisted. "Better not to get our hopes up too high."

It wasn't long before Jaid left to go back to her husband, currently being watched over by a guard she'd dragged from duty. Georgianna had grinned in amusement, not only wondering what Beck would think about one of his guards being pulled off duty, but also what the guard themselves had thought about being used as a glorified babysitter. She decided it was best not to comment though. If Jaid hadn't been there, who knew what would have happened. Georgianna also doubted that any Belsa would comment on it so soon after Jaid had partially lost her husband to the madness of the heat thanks to a Belsa mission nobody knew the details of.

With Wrench passed out on the bed, Georgianna cleared away the bucket and cloth. She closed the wooden box of hyliha powder and tucked it into the top of her bag. She would ask Lacie to make another batch, knowing now how useful it could be. She'd probably test a few other things, but as hyliha was so readily available throughout most of the year, it seemed an incredibly useful trick to know.

Taking a seat on one of the beds, Georgianna pulled out a journal from her bag, its horse-hide cover no longer crinkling in protest the way it used to, worn and supple with years of use. Her brother had given it to her as a present when she chose to take her training as a medic, a place for her to record all she had learned. The inside paper had been changed out three times since she had received the gift. Once when Georgianna was fifteen and the book had been so full of notes that she couldn't fit any more into it, not even around the edges where she scribbled tiny things to remember. Georgianna had spent an entire freeze down in Nyvalau organising and rewriting the notes in order.

The next time had been when she completed her training and now, once again the book was full. Georgianna had separated the journal into different sections, one for procedures, one for supplies and their uses, a section for things Georgianna wanted to learn how to do, and one for everything else. Flicking through to the supplies section, she noted down hyliha's use for copaq wounds before she found the section on copaq wounds and added hyliha, circling it a couple of times.

Georgianna looked up, her gaze landing on Jacob who was swirling his finger around in the hyliha paste, leaning against the wall. Moving herself to the end of the bed, Georgianna smiled at Jacob and nodded to the space next to her. He considered for a moment before he walked slowly over, perching himself delicately on the edge.

"How did you know about the hyliha, Jake?" she asked, closing her journal and replacing it into her bag. "Have you..."

"Not with a copaq," Jacob answered, cutting her off, though he didn't look up from the paste. "The cinystalq has the same sort of charge as a copaq."

Georgianna glanced at the burn on Jacob's neck, a white scar running down from beneath his ear until it disappeared under his shirt.

"Will his be like that?" Georgianna asked, nodding towards his neck.

Jacob rested the bowl in his lap and reached up,

covering the wound protectively.

"No," he answered. "This wasn't nearly as bad before they removed the collar."

"It wasn't made by them removing it?"

"That made it worse," he explained. "But I already uh... I had a number of burns there from... from Uyinagh."

"Is that," Georgianna paused. "Was that your owner?"

Jacob nodded.

"They can give you shocks through the collar. If you do something that displeases them."

Georgianna frowned gently and carefully reached out. Jacob flinched, cowering a little as she came closer. She took her time, moving forward to take the bowl from his lap. The young man became as still as a statue until she moved a little further away.

"Do you mind?" Georgianna asked, holding the bowl up towards him.

Jacob kept his head down, but he glanced at her curiously. Georgianna indicated his wound.

"It's older, but maybe this will still work for you."

Staying still for a moment or two, Jacob finally nodded. Georgianna carefully scooped up some of the paste on two fingers and placing the bowl between them, she used her other hand to reach out and gently brush the hair back from Jacob's neck before she smeared the paste over the wound. The entire time Georgianna was touching him, Jacob remained as still as if he had been made out of the stone his name spoke of.

"I don't know anyone who has been through the things you have," Georgianna lamented quietly as she scraped the last of the paste from her fingers into the bowl, taking a dressing and placing it carefully onto his neck. Gently, as to not restrict his breathing, she wrapped a thin bandage loosely around his neck to keep it in place.

Jacob didn't say anything.

Finally pulling back, Georgianna held out the bowl for him to take. Jacob took it, a small smile flitting across his lips.

"So, when you got those wounds," Georgianna said slowly. "How did you know about the hyliha?"

The smile, so small and inconspicuous at first, split into a broader grin. He seemed proud, something she had never seen in Jacob before. The only time she'd seen him smile was when he was playing Erpal with Lacie. This was more measured. It wasn't a sudden smile of enjoyment, but of memories.

"I was training as a herber," Jacob answered, finally turning his head to look at her.

"Really?"

Jacob nodded.

"That's great. You know, we've been looking for someone to help out," Georgianna suggested suddenly. "Maybe once you're feeling better, once you're up to it, you could take the job?"

Dropping his head immediately, Jacob looked like the young boy again, so scared and unsure of himself. He dipped his finger back into the paste and began drawing patterns into it, smearing it against the bowl.

"I only trained for three years," he answered. "I'm not…"

"You're more than what we have, Jake, and I know a couple of people in the camps. I could bring them here, maybe make a deal for training."

"I… I don't know where my parents…"

Georgianna shook her head. The usual arrangement for training was that parents would accept someone to train in exchange for another family accepting their own child for training. Either that or payments in trade were made every season. Georgianna's parents had paid highly in furniture for Georgianna to be trained as a medic. Not to mention that her father took in two boys to train in carving and carpentry.

"I'll do it," Georgianna declared. "I'll take a trainee so that you can train."

Jacob's shy nature seemed to vanish for a second as he stared at her, open mouthed, his eyes wide in surprise.

"You'd do that?" he asked.

Georgianna smiled and nodded.

"Of course I would," she answered.

"What are you doing?"

Georgianna turned in surprise as Keiran climbed into the car. Smiling brightly, Georgianna got to her feet and moved over to him.

Keiran looked down at Wrench in concern for a few moments until he realised Georgianna was next to him. Turning his head, he pressed a soft, slightly absent kiss against her lips, quickly turning back to Wrench.

"What happened to him?"

"Hit with a copaq," Georgianna explained, reaching up and touching her fingers to Keiran's arm.

"He okay?"

"He's going to be fine. Turns out, we've got a pretty great herber here."

Keiran threw a glance over to Jacob, who, at the appearance of someone new, had retreated into himself again, keeping his attention on the bowl in his lap. Georgianna gave Keiran's arm another squeeze.

"You alright?" she asked. "What you doing here so late?"

Keiran frowned distractedly, his tongue swiping out to wet his bottom lip. Georgianna wondered why he was even awake at this time. She knew he hadn't been on duty, they'd discussed it the night before, so why wasn't he asleep?

"I had to go meet a friend," he answered. "Heard about Wrench as I was coming back into the tunnels."

"Bit of a late meeting," Georgianna said with a snort.

Keiran's gaze flickered over to Wrench and he remained silent for a moment, as if he didn't want to comment on why he had been out so late. Georgianna frowned and quickly looked away. She was pretty sure she knew who he'd been meeting. Well, not who, but at least what kind of meeting it had been... most likely one that didn't involve a lot of words. If that was the case, it wasn't really surprising he was coming back so late. Georgianna moved over to Wrench and placed the back of her hand against his forehead. His temperature had come down drastically since they'd put the paste on and given him the water. Jacob really did know his stuff.

"He'll be fine," she reiterated. "Jacob gave us a new method which is working far better than our usual."

Keiran nodded.

"That's good!" he answered. "You know how he got shot in the first place?"

"Cornered on a scout."

Georgianna, Keiran, and Jacob all looked at Wrench in surprise as he groaned the words, his eyes fluttering open. He reached up, rubbing his hand delicately over his face, and his lips curved into a smile.

"Hey," Georgianna muttered, brushing her hand over Wrench's forehead again. "How're you feeling there, hero?"

"Like I was trampled by a horse," Wrench answered. "But better. That kid's a genius."

Georgianna glanced over her shoulder at Jacob, smiling at the young man. Back to staring at his knees, Georgianna saw Jacob grin briefly.

"You were on a scout?" Keiran asked.

"Yeah."

"Why didn't I know about it?" he asked, frowning as he took a seat on the edge of Wrench's bed, down by his feet.

"Casey's orders," Wrench explained in a gruff voice. "Needed a couple of guys to see what was going on at that new building."

"The one on the way to the Camps?" Georgianna asked. "What is it?"

"Dunno," Wrench answered. "I was hit before we had a chance to get a decent look."

She frowned. What was it that would be so important in an unfinished building that Beck would want people scouting it out? The Adveni erected dozens of buildings every year and hardly any of them were ever scouted. Well, as far as she knew, anyway. Perhaps Beck sent scouts to each of them, but usually there were no problems?

"Well, your temperature has come way down," Georgianna explained. "You want to try sitting up for me?"

Wrench nodded, but it was a difficult process getting the man upright. In the end, Keiran had to get up off the bed and take hold of Wrench's hand, placing his other arm behind the man's shoulder to help him sit up.

"Aww, you two look so cute together," Georgianna mocked, bringing another small smile from Jacob in the corner.

Keiran and Wrench glanced at each other before looking at Georgianna, Keiran quickly moving away as Wrench adjusted his position on the bed, leaving room at the end for Keiran to take a seat again.

"Fuck off, George," Keiran scoffed under his breath, leaning back against the wall.

"No, it's adorable that you worry," she assured him.

"Only 'cause Casey'll have his ass if I keel over," Wrench chuckled, quickly regretting it and holding his hand to his injury.

Georgianna rolled her eyes as she took a seat, perched on the edge of the bed next to Wrench's legs. She took a rough count of his pulse. He already looked so much better. The sweat was gone and his breathing much more even. The hyliha was definitely working better than anything Georgianna could have done.

"Hey," Keiran piped up from behind her. "What happened down the dwellings? I haven't seen you."

Wrench gave Georgianna a curious look, and Georgianna knew immediately that despite the fact Keiran and Wrench were friends, not to mention Keiran being Wrench's superior, Keiran had not told his friend about Georgianna being tangled up in a drysta escape attempt.

Georgianna waited a few more seconds, keeping a track of how many thumps of blood she felt passing beneath the skin before she finally released Wrench and noted down the number on the papers Jaid had set up.

"We saw her," Georgianna explained. "She's got a collar on. Taye wasn't happy."

"Yeah I bet," Keiran grumbled.

"Who we talking about?" Wrench asked.

"Pretty thing. Carae that used to sell down Rion," Keiran answered. "What's her name?"

"Nyah," Georgianna offered.

"Oh yeah, I remember her."

"She was sold, her boyfriend wants to get her out."

"And she's got a collar?" Wrench asked, sucking in a breath. "Tough break."

Georgianna frowned and nodded, looking absently down at the notes for a few moments before she glanced back up at Wrench.

"Weren't you the one who got Lach's off?" Georgianna asked.

"And mine," Jacob piped up.

All three looked at him. When he realised they were all watching him, a deep pink blush rose almost immediately into Jacob's cheeks. He kept his gaze fixed on Georgianna instead of the two men he didn't know properly.

"Well, he did," he assured them.

"Yeah, I've done a couple," Wrench confirmed.

Georgianna pushed herself off the bed, chewing on her bottom lip as she began pacing. Since discovering that Nyah had been given a cinystalq, she'd assumed it would be much more difficult to get her away from Maarqyn. The whole point of a cinystalq collar was that it could be tracked to a location. They'd need it off before they even considered bringing her back to Belsa or Carae territory. However, if Wrench could disable it and get it off, maybe it would be easier than they thought. Wrench was a good friend of Keiran's, and the fact that Keiran was his superior would mean convincing him to remove a drysta collar would be much easier.

"How long does it take?" Georgianna asked.

Wrench shrugged.

"Depends. It's difficult and quite precise, so I'd need to see it."

"But you can do it?"

"Can, yes," Wrench answered sceptically, narrowing his eyes.

"What does that mean?"

"Will you do it?" Keiran asked, reaching out and slipping his arm around Georgianna's waist, pulling her a little closer.

Wrench gazed at them, glancing occasionally over to Jacob before he sighed and threw his hand up on the side that hadn't been hit.

"Well, I guess I owe you now, huh Med?" he answered.

It was only because she was sitting on Keiran's other side, and his arm was wrapped around her, not because she would have hurt Wrench, that Georgianna didn't leap into his lap and throw her arms around his neck. Suddenly, getting Nyah out didn't seem quite as impossible as it had before.

"I take it this means that you're not done helping your friend," Keiran suggested.

She shook her head.

"I have to help him."

He nodded as if he'd expected as much. He knew who she was, that she couldn't stand to see people needing help and doing nothing about it. It was who she'd been when she met him, and it was still who she was now.

The first time they'd met, she'd helped him even though she wasn't supposed to be working. The fact that it had been her fault he needed treatment in the first place was neither here nor there. He should claim some of the responsibility there since he'd been the one sneakily trying to grab a feel of her ass and had accidentally grabbed hold of the knife in her belt. Still she felt bad that she'd forgotten to make him aware of the weapon in the first place.

Keiran pushed himself up a little and pressed a kiss gently against her temple, brushing her hair out of the way. Yes, he knew who she was. She helped Wrench, she helped the Belsa, and she would help Taye now that she knew that they might be able to pull it off without all being carted into the compound as criminals.

23 Pillars of a Plan

Heat still rose in chest-tightening waves, even after the sun had set. Out of the city and away from the towering buildings the Adveni had erected in its centre, there was nothing to shield the ground from the baking rays, leaving it to expel the heat throughout the night once the sun had disappeared over the horizon. Georgianna lay on the ground, her head resting on Keiran's shin as he cleaned a pistol in his lap. Wrench, still a little sore from his injury, but doing better than anyone would have expected after a copaq wound, was sipping dark berry wine, swirling the liquid around in the bottle every time he lowered it.

They'd decided on a spot outside the city to talk to Taye. While the tunnels would have been acceptable, Wrench had been antsy to get out of Medics' Way and Georgianna had been cooped up underground most of the day. This wasn't the type of thing you could discuss in the Oprust district, not knowing who would turn you over to the Adveni for a few coins. So they had left instructions for Taye and headed south out of the city, a good half-hour's walk towards Keiluck Forest. They had considered going as far as the forest, but even to the wary Belsa it seemed overcautious to walk two hours out of the city in both directions just for a conversation. Instead, they had chosen to meet under the southern Mykahnol pillar, knowing that most gave the towers as wide a berth as possible whenever they could.

The Mykahnol pillars weren't actually dangerous. If anything, the towers themselves were a safety measure. However, no Veniche living in Adlai could think of the pillars without thinking of the device that they were installed to control. Aimed at the centre of Adlai, at the centre of every city in fact, the Mykahnol weapon was more destructive than any that the Veniche had ever seen before the Adveni arrived. It was capable of wiping out a city in a single blast and, if the Adveni were to be believed, without the pillars reigning in its power, the force of the blast would continue until it consumed the whole of Os-Veruh. The four pillars, installed equidistantly around Adlai, provided some kind of electrical lasso, or unseen force that held in the blast.

No Veniche person had proof that the destruction would continue without end if the pillars were not in place, but many had seen the pillars contain a Mykahnol blast, Georgianna included.

It had been near the end of the fighting, when most

people were giving in to Adveni rule. Many fled south, hoping that they would be able to find their own small corner to live out their days. However, as they neared Nyvalau, the weapon was detonated. Even from two days' travel away Georgianna had seen the blast, a humungous cloud that rose into the air like a field mushroom, the crackle of electric green lightning flashing in a sphere below it. They'd sheltered for three days, waiting out the aftermath that was sure to come, but when no such force hit them, they continued south only to find that their entire southern lands had been levelled, a great canyon in its place where some began to rebuild their lost Freeze homes.

From the information skittering through the different tribes, the Mykahnol was the last resort of the Adveni. Should they choose to leave Os-Veruh for good, they would detonate every Mykahnol as they left, destroying everything they had ever built on the planet in the fast-growing cities. The pillars weren't something people talked of often, not wanting to think about what would happen if the Adveni made good on their threats. However, staring up at this one, as it towered ominously, silhouetted against the sky, Georgianna wondered if the force of the blast would continue past their world if the pillars were not in place. Perhaps it was not for Veniche protection and survival that they had been put in place, but for that of the Adveni.

Keiran had picked up some bottles of dark berry wine. Though Georgianna thought it was best they all remained sober while they sorted out a plan, Keiran and Wrench had talked her down because surely liquid was good while out in the heat. She had tried to explain that actually, berry wine made the heat's effects on the body worse, but before she'd even finished talking, Wrench had one of the bottles open and was drinking large, unhealthy mouthfuls. So, she had instead resorted to staring up at the pillar as they waited for Taye to arrive.

"Took me a long time to find you guys!"

Georgianna lifted her head, spotting Taye walking towards them. His lightweight jacket had been shrugged off and he carried it instead, swinging it from one hand.

"Well, didn't want to make it too easy by sitting right on the path next to a giant erection," Keiran answered sarcastically, glancing first at the pillar and then off to his left where the path was trodden into the ground not ten feet from where they had camped out.

Taye threw a glare in Keiran's direction before coming over and slumping down next to Wrench. Wrench, far more cheerful now he'd drunk a decent amount of berry wine, offered the bottle. Taye looked at it sceptically before he shrugged and took it, glugging down a mouthful as he reached into his pocket and tossed Wrench a small linen pouch.

The other opened it and peering in, let out a laugh.

"Oh, brilliant!" he cheered, lifting the pouch and taking a deep sniff. "Yapoque?"

"Foinah," Taye corrected, glancing at Keiran. "Your usual, right?"

Georgianna turned her head, glancing up at Keiran as he looked at Taye in surprise. She blushed and quickly looked away. She'd told Taye that Keiran smoked cigarettes made from foinah leaves when he could get it. Of course, they were harder to get than yapoque, but better.

"Uh, yeah," Keiran answered. "Thanks man."

Taye shrugged and took another mouthful of the wine, glancing sideways at Wrench. Georgianna didn't know how well the two knew each other, she was even sure that Taye didn't know Keiran that well. He knew him enough to know his name and a few other choice pieces of information, gathering from their conversation in the Adveni dwelling quarters, but whether the two had ever actually held a conversation, she didn't know.

"So, how're things going?" Taye asked awkwardly.

Leaning forward, he placed the bottle between them as Georgianna pushed herself up off the ground, turning around to face the centre of their little circle. Crossing her legs, she sat comfortably next to Keiran, his arm brushing against hers as he continued cleaning out the pistol. After Wrench's injury, he'd been unwilling to travel so far without it.

"Wrench was hit by a copaq," Keiran announced, as if that explained how they were doing.

"Fuck, man, you alright?" Taye asked, glancing to Wrench.

Wrench nodded, a cigarette paper on the ground in front of him as he sprinkled the foinah into it.

"Yeah, thanks to Med here," he answered. "And that kid, Jake."

"Jake?"

"Escaped drysta," Georgianna explained. "Was in a

pretty bad state when he was found, but turns out the guy is a herber, knew enough to change the way we treat those things."

"Ah, well, that's good then."

Wrench and Georgianna nodded. For a minute there was silence, no one really knowing what to say. It wasn't like this was any ordinary meeting. How were any of them supposed just to blurt out a plan to free a drysta?

"So, your girl's been sold, huh?"

Georgianna looked at Wrench in surprised amusement. Apparently, that was how it was done. Taye looked at the ground between his legs, nodding to nobody in particular.

"I found out he's military," Taye answered, glancing to Georgianna. "Maarqyn."

"They're all military," Keiran answered. "Hence their… their… dickishness!"

Georgianna snorted.

"Coming from someone who could be considered to be involved in a Veniche military organisation…" she suggested, leaving her comment hanging in the air between them.

"Yeah, well, I wasn't brought up saluting and bowing to Casey's every demand, now was I?" he asked, grinning back at Georgianna.

"Okay, so he's military," Wrench interrupted. "Makes sense about the collar then."

Taye picked up the pouch of foinah leaves and began dealing out portions for three cigarettes into papers, evening them out before he dropped the pouch onto the ground in front of him.

DEAD AND BURYD

"He's some kind of commander," he explained.

"So, we're gonna need a solid plan with backups," Keiran agreed.

"What do you suggest?" Georgianna asked.

Out of the four of them, Keiran had the most experience in these sorts of things, closely followed by Wrench. The two had been in the Nerrin together. From what Georgianna knew, both from Keiran and from Liliah, who had taken the opportunity to tell Georgianna about their tribal days, the two men had been hunters, meaning that they had a lot of experience in planning attacks, even if those attacks had been against animals. Once the Adveni arrived, it was only natural that the two joined the Belsa, though Georgianna also knew a lot of hunters who had preferred to keep their heads down and avoid joining the rebel group. More recently, however, a hunter had come to mean something completely different to most people. A hunter was an Adveni whose job it was to track down Veniche who had escaped punishment for a crime. From the Adveni perspective, Keiran and Wrench were no longer hunters, they were very important prey.

"She's got a collar on, right?" Wrench reconfirmed. "We're gonna need somewhere to get rid of it. Can't risk one of those coming into Belsa, not for anything."

"She'll be coming to the Carae!" Taye corrected fiercely, looking up from the papers in his lap.

"You want one of those collars in the Carae?" Keiran asked, raising an eyebrow as he looked over at Taye. "Good luck keeping the Adveni off your ass, you do that."

"Where she's going isn't the point," Georgianna interjected. "Wrench is right. We need somewhere else, somewhere we can remove the collar before she goes underground."

"Where?" Taye asked.

"Oppression City," Wrench suggested. "Busy as hell, especially if we get it at the right time. Even the Adveni will have trouble getting through quickly."

"Alright," Keiran agreed slowly. "Wrench, can you find a place? I would suggest the Trade, they're always willing to help, but Oz won't appreciate an Adveni battalion bearing down on his ass. Get somewhere central enough that it'll hold the Adveni up."

"Doesn't that mean we'll be held up?" Georgianna asked in concern.

Keiran glanced at her, his tongue flicking out to wet his lips.

"Well, yeah, but we ain't got a lot of choice."

Georgianna nodded. She didn't exactly know a lot about battle tactics. Keiran probably knew best.

Taye leaned forward, offering one of the rolled cigarettes out to Keiran. He accepted it gratefully, holding it up in a toast to Taye before he stuck it between his lips, but he didn't light it. Almost immediately, he plucked it from his lips and used it to point at Georgianna.

"Oh, and another thing," he announced. "We're doing it on a day you're at the compound."

"What?" Taye and Georgianna demanded at the same time.

"Why?" Georgianna asked.

"We need her!" Taye exclaimed.

Keiran dug into his pocket, pulling out a lighter, a convenience the Adveni had brought to Os-Veruh with them. Lighting his cigarette, he inhaled before bringing it down from his lips, blowing the smoke up into the dry air.

"You asked that guard about the girl," he explained, looking at Georgianna squarely. "Minute she goes missing, you'll be suspected of being involved. We need to make sure they got nothing on you, that you're somewhere the Adveni can recognise you."

"But, what if we need her?" Taye asked, holding a cigarette out to Georgianna.

"The first priority is going to be that collar," Wrench said. "No matter who needs what. The longer that collar stays on, the more likely we're carted off to Lyndbury to be sold with your girlfriend. I say George meets us later. We get to Oprust, we remove the collar, everything else comes after."

"Do you think Beck could get some Belsa to help?" Georgianna asked, turning the unlit cigarette over and over in her fingers.

Wrench watched Georgianna as he sucked in a lungful of smoke and let it flow lazily past his lips.

"Jobs like this, the less people the better. More people that know, the more likely someone will talk."

"A Belsa talk to an Adveni?" Taye asked. "Come on."

"No, to a friend," Keiran answered. "Guy talks to his buddy over a drink about how they're helping break out a pretty little piece of ass from the Adveni. The friend talks to another friend. That guy tells an Adveni for a few coins."

Georgianna wasn't sure which Taye looked angrier about, that Keiran had proven his scepticism wrong, or that he had called Nyah a pretty little piece of ass. Even Georgianna felt a stab of annoyance at the latter. She didn't mind jokes about him seeing other women, she didn't even mind that it happened. But it didn't mean he had to talk so openly about it in front of her.

"What if we don't tell them what it's for?" she asked. "Just a couple of guys to hang out around the place where Wrench'll remove the collar? So they can warn you guys if Adveni show up?"

Wrench thought about it for a minute before looking at Keiran.

"She has a point. A few lookouts might be helpful, especially if this collar proves difficult."

"Alright," Keiran answered. "We'll try to get some men to look out."

Though, for some reason, he didn't seem too happy about it, quickly taking a swig of the wine.

"George, you got some paper?" Wrench asked suddenly.

He reached out and took the bottle of berry wine from Keiran, drinking down a mouthful as Georgianna tucked the cigarette behind her ear and dug into her bag, pulling out her journal and a pencil. Placing the bottle down between them, Wrench took the journal and opened it on the back page, checking both sides before he began scribbling something down. Georgianna picked up the bottle as she watched him, sipping the wine thoughtfully.

"When can we do this?" Taye asked hopefully.

Keiran glanced at Georgianna expectantly, but she could only shrug.

"This is a list of things I'm gonna need," Wrench explained, placing the journal down between them. "Once we have those, we can go the next time George is in the compound."

"And I'll meet you after," she added, glancing at Keiran.

As Taye reached out, holding the journal open at the back page to get a good look at the list, Keiran reached out and brushed some of her hair back. Smiling, she leaned in as he placed a soft, simple kiss on her lips.

"And you'll meet us after."

24   THE SUPPLY SCOUT

Despite the fact that Taye and Keiran seemed intent on not getting along with each other, they ended up having a pretty good night. Keiran had brought berry wine and a bottle of Adveni-brewed liquor that Georgianna had given him to get them significantly merry, and Taye had enough foinah leaf to last them until the early hours.

In the predawn they made their way, admittedly with some wavering along the path, back into the city, Taye peeling off when they reached the entrance to the Carae. Georgianna knew that really she should go back home. Though, seeing as she needed to speak to Beck, she accepted Keiran's rather blunt and dirty suggestion that she come to his place instead. Wrench made the usual jokes of course, but in all reality, by the time they got back to Keiran's shack, Georgianna was so tired that Keiran just slipped an arm around her under the blankets and pulled her close. Georgianna was asleep within moments.

Later that morning, she set about locating Beck. His tunnel car was empty and no one had seen him since they emerged from their own homes. In the end, she stopped by Medics' Way to find Lacie in the hope that she might know where her adoptive father may have gone. Lacie informed her somewhat distractedly, as she sketched in a notebook, that Beck had been gone before she woke that morning.

The sun's highest peak had been and gone before Georgianna found Beck, sitting with a group of men, plans lying across a couple of crates in front of them. One of them, an older man Georgianna didn't recognise, glared suspiciously at her, but Georgianna waved him off.

"I'm not staying," she explained. "I just, uh, need to speak to the marshall."

Beck took hold of Georgianna's elbow, leading her down the tunnel a hundred yards or so before he turned to her. He looked tired, lines that previously appeared and vanished depending on his expression slowly wearing their way into his skin. The circles under his eyes were darker than normal and Georgianna gazed at him in worry for a few moments, even after Beck indicated that she should start talking.

"Georgianna..." he urged, his eyes widening expectantly.

"Oh, right, yeah. I uh, I wanted to ask if there was any chance of getting a few Belsa to stand guard for us."

Beck looked at her, puzzled as he shifted his stance, crossing his arms over his chest.

"For?"

Shuffling her feet awkwardly, she didn't know why she felt so nervous asking this of Beck. She'd asked favours of him before and never felt this knot in the pit of her stomach. The only thing she could think of as the cause was that Beck was a friend of her father's and she already knew that he would not be happy about what his daughter was planning to do.

"A friend's partner was taken by the Adveni a few months ago. She was sold to a man living in the Adveni quarter and we want to get her out. We need a few men to stand guard in Oprust while we remove her collar to let us know if any Adveni are coming."

Beck frowned as he looked down at her, pushing his lips into a thin line, his expression thoughtful. For a moment, Georgianna thought she saw a hint of anger in his face and wondered if she should say more, if she should explain that Keiran and Wrench had already agreed to help them. She considered telling him that they had a plan in place, or at least, the beginnings of one, but she quickly decided against it, standing silently as Beck considered what she'd said.

"I'm sorry, George," he said, letting out a low sigh. "I can't risk a number of men for the freedom of one girl. If they were discovered to be Belsa, they would face the rope."

Georgianna sighed and looked down at her boots, but she couldn't fault Beck on his logic. If they were discovered, the people who stood to lose the most were Wrench and Keiran. They would be executed for Belsa affiliations if it became clear the Belsa were involved. Having a group of men standing guard would make it obvious that this was a Belsa operation. Nyah would be sent back to her owner, Georgianna and Taye to the yard. The Belsa faced a much fiercer penalty.

"I understand," Georgianna answered sadly.

She immediately felt bad that her tone was not cheerier, that she was possibly making Beck feel guilty about not being able to help. While she'd hoped he would, it would be stupid to have expected it.

"Look, if I can help in some other way…" he suggested.

"No, no, it's okay," she interrupted, trying her best to sound more cheerful. "I understand that you need to look after the Belsa. I was only hoping anyway."

Beck nodded slowly. Suddenly remembering Wrench's list, Georgianna tugged the book from her bag. She opened it to the last page and turned the book around so that Beck could see.

"Can you get any of the things on this list? Wre… We need them to get the collar off."

Studying the list, Beck's brow furrowed. He tapped a finger against his jaw until he pointed to two of the items on the list, one of which, Georgianna had been sure would be the hardest to find.

"I can get the absorber," he answered. "Managed to get a couple from a raid a while ago. I'll keep the other bits in mind."

"That would be great, thank you!"

"When do you need them?"

"Soon as possible," Georgianna answered shyly.

Beck nodded.

"Alright, stop by my car tomorrow, I should have them for you," he said. "Now, I'm sorry, Georgianna, but I really need to get back."

Georgianna nodded gratefully, closing the journal and slipping it into her bag.

"Thank you again, Marshall."

Beck had already turned and taken a few steps back towards the other men when he waved a hand above his head dismissively.

"Beck!" he called back.

Georgianna laughed as she made her way back down the line.

* * *

She had promised to meet Taye that afternoon in the hopes that they'd be able to find some of the items on Wrench's list down in the Junkyard. While she had considered ripping out the list and simply giving it to Taye, she was now glad that in their slightly drunk state, she'd completely forgotten.

As she walked, she took the journal from her bag, placing marks next to the items that Beck had said he could find for them. They really were lucky that Beck thought he could get an absorber, as the likelihood of finding one in the Junkyard, or anywhere, was going to be slim.

The small device was Adveni by design and practically impossible to pronounce in Advtenis, so it had been dubbed "absorber" by the people of Os-Veruh. It was only a small tab, the size of a coin, but when attached to a sheet of metal it absorbed the charge of a copaq weapon, or a less powerful cinystalq collar, rendering the shock administered useless. The Adveni had them attached to their shields when they fought to protect against being hit by their own weapons. Obviously none were offered to the Veniche, so the only way to get one was take down an Adveni in full combat gear. When Taye had asked Wrench, the Belsa explained that it was to do with the charge of an Adveni weapon, neutralising it by sending out an equally powerful counteractive charge.

Wrench had drawn a rough sketch on the back page of Georgianna's journal of the collar, showing that when the collar was detached, the charge constantly flowing through it, usually administered in small doses to send a jolt of pain through the wearer, escaped and jumped into the nearest compatible substance, the neck of the person it had been fastened around. That amount of charge jumping straight into the body was enough to kill instantly, so the absorber was used to take away at least a portion of the charge. He couldn't promise that Nyah would be completely unharmed. She might receive a burn from the overflow, but at least it wouldn't kill her.

It was only as Wrench explained these things, how he would detach the collar and ensure that the charge went into the absorber and not Nyah, that he would need to be very careful to cut the right parts at the right time, that Georgianna fully understood how Wrench had earned his nickname.

Finding Taye in his tent, idly strumming on a guitar Nyah that had scraped money together for months to buy him, Georgianna slumped down onto the thin mattress he used as a bed.

"Beck can't give us men for a guard," she explained. "But he got two items off the list, including the absorber."

Taye looked disappointed about the guard, but he couldn't exactly be angry when Beck was offering them an absorber to use.

They made their way down to the Junkyard, though this time, instead of leaving Georgianna at the outer fencing, Taye took full responsibility for her with the guard and led her inside through the stacks.

The place was a maze, and an exciting one at that. Every way Georgianna looked there were different things to see. Every few seconds she had to stop herself from squeaking in excitement as she spotted something that she could use, and every thirty seconds or so, had to hold her tongue from asking Taye what the hell something was.

Finally coming to a break in the stacks, Taye turned to her.

"Ok, so what do we still need?"

Georgianna tugged the journal back out of her bag and opened it up. She counted down the list once before she went back to the top, glancing around her as she did.

"Ok, a silver or gold knife, a pair of hide gloves."

"He doesn't have gloves?" Taye asked, cocking an eyebrow in amusement.

"Burned out, apparently," Georgianna explained. "Shows

he's done it enough times, I guess."

"I guess," Taye repeated. "What else?"

"Umm," Georgianna murmured, scanning down the list. "Rubber sheeting."

Taye nodded, glancing in each direction leading off from the gap in the stacks before he nodded more firmly. Setting off down the gap in front of them, he walked a few metres before stopping, looking at the shelves in front of him. Georgianna had to admit, it was pretty cool that they'd managed to build shelves in here. She could only imagine how it would have been if they hadn't: piles of objects and supplies, with the thing you wanted down at the bottom. The problem, however, quickly became apparent as Taye looked up, and realised that even he wasn't tall enough to reach the top shelf.

"Here," Georgianna suggested, slipping the strap of her bag from her shoulder and dumping it on the floor. "Give me a leg up."

Taye stepped away from the shelves, interlinking his fingers into a cradle, which he bent down to hold at a decent height for Georgianna to put her foot in.

"Ready?"

"Ready."

"Alright, up!"

Georgianna was pushed into the air. Kicking out, she placed her other foot on one of the mid-level shelves, pressing more weight onto that foot and using Taye to merely keep her steady as she picked up a box and lifted it from the shelf with one hand, peering in. She quickly replaced the box and took the next one, finding that it had the knives they wanted. A little blunter than perhaps would have been useful, Georgianna glanced down at Taye.

"Solid?" she asked.

Taye shook his head, and Georgianna sighed, placing the box back on the shelf and grabbing up the next. The knives in the next box looked much sharper. Thin and small, she had no idea what they were usually used for, but she took one out and placed it on a reachable shelf before putting the box back.

"Ok, I can come down," she said.

Taye slowly lowered her back to the ground, Georgianna walking her hands down the shelves until she could place a foot on the ground and lift her other from the cradle of Taye's hands.

"Alright, so that's the knife," Georgianna said, picking up the knife from the shelf and collecting her bag from the floor.

Luckily, the gloves and the rubber sheeting were much easier to find, and didn't involve any more lifting on Taye's part, as he insisted on making jokes about straining his back from lifting her for that short time. The first time, Georgianna was worried that he was serious, but when he grinned, she smacked him and moved along.

Once out of the Junkyard, Taye noted down what he'd taken, paying with some coins he'd earned from selling down in Rion district. It was tough, the money the guard asked for was easily enough to have cost Taye half a month to scrape together, even without having to feed and clothe himself. Still, Taye barely batted an eyelid and Georgianna realised that it wouldn't have mattered if it were ten times that amount, he would have figured out a way to pay.

"You should keep those," Georgianna said, handing over the items. "Seeing as I won't be there."

"I've been thinking about that," Taye said slowly. "And I think I agree with Keiran, surprisingly enough."

"Surprisingly enough, huh?"

"Well, yeah, alright, he isn't as bad as I thought," he admitted. "I really do appreciate him helping."

"So you'll stop badgering me about finding someone better?" She raised an eyebrow at him as they made their way down the tunnel.

"Yeah," he said before smirking. "For a month at least."

Georgianna laughed, step in step along with Taye.

"Make it three and we have a deal."

"Deal."

When they reached the tunnel entrance that led back down to the main line, Georgianna paused, expecting Taye to go back. However, from the way he was looking down the tunnel, Georgianna frowned.

"What's wrong?"

"Nothing. I was just thinking that I should go see Nyah. Try to talk to her."

Georgianna's eyes widened and she reached out, taking hold of Taye's arm.

"Taye, you can't! What if you're caught?"

"I'm smarter than that."

"Yeah, and Nyah was smarter than attacking an Adveni. Things happen!"

Taye didn't look convinced, which worried her. What if she left him and he went over there on his own? As awful as it was to think, she didn't actually trust Taye to be able to hold himself back.

"We need to tell her, so she can plan," he insisted.

"We don't even have a plan on how we're getting her out of that house! What's the point?"

"I have to see her!"

"Taye…"

"Come on, Gianna! You know she'll need to know what we're planning."

Georgianna's brow furrowed as she dug her hands into her pockets. She glanced towards the exit into the main line. Taye did have a point that Nyah would need to know about it sometime, but she still didn't like the idea of Taye going over there alone. If he actually managed to speak to Nyah, if he saw her, would he be able to convince her to go back inside until they were ready? Would he even want to, or would he think that running that second might be better? Georgianna took a deep breath.

"Alright, but not now!"

Taye opened his mouth to argue but she placed a hand on his chest.

"No!" she insisted. "Not until we know when it's going down and how we're getting her out. Just a few days Taye, I promise!"

Taye finally nodded.

"Okay, but if you've not agreed in three days, I'm going."

She didn't like that ultimatum, but nodded just the same.

"I'll see you in less than three days then."

Taye didn't wait for any long goodbyes. He turned away from her and walked down the tunnel back towards the Carae. Georgianna watched him until he disappeared into the darkness before she sighed and started down the thin tunnel towards the main line, for the first time in what felt like weeks, towards home.

25 THE OTHER ONE

As it turned out, by the time it was finally decided that they would go out to the Adveni quarters with the hopes of seeing Nyah, Keiran had decided to come along as well. Because Georgianna would be at the compound when they went to get Nyah, Taye would need someone with him as a lookout. Wrench, it had been agreed, would be waiting in the Oprust district, keeping watch to check that no Adveni were on the scene and to set up the things he needed to remove the cinystalq collar.

Walking through the Adveni dwelling quarter, Georgianna looked around her every thirty seconds until Keiran snapped at her to calm down and cut it out. They weren't doing anything now, they were just taking a look, so she didn't need to look so worried. Georgianna had taken a trip down to Park Street, a centre of Adveni trade, going into one building after another asking if anyone had any deliveries that she could make in exchange for a few coins. Most had kicked her out pretty quickly, but finally a woman agreed that Georgianna could deliver a new tsentyl to an Adveni out in the dwelling quarter. Of course, Georgianna had been forced to give blood and the code to her own tsentyl to ensure safe delivery, but as she was perfectly happy to make the delivery, and had no intention of trying to steal the device, she happily accepted.

The walk was faster than before, no need to count houses or wonder at every junction whether they were taking the correct turning. The Adveni they were meant to deliver the tsentyl to lived right at the edge of the quarter, but instead of dropping it off when they passed, the device was still safely nestled in her bag, ready to use as an excuse if Nyah's owner should see them.

It was lucky that Nyah had such bright, fair hair, for they saw her from a couple of hundred yards away, sat on the doorstep, a piece of Adveni armour across her lap and a device Georgianna didn't recognise in her hand. Taye stepped forward to go to her, but Georgianna stepped in front of him.

"I'll go," she said firmly, earning herself surprised looks from both men.

"No, Gianna, come on," Taye begged. "I've done everything you've asked, I've stayed away. Please, just let me talk to her?"

Georgianna shook her head resolutely. She felt bad,

keeping Taye away from Nyah. She knew how much he wanted to see her, but she held her ground.

"George, why not just let him go?" Keiran asked.

"I asked about her in the compound. It would make sense for me to be seen. Plus, it's for the same reason that I'll not be here when you actually get her out: because they'd know I was involved. If anyone sees Taye talking to her, they'll know who to look for."

Georgianna placed her hands on her hips. She had to say she was rather impressed with her reasoning, especially when neither Keiran nor Taye could think of a reason to argue. Agreeing to wait on the turning to the next street, Georgianna walked with the men to the turning before she peeled off, crossing the street and making her way up towards the house.

She moved slowly, making a point to look at the numbers in Advtenis written next to each door. Even turning back a few times, she finally approached Nyah.

"Excuse me?" she asked, stepping forward.

Nyah jumped and looked up.

"'Gia…"

Georgianna gave her a quick glare and shook her head.

"Did the Adveni of this house order a tsentyl?" she asked, keeping her gaze fixed obviously on Nyah.

Nyah stared at her in confusion for a moment and finally smiled a little.

"No, he didn't," she answered. "But he's not here right now. It's just us."

Georgianna's expression split into a wide grin, but while

she wanted to fling her arms around Nyah and hug her tightly, she restrained herself to simply reaching out and clasping Nyah's hand.

"How are you, Nyah?"

Nyah put the armour on the step next to her, resting the device on top before getting to her feet. She gave a small smile and shrugged. Georgianna didn't need more than that. No words would be able to explain how Nyah was coping with her current situation, certainly not "fine" or "okay".

"And you?"

"I'm doing well," she answered. Glancing over her shoulder for a moment, she turned back and smiled at Nyah. "Taye is here. He's down at the next road."

Georgianna nodded her head back in the direction where Taye and Keiran were waiting. Nyah glanced towards the house before sidestepping, looking down the street. From the longing that slipped into her expression, Georgianna knew that she had spotted Taye.

"How is he?"

"He's fine. He misses you."

Nyah gulped, and darted a glance at Georgianna. She got a worried expression and looked at the house again, taking a step back towards the doorway.

"Ny'," Georgianna urged, making no move to reach the woman, but the desperation clear all the same. "We're getting you out."

The panicked look on Nyah's face at those words was certainly not what she had expected. Her hand came up, touching the collar around her neck.

"No, it's okay, we know. We saw you before. We have a plan," Georgianna explained quickly. "We have someone who can remove that. He's agreed to it already."

"Really?" Nyah's gaze fixed past Georgianna and onto Taye. "When?"

"Eight days," Georgianna answered. "Sun-high."

Nyah almost looked like she was lost in a daze as she nodded. Something was bothering her, though Georgianna couldn't be sure whether it was simply the worry that something would go wrong. Glancing over her own shoulder, she spotted Taye and Keiran at the turning. Keiran looked like he was at least trying to appear natural, standing on the street corner. Taye, on the other hand, was staring in longing, shifting his weight continuously, like he might suddenly break into a sprint towards them. Georgianna quickly turned back to Nyah.

"You need to get outside. They can't come into the house, but they'll protect you as you run," she continued. "Can you do that?"

Fixing her gaze onto Georgianna, Nyah nodded.

"I... I can, but Georgianna... Gianna I'm not the only one here."

Georgianna frowned. She took a deep breath, ready to tell Nyah that no, they couldn't get a lot of people out. However, when she opened her mouth, the words she was expecting didn't come out.

"How many?"

"Just one other," Nyah said. "I can't leave him. He's been... he's been all I've had to keep me going."

Georgianna rubbed her hand over her face roughly. She couldn't agree to this, not without talking to Taye, Keiran and Wrench. If Nyah was wearing a collar, then she could be fairly certain that this other drysta would be as well. She wasn't even sure whether Wrench would even be able to remove two collars in the time they had. He would probably need more supplies, maybe even another absorber. Getting one had been lucky enough. She had no idea if Beck would be able to get his hands on another.

"Nyah, I..."

Georgianna swallowed back the lump rising in her throat. Under Nyah's desperate gaze, she frowned and glanced back at Keiran. He met her gaze, a curious expression on his face as he took a step towards them. Holding up her hand, telling him to wait, she turned back to look at the house. The man was probably inside right now. She searched the windows, almost expecting to see him watching them.

"If we can't find the supplies, if we can't get help..."

Nyah grabbed her arm, holding on in a vice-tight grip.

"You have to find a way," she exclaimed in a pleading breath. "He suffers far more than I do."

Scuffing her foot against the dry grass, Georgianna bit on her lip, trying to think of a solution. Nyah glanced at the doorway, a panicked look on her face.

"Gianna... he's a Belsa!"

26   One of Their Own

"Absorbers are rare, George. Why under the sun would you need two?"

Georgianna stepped further into the car and perched on the edge of the seat next to Beck.

"We went to see Nyah, the girl we're trying to help," she explained. "She says that there is another drysta there with her."

"That's risky. Those collars aren't easy to remove and doing two in one go?"

"I know, but, Beck... He's a Belsa. I can get you his name. The Adveni is a commander called Maarqyn Guinnyr. Nyah says he's suffering."

Beck didn't meet her gaze as he rubbed his hand through his hair, a heavy furrow in his brow. He shifted in his seat and leaned forward onto his knees, staring at the crate in front of him.

"I'm sorry."

Georgianna blinked and watched him in confusion. He was sorry? She didn't understand why he would be saying sorry to her, unless it was an abstract apology to the Belsa under Maarqyn's control.

"I don't…"

"I can't help you."

"You can't… You're saying no?" she spluttered.

He glanced up, disappointed but resolute.

"I have to. It's too high a risk."

"But he's one of yours!"

"You don't know that," he sighed. "This man could be lying to seem important to your friend. You know that Belsa are not sold."

Georgianna turned, leaning across the gap between them. She grasped his arm, looking up at him, pleading.

"Beck, please."

"Geor…"

"Why?" Georgianna cried. "I don't understand!"

"Because I'm fighting a war, Georgianna!" he snapped. He shook her from his arm, getting to his feet so fast that he kicked the crate away from them and into the opposite wall. "I can't risk a dozen good men to save one. You think I want to leave him there? I have no choice."

She was on her feet right after him.

"You do. You could help us!"

A steely glare met her.

DEAD AND BURYD

"I need to think of the people I have here. Those absorbers are hard to get hold of, and the time it would take to remove two collars would get all of you killed. I will not lose more men than I would save over this." His glare, if possible, hardened further. "And you will not drag them in against my orders. Are we understood?"

The silence was bitter. She had always trusted that he was doing the right thing. Not anymore. This was not the man who had snuck them from the camp and taken them to see a mother bear with cubs, even though her father had told her that it was too dangerous. This was not the man who'd sat with her parents long into the night around a campfire.

Georgianna stepped back to the door.

"Not doing everything you can to save one of your own," she muttered, throwing a glare over her shoulder. "Only thinking of the mission?"

She snorted in derision.

"You fight the Adveni, but you know, Beck... You're just like them."

* * *

"Shit!"

Georgianna leapt away from the shattered glass as it bounced across the floor. Sitting on the side of the bed, she groaned and flopped backwards.

Keiran grinned as he leaned over, picking up another wheat beer and dangling it over her head. She glanced at him and reluctantly accepted it.

"The drink ain't gonna calm you down if you keep throwing it around like that," Wrench said, swigging a mouthful of his own beer.

"I don't want to calm down."

"Well, can you throw empty bottles instead?" Keiran asked, patting her on the head. "Some of us might still want to drink those."

"He won't help!" she screeched, launching herself back up off the bed. Placing the new bottle down, she crouched in the middle of the small shack and began gathering up the bigger shards of glass.

"We hear you, girl. The marshall's a bastard."

The glance Keiran threw in Wrench's direction at his words was surprised but thoughtful.

"He's one of our own. We should be helping," he added.

Georgianna placed the shards of glass on the upturned crate next to the bed. She stared down at the men lounging on the bed, and frowned. Them saying that Beck was being unreasonable was all well and good, but unless they could find a way to convince the marshall to change his mind, they wouldn't be able to do anything. Even freeing Nyah was looking less likely. Would she be willing to leave without the Belsa held with her?

"Look, Casey not being on side is a setback, but it wasn't like he was all giddy to help in the first place," Keiran said dismissively.

"We only have one absorber."

"So we find another one," Keiran answered.

"It'll take longer."

"Move faster," Wrench replied.

Georgianna wasn't sure that they were taking her seriously. How was it that they weren't more worried? Their plan had just fallen flat. Beck refusing to help had devastated her. She'd been so sure that he would say yes, that he would be keen to save a Belsa, one of his own. She couldn't go back to Nyah and say that they couldn't help the unknown man.

Wrench and Keiran had debated the identity of the Belsa, but they'd lost so many, both to the compound and the ground, that names and fates became muddled together.

"Who will I get to help Taye?" she asked finally.

"Are we not good enough anymore?" Keiran asked.

"Beck said I couldn't drag any Belsa into it."

Keiran and Wrench exchanged an amused glance.

"Good thing we offered then, isn't it?"

* * *

The dappled light from the oil lamp flickered across the roof of the tunnel above their heads. The oil was getting low, the bright flames slowly receding towards the wick. Georgianna watched the light play in the darkness, frowning.

"It doesn't matter who it is, George," Keiran murmured, brushing some hair away from her face.

"We still have to go back."

She glanced at him to find a frown on his lips. He rolled further onto his side, shaking his head.

"It's too dangerous. You've been there twice already."

"But we have to tell them, they have to be ready."

Keiran cocked his head to the side as he considered it. Turning towards him, Georgianna propped herself up on her elbow, resting her head in her hand. She wasn't sure whether Keiran was worried about her, or the plan failing, but either way, it felt nice knowing he thought about those things. She'd been spending more and more nights with him recently, and when she wasn't there, she missed the familiarity of having him next to her. She was quickly finding it harder to sleep when his breath wasn't there to lull her into her dreams.

"Taye's too jumpy," he said slowly. "It was difficult convincing him to stay back last time, he won't again."

Georgianna nodded.

"We don't tell him then."

Keiran raised an eyebrow, his frown melting into a smile.

"You'd be a good Belsa, all secrets and sneaking around."

"Maybe I've just known you too long. You're a bad influence."

He laughed, an infectious chuckle that soon had Georgianna giggling with him. They melted back into the bed, and as fast as the laughter had come, it was gone.

"I could do a delivery again," Georgianna suggested.

"Too suspicious," he answered, shaking his head. When Georgianna turned her head to look at him, he was staring at the ceiling with a faraway look. "I've got some contacts. Maybe I can find out Guinnyr's schedule, get a time when he'll be out."

"Is it a girl?"

Keiran didn't answer, but as Georgianna was considering whether or not to push him on the subject, the oil in the lamp finally gave out, and they were plunged into darkness.

27 One Dead, One Drysta

"Did she tell you where he was going?" Georgianna asked.

She didn't look at him, her gaze fixed on her boots. As it had turned out, she'd been right, Keiran's contact had been a woman. She cleaned floors in the Headquarters, and according to Keiran, had a keen ear for secrets. Georgianna appreciated the help, even if she hadn't appreciated standing ten feet away while the woman flirted and asked when she could see Keiran again.

"Had some big-shot meeting."

"You know who with?"

"Does it matter?"

Georgianna raised an eyebrow as she lifted her head to look at him. It was his turn to avoid her gaze, his lips set in a resolute line. She frowned.

"Who is it?"

He huffed and shoved his hands into his pockets.

"Volsonnar."

Georgianna forgot to walk. She stood in the middle of the path, staring after him as Keiran took a few more steps before realising she was no longer with him. He turned around, curious, as she gaped.

"The Volsonnar? He's important enough to have meetings with the leader of the Adveni?"

He hurried back to her, shushing her as her voice cracked. He slipped his hand into hers, entwining their fingers, and tugging her into a steady pace.

"We knew he was a big shot, George. Keep your…"

"Stop there!"

They froze, hand in hand on the path, not even daring to look behind them as a pair of boots approached. Keiran squeezed her hand, and she could feel the beads of sweat dripping down her wrist and between their palms.

The Adveni stepped around them, eyes narrowed and suspicious as his gaze travelled over them both.

"What are you doing out here?" the Adveni asked.

His moss green uniform was plated with dark grey armour that glinted and shone in the sunlight as he moved. Georgianna licked her lips. Agrah.

She wished they'd brought a delivery with them, or they'd told Taye so that he could have brought some product along. As it was, they didn't have anything. She didn't even have her medic's bag, not that it would have made a difference. The Adveni had their own medics, they wouldn't have called a Veniche.

"Personal call," Keiran answered as smoothly as if it had been the truth.

The Adveni raised an eyebrow.

"You know people in this district?"

Keiran chuckled, a deep and knowing laugh. His grin spread broadly across his lips, and he nodded. He released Georgianna's hand and slipped his arm around her waist, pulling her against him.

"Not yet. She was purchased."

"You're olcinyty?"

The Adveni gave her all his attention as his gaze slipped down her body. He smiled briefly, but his eyes remained cold and suspicious. Georgianna gulped as she tried not to sneer at Keiran for suggesting that she was a prostitute.

"Yes, Volsonne," she nodded.

The Agrah didn't look convinced, he reached behind him, digging into his pocket.

"Come on, wouldn't you hire this if you got the chance?" Keiran suggested, hugging her a little tighter. "She's very good."

"And why are you here?" the Adveni asked, looking at him.

Georgianna beamed suddenly.

"We work as a pair." She stepped between Keiran and the Adveni guard, reaching back and grasping Keiran's hips. "Our clients have an... eclectic taste. One they'd rather keep private from the Adveni-run places."

If the Adveni was shocked, he didn't show it. In fact, as

he looked at Keiran, his smile became almost curious. It took everything Georgianna had to keep herself from letting out her nerves by laughing.

"Can we pass, Volsonne?" she asked.

He looked back at her for a moment before nodding. As Georgianna passed him, she trailed her finger down his arm, putting on a giggle as Keiran took her hand and tugged her along.

"You made me gay?" he hissed as they rounded the corner.

Georgianna sidled up against him.

"Bisexual," she giggled, kissing his shoulder. "And you started it by saying I was olcinyty."

Keiran grinned, and dropped the conversation.

* * *

Keiran wiped the sweat from his brow and flicked it from his hand into the dry dirt. They'd been outside the house for over an hour, and hadn't seen evidence of a single person inside. Knowing that there was an Agrah patrol out, they'd switched locations four times already, including once ducking into a bush to avoid an Adveni rounding the corner.

"I'm just going to have to knock on the door," Georgianna said, picking a twig from her hair.

"You can't be serious."

"We can't stay here all day just waiting for someone to happen to come out. Plus, Maarqyn will be back soon."

Keiran reached out to grasp her wrist, but missed as

Georgianna hurried across the road towards the house. He swore under his breath and ducked back.

A panel was mounted on the wall next to the door with a dozen buttons, each marked with a different Adveni symbol. She stared at it for a few moments, finger hovering over the buttons. In the end, she banged three times on the door instead.

"Get that!"

Even though it was distant, Georgianna could hear that it was the same man who had called Nyah back from the window on their first visit. Her eyes widened in panic, and when she turned to look back at Keiran, he was shifting his weight from foot to foot, looking like he was ready to run.

She took a step back, ready to run herself, when the door opened.

Nyah's expression mirrored Georgianna's panic as she stepped forward, pulling the door behind her, leaving just a crack open.

"Gianna, what are you doing?" she breathed.

"We were told that your owner had a meeting."

Nyah shook her head.

"Cancelled. He's furious about it."

Georgianna grimaced, but shook it off. They had to be quick.

"I had to see you. We're doing it. Six days."

Nyah checked through the crack of the open door.

"You can get us both out?"

"Yes," Georgianna whispered. "You have to be ready to run, Nyah. Both of you. Can you do that?"

She nodded.

"Is Taye…"

Georgianna waved her hands, cutting Nyah off.

"He's fine, Nyah, look, I have to go. I can't be caught here."

A voice echoed down the stairs, and Nyah pushed the door open again.

"Who is it?"

"Sales person, Volsonne," she called sweetly.

"Get rid of them. Unless it's the Volsonnar himself, get them the fuck off my land, girl."

"Yes, Volsonne."

Nyah glanced to Georgianna with an apologetic frown. Reaching forward, Georgianna squeezed Nyah's hand.

"Six days, sun-high," she reminded her in a whisper.

"CARTWRIGHT!"

Nyah almost had the door closed when Georgianna's hand slammed into the wood, stopping her. They stared at each other as the call echoed around the house. Footsteps followed, and Georgianna stared through the gap, trying desperately to see up the stairs. Without stepping into the house, it was impossible.

Finally gathering her senses, Georgianna mouthed an apology to Nyah before hurrying away from the house, back towards Keiran. He watched her approach, falling into step with her as Georgianna didn't even pause. He grasped her hand, pulling her into an alcove.

Georgianna's breath was ragged. She should have known. She'd seen him in the compound, seen him standing in line to the podium in the drysta yard. That had only been a few days before Nyah had been sold.

Keiran manoeuvred her against the wall, letting her splutter and gather her breath.

"Did I hear right?" he asked finally. "Did he say…"

"Cartwright," Georgianna breathed.

She looked up at Keiran, gulping.

"The Belsa in that house is Landon Cartwright," she confirmed. "Alec's little brother."

28 Colourful Truths and Excuses

The day after learning the identity of the second drysta in Maarqyn's house, Georgianna was unable to stop thinking about him, or about the brother who had left him behind. A variety of scenarios had played through her mind, of Maarqyn keeping him locked up, or of Landon being subjected to the most despicable torture while Nyah was forced to listen.

With Crisco closed until later that evening and Jaid watching over Medics' Way, Georgianna slipped from the tunnels and her thoughts, walking the long path that led out to the camps. She was certain, yet again, that she would receive a strong word or ten from her father. Yet as she walked, she found she could not be concerned about it. It was better to meet his worries with silence than tell him into what she had got herself tangled. Georgianna could already imagine her father's reaction. She could picture the way his eyes would bulge and the way he would keep an eerie calm as he ordered Halden and Braedon from the room. Once alone he would shout and get angry, only quietening when he had shouted himself out, a deadly calm resolution that was not to be argued with. It was smarter not to tell him.

The heat did little to keep the Veniche from the path, unlike the Adveni who were taking every opportunity to shield themselves from it. Out on the building constructions, Adveni forced to oversee their creations stripped to as little as possible in the hopes of cooling their burning skin in the breeze while the skilled Veniche workers kept themselves covered to avoid the harmful rays.

Out in the camps, trade and chores continued as usual and Georgianna was held up from her destination three times by those hoping that she would trade for medicines. By the time Georgianna reached the Lennox home, she had a supply of beans enough for three stews, and had picked up some hyliha leaves. Their seller had been most impressed with the price she offered for them.

Away from the open door, the house was dark with creeping shadows. It wasn't until she had called twice that her brother appeared from the kitchen, a hide bag swollen with liquid dangling from his fist.

"Well, if it isn't the girl I used to call sister," he mocked, giving Georgianna a stern look that was more and more reminiscent of their father every day.

"I don't know, brother. I remember you would give me far more colourful names."

"Yes well, were Da' here, I'm sure he would think of something colourful for you."

"He's not here then?"

"Luckily for you, no."

Georgianna smiled and slipped past Halden into the kitchen. Dropping her bag into the corner and the beans into the trunk, she turned to her brother, glancing down at the hide in his hand.

"You have a foal?"

Halden didn't use the hide for anything but foals, though he had not had one to tend for a long time, even considering that it was the wrong time of year for it.

"Yeah, got him a few days ago. Ikal was in no place to take a foal, promised him to me soon as he knew the mare was carrying."

Georgianna's eyes widened. Foals fetched a hefty price, and Halden reared the best. It would easily keep them fed down the trail. That was, if they were planning on making it. She had shared her wish with Keiran to go, but it only occurred to her now that she had not asked her family. While the south would be much more manageable than Adlai once the freeze set in, they may already have chosen to stay where work was more readily available.

"Come out," Halden said, moving to the back door. "He still needs the rest of this."

She followed him to the back door, taking a seat on the step as she watched Halden urge the bandy-legged foal back to the hide. The gentle sound of the foal suckling lulled them into silence, Halden carefully brushing the foal's neck while Georgianna picked absently at the grass between her feet.

"What's the excuse this time?" Halden asked, with the same smirk as Georgianna offered when she chose to mock someone.

"What excuse?"

"The one you're going to tell Da' to cover why you've not been home."

Georgianna rolled her eyes, taking a blade of grass between her fingers and carefully pulling it into two.

"No excuse. Work."

"It is a classic," he answered. "But you've used it far too often to be considered truthful."

It wouldn't matter whether she really was in Medics' Way every day and the Rion every night, she knew her father would assume something different. She had been absent too many times before with too many different excuses. Plus, she figured she could probably have been a little more secretive about her off-work hours. It was just that she had always been close to her father, especially after her mother's death. She didn't want to lie to him.

"How about you tell me what you've really been up to and I'll help you find a suitable cover?"

Georgianna glanced up at Halden, her dismissive smile faltering. As much as she hated lying to her father, she hated keeping things from Halden even more. Halden had always been there and had always told her the truth, even when he had told her before their parents that he was in love with

Nequiel. She didn't want to lie to him, but she couldn't bring herself to tell him that she was risking her neck after what had happened to his partner. Maybe Keiran had been right after all: she should have thought of her family before this all became so messy.

"I wasn't lying, Hal," Georgianna insisted slowly. "I've had work in the Rion, and Keinah is too big to cover the Way much anymore, so I'm covering her shifts."

Halden looked suspicious and she knew he was trying to sniff the lies out. However, having not been underground except in the main lines, there was no way for him to know. He frowned, weighing the hide in his hand, giving the foal another distracted pat on the neck.

"Jaid also had a thing," Georgianna added quickly. "Si got caught out in the heat. Three days. He was pretty bad, so she's been looking after him."

Halden's suspicion faltered as he let the hide hang by his side. He frowned, keeping his gaze on his feet.

"That's bad. Is he doing okay?"

Georgianna shrugged. Si had improved since his return, but Jaid had been right, he wasn't the same man who came to check if she wanted dinner. The glimmer in his eyes had faded and the transformation was taking its toll on Jaid too. She was more serious, less likely to share a joke. Her husband had gone, and in some ways, had taken a part of her with it.

"It'll get better," Halden said. "Everything else is good though?"

She probably shouldn't, not before the escape when so

much could still go wrong, but Halden had been friends with Alec, the two had grown up together. Landon was a younger brother to Halden almost as much as Alec. She felt it was wrong to keep that news from him.

"Halden... I found out that, uh..."

"Out with it Gianna," he chastised. "I promise it won't be nearly as awkward as telling me you'd had sex."

Georgianna grimaced, but was grateful for the intervention. He was right, there was no reason this should be awkward. She had told Halden far worse things. As he'd rightly pointed out, telling him that she had lost her virginity had been far more daunting a conversation.

"You know how I told you... I said about Nyah?"

Nodding, he gazed at her suspiciously. She looked down at her feet, scuffing her toe into the dry grass.

"I took the note into the compound."

Halden looked back at her, silent. Georgianna wondered, if like Keiran, he had expected it of her all along.

"She had been sold, so I... I went to the house of the Adveni..."

"Oh, Gianna, what were you..."

"Landon was there."

He frowned, but didn't reply, his accusation dead in the air. Well, it was pretty much as she had expected. She had not exactly been a gaggle of words at the news either.

"He's a drysta."

"You're sure it was him? You saw him?"

She shook her head.

"Then Gianna, you can't be..."

"I heard his name. There is no one else, Halden."

He didn't answer her. He rubbed his hand over the foal's head and down its neck. Georgianna leaned forward, resting her chin on her knees.

"What were you even doing there?"

She watched the foal instead of her brother. She couldn't bring herself to look him in the eye as she lied.

"I was checking on Nyah, nothing more."

"Taye made you?"

Halden's voice was restrained, but she could hear the anger in his tone, the accusation. She shook her head.

"He wasn't there."

"Then who, Gianna? Who are you doing this for?"

"For myself, Halden. I want to make sure that she is safe."

"She's a drysta! She isn't safe and you know it, so why go?" he demanded. "If you were caught…"

"I wasn't."

"That isn't the point."

Halden sighed. With his free hand, he reached up, scratching behind his ear, his gaze settled on something far more distant than his sister or the open doorway. Picking at a blade of grass from between her feet, Georgianna began pulling it into ever thinner strips.

"I don't want to make you worry," she said.

"You make me worry every time you step into those tunnels."

She watched him as he pulled the hide from the foal. He tipped the hide, feeling the weight.

"You know why I do that."

"Sometimes I wonder."

"About?"

"Whether if it is more about that man you're seeing than it is about the work. Wanting to be close to him."

"What? No, I was there long before I met him."

"I never said you didn't begin it with the best intentions," Halden assured her. "But you could do the same work out here."

"I know, but…"

"You don't need to associate with the Belsa, Gianna, you choose to," he argued. "This new man, Keiran? He is more than a friend, isn't he?"

Georgianna sat up straight again, stretching her legs out in front of her.

"No," she answered, regretting it immediately. "I'm not sure."

She didn't know where the regret came from. It had lodged itself in her chest and refused to budge. Knowing that Landon was suffering had thrown her emotions into the air. She felt a responsibility to help the boy after she'd been so entangled with his brother. However, with it came guilt telling her that she shouldn't feel so strongly about helping Landon while she was with Keiran. Had Alec been nothing more than a friend like she had always said he was, like she had always told herself he was, she wouldn't have felt this way. She'd still not dared tell Keiran about her connection to the other Belsa, which only fuelled the guilt more.

The foal whinnied and skittered slightly on its bandy

legs. Halden brought the hide back down, offering it to the young animal. It took it cautiously, gaining in confidence when it once again discovered the sustenance inside.

"You say you're not sure if he's a friend, but what if he ended it? Right now, said he couldn't see you anymore because he'd found someone else."

A spasm clenched in her stomach, and staring at the grass, Georgianna couldn't answer him.

"Would you just move on to a new guy, or would you maybe be upset about it because you, oh, I don't know... like him?"

Georgianna frowned and kept her gaze fixed as far from Halden as she could manage without turning away like a stubborn child. She wasn't ready to make commitments, but Halden was right in some respects. She would be upset if Keiran suddenly cut all ties. What was worse, as she sat there, trying to think of something to say, she realised that it wasn't the physical stuff that she would miss the most, it was everything else.

Alec had never been like that. While Liliah had once accused Keiran of using her for his own benefit, Georgianna knew that Alec had been far the worse offender. He had cared about her, she knew that, but her uses to him had outweighed the things he had given her. As she thought about it, even their arguments seemed more about his own loss than her safety. He had lost his wife to the Adveni, and no matter what Georgianna had done, he would never have let go of that.

"I should go," Georgianna mumbled, getting to her feet.

Halden reached out and took her hand.

"Gianna," he murmured. "Come on, don't…"

"No, it's… I need to look for a herber for Jake. He's good and he can learn."

Raising an eyebrow, Halden gazed at her. He shook his head. Georgianna wrapped her arms around him in a brief, tight hug.

"Honestly, we're fine. I'm fine. I'll… I'll think about what you said."

Think about it, she wouldn't stop thinking about it.

"Well, come back after you're done. I'll keep my mouth shut," he said, brushing her hair back behind her ear.

She nodded, giving him a small smile before she turned and went back into the house to collect her bag and set out to find someone who would willingly go down into the tunnels to train Jacob.

29 Keep Him Dead

"I should go, yep, definitely should go."

Georgianna leapt up off the bed, the Way notes slipping from her knees and littering the floor. Jumping over them and colliding with one of the metal drawers she'd not completely closed, she yelped, pain shooting through her hip. Pushing the heel of her hand against her throbbing flesh, she reached for Si's elbow, gently urging him to stay put.

"We talked about this, Si," she breathed, another gasp as she eased her hand over the curve of her hip. "Jaid wants you to stay with me for a while."

A damp lock of hair slapped across Si's nose as he shook his head. Pulling his arm out of her grasp, he took a step away from her towards the open door of the tunnel car. He wrinkled his nose and snorted, dislodging the hair.

"No, no, need to get going," he insisted. "Counting on me, expecting me."

He took another step and picked up one of the cantinas from the shelves along the wall, wrapping both hands around it and clutching it to his chest.

"Need to take water... long walk. Jaid... Jaid says long walks need water."

Georgianna watched him cautiously, sidestepping until she could stand in front of the open door, a barrier to dissuade Si. He'd been much better once the pain of his wounds had subsided, but they'd been right about the damage the prolonged heat had done to his mind. Of the few times she had seen him, Jaid bringing him to the Way when she was on shift, he seemed agitated and confused, but thankfully, not often violent.

"Where do you need to go, Si?" she asked. "Wouldn't you rather stay with me?"

"Can't." He clutched the cantina tighter to his chest. "Need to check on him, need to make sure. My job."

Shifting her weight from one foot to the other, Georgianna pursed her lips, her eyes narrowing.

"Your job? Is this the job Beck gave you?"

His gaze finally settled, staring at the door as he nodded. His finger drew around the mouth of the cantina, feeling the screw threads on the cap.

"What was the job? Maybe I can help?" she asked hopefully.

He shook his head violently, locks of hair slapping across

his face. She stepped back, balancing on the lip of the doorway.

"No help. No one to know," Si muttered. "My job. Casey trusting me to keep him dead."

Georgianna lifted her foot to step back, her boot finding nothing but air beneath it as she teetered back in the open doorway. She squealed, catching Si's attention, and grabbed the edge of the doorway, clinging on as she righted herself back inside the car. Si watched her. His finger paused in its progression around the rim, his brow raised.

"Keep him dead?" She was confused. "Beck is alive, Si."

"I know that!" he snapped before turning away, trampling the notes on the floor with his dusty boots. He lifted the cantina on his chest, resting his chin against the rim of the mouth. "Marshalls remain marshalls, dreta remain dead."

"Dreta?"

The breath of a word slipped through her lips. She stared at Si. Her mind raced around Si's words. Memories fell into place. She blinked, wondering how she had missed something so obvious.

"It was Cartwright," she whispered. "Your job, it was Cartwright!"

Si spun on his heel. The cantina slipped from his fingers. In an instant he was before her, fingers grasping her wrists.

"You…" he sneered.

Georgianna wrenched her hands back. Yet he tightened his grip, tugging her towards him.

"Si, you're hurting me!"

"You sold me out!" he snarled, ignoring her pleas.

Georgianna trembled in his grasp. She tugged away from him fruitlessly, shaking her head.

"No. No, Si, I didn't," she pleaded. "I heard about Landon the other day. Please, Si, let go."

His grip on her wrists faltered, a spasm of uncertainty, or confusion, that gave her the chance she needed. Tugging herself free, she overbalanced, landing with a thump on the floor. Her breathing was ragged. Tearing her gaze from Si's, she glanced around the car, making sure that there was nothing within reach he could use as a weapon. As she looked back at him, she cradled her hand in her lap, rubbing her fingers against the sore skin where she knew bruises would appear.

"Saw Alec?" he asked.

Georgianna shook her head.

"No, not Alec," she corrected. "Landon, Si. Alec's little brother. You remember, right?"

Si glared at her, but remained silent.

"There's another drysta in the house with him. Her name is Nyah."

"No, no others," Si rattled. "Only Alec dead."

Georgianna shifted her legs out from underneath her, moving herself into a more comfortable position. Between them, the papers lay scattered and crumpled on the floor.

"Nyah was bought after you were found," she said, her panic subsiding as Si slipped back to sit opposite her.

He buried his head into his hands, hunching over his legs, and whined into his skin, rocking his body in a rhythmic bobbing. Tentatively, she reached out and laid her hand on his knee. Si froze, still as stone, but did not push her away.

"You're confused, Si. It wasn't Alec you saw, it was Landon."

Si didn't move, didn't even breathe as Georgianna shifted a little closer.

"He was your job? Watching out for him?"

Finally, in a motion so small that she would have missed it had she not been staring at him so intently, Si nodded.

"Be... Beck told you where he was, that he'd been captured, didn't he?"

"Safer," Si breathed. "Stay dead, no one looks."

He lifted his head, peering at her through his splayed fingers.

"No one helps."

Georgianna let out a timid breath, staring at her fingers against Si's knee. She had taken a guess, but never actually thought she might be right, that Beck would have known about Landon.

"Do you know his owner?"

"Maarqyn," Si breathed. "Maarqyn Guinnyr. Mean. Cruel. Vtensu."

She pulled her hand back from Si's knee, her thumb coming to her lips where she chewed on the nail. Something wasn't adding up. Si had been found the day after she'd seen Landon in the compound. Si had been missing for days; there was no way that he would know where Landon Cartwright had gone. Not unless someone knew before the sale that Maarqyn would buy the young drysta.

Were there more? Belsa they believed dead who had been sold in secret? Had Si been checking on all of them, and the damage of the heat had merged them into one singular assignment? Georgianna just knew one thing for certain: Beck had lied to her about more than Landon Cartwright.

30 Avoiding the Arrangement

Since her conversation with Si, Georgianna hadn't been able to get his revelations out of her head. She avoided the Belsa encampment as much as she could. The moment Jaid had returned to take over her shift on the Way, Georgianna had excused herself, heading out into the camps. While her pride still smarted from Halden's accusations, she figured that facing those feelings had to be better than confronting the Belsa marshall.

She couldn't understand why Beck would be so keen on keeping these people hidden. She'd been suspicious since he told her that he wouldn't help in Landon's escape from Maarqyn. Now she could only wonder how many other Belsa out there had been captured instead of killed, and how many of them Beck had kept secret.

She hadn't been able to get any more information out of Si, he was too confused and agitated by the time she tried to press him for more information. Georgianna knew that she needed more evidence before she approached one of the other Belsa about her suspicions, she couldn't accuse Beck without proof. She realised that the only way she could do it was to wait until Landon was free. With Landon free, he would be able to tell the other Belsa what Beck had done: how Beck had left him with an Adveni to be tortured. Just a few more days, then all the lies would be out in the open.

While Halden was home—those few moments between him returning from work and Georgianna disappearing to return to it—questions bubbled silently between them. Halden didn't dare mention Keiran or Alec, not in front of their father, and Georgianna didn't want to share her confusion. Instead, they avoided it, and avoided each other.

Unfortunately, avoiding Halden didn't do anything to wash his words from her head. She didn't want her brother to see her as a child, only doing things that made her happy. However, the more she thought about it, the more difficult it became to dismiss his opinion as big-brother ramblings. Even Liliah had claimed that she only did things until they stopped feeling good, and while Georgianna wanted to argue, she wasn't sure that her friend was wrong. She'd tried using the fact that she went into the compound, that she was helping Nyah and Landon, but in the end, those things made her feel good about herself. She was even letting others take the risk by not being the one to actually get Nyah and

Landon from the house and remove their collars. She would be in the compound, safe and sound, feeling good about it all.

What was worse though, as helping Nyah and Landon had good repercussions for other people as well, was that she'd not been able to stop thinking about what they had both said about Keiran. She didn't want to admit it, but she did really like the man, more than she'd originally intended. She'd thought she could handle the no-strings, casual thing that they had going. However, more and more, she realised that she didn't like knowing that Keiran was seeing other women when she wasn't around, or wondering if he liked them more than her.

She wasn't ready for a joining ceremony, that was ridiculous, but maybe someday she would be. Hard as it was to imagine, she was suddenly very scared that when that day came, Keiran would be gone.

As such, Georgianna had done the only thing she could think of that left her some semblance of control. She avoided him. She blamed it on avoiding Beck, she told herself that it was safer this way, but the hope constantly nagged at her that surely, if she didn't see him, if she didn't remember how well things worked between them, then it wouldn't be as difficult to move on.

So far, the plan had fallen flat on its face. Every time she let her mind wander, it went straight back to Keiran. Georgianna knew that she'd have to see him eventually, especially since their plan was set for the next day, but she didn't want to have to have that conversation with him that ended in "I think it's best that we don't see each other anymore". Before they had that conversation, she could at least pretend that everything was fine.

Medics' Way had been quiet, too quiet for Georgianna's liking. She didn't want to see people injured, but the lack of patients to check on or tend to was giving her far too much time to think, not only about Keiran, but of everything that could go wrong the following day. With each new scenario that came to mind, she came one step closer to backing out completely.

"Hey, George!"

Georgianna turned, her arms filled with bandages she'd been reorganising. Wrench was climbing into the car, a tyllenich rifle hung over his shoulder.

"Hi Wrench, how's things?"

Wrench dropped himself heavily onto one of the makeshift beds, adjusting the tyllenich by his side.

"Good. Nervous about tomorrow."

She wasn't sure whether it was a statement of his nerves or a question about hers so she simply nodded.

"Anyway, I just came to get some more of that paste."

"The hyliha." She nodded.

Moving to one of the lined crates, she dumped the bandages into it without bothering to organise them. She picked up the box with the hyliha powder in it, and taking one of the small cloth bags, poured in a generous amount.

"You just need to add a little cold water," she explained, tying the strings from the bag around it and grabbing the first dressing her hand found.

Wrench nodded, placing the bag and dressing in a jacket pocket. Giving her a grateful wink, he got to his feet.

"We're all ready for tomorrow."

"You found another absorber?" Georgianna's voice filled with excitement and relief. Of the things Beck had refused to help them with, the second absorber had proved the most difficult to find.

Grimacing, Wrench shook his head.

"What are you going to do?"

"The charge might last enough for two collars," Wrench explained. "They're designed for copaqs, which give off a stronger charge."

"It might last?"

Wrench shrugged.

"Can't promise. Only thing we can do, I guess, is hope for luck."

Georgianna nodded, but it didn't ease her fears in the slightest. Wrench moved towards the door, stopping just as he was about to jump out, and glanced back.

"See you when it's done, George," he said with a cheerful smile.

Once Wrench had disappeared down the tunnel, Georgianna went back to her counting. However, the task was pointless, as she never got all the way through the box before she became distracted by her thoughts, and lost count. In the end, she gave up and simply organised them by size, which she could do without distraction.

The afternoon was slow going. Jaid was meant to take over at sundown, but Georgianna was considering telling her not to bother. After all, Georgianna would need to be here in the morning because it was easier to get to the compound from the tunnels than the camps. She didn't have a shift in the Rion district, and didn't exactly want to go crawling into Keiran's shack. However, knowing that she needed sleep if she was going to be alert the next morning, Georgianna decided that she would simply sleep at the back of the train car with Jacob.

The young man was practically healed. While he still had his scars and anxiety levels to rival a rabbit being chased by coyotes, he was physically fit enough to leave Medics' Way. The problem was that he didn't have anywhere else to go. So, instead of kicking him out, Jaid had agreed to let him stay as long as he needed, on the condition he pulled his weight.

She wasn't sure what kind of weight that might be: he was still rather skinny and didn't like touching other people. But as it turned out, he was good at inventory and slowly coming out with more and more information from his training as a herber. Georgianna had yet to find anyone who would take him on. Funnily enough, it wasn't that she couldn't match the price they were asking, or that they didn't want an escaped drysta (she had left that part out for now), but just that they didn't have the necessary supplies to do a good job. Despite her disappointment, she was impressed with their honesty. Some people would just have made the deal anyway, but the ones she'd asked seemed like nice people.

She hadn't yet asked Liliah. Georgianna trusted her

friend to see that Jacob would be expertly trained, but she hadn't wanted to put that sort of pressure on her. Liliah would immediately know how Georgianna knew the young man, and once that knowledge was there between them, Liliah would have no say in whether she even wanted a secret like that.

"You avoiding me, George?"

Georgianna jumped. She glanced over and gave Keiran an anxious smile.

"No, just busy, you know."

He pulled himself up into the train car, an amused smile on his lips. She was sure that he didn't believe her. Even as busy as Georgianna usually was, she found time to see him. In fact, it was usually when she was busiest that she saw Keiran the most, because his shack was rather conveniently located.

"Yeah, those stocks look riveting."

Keiran's tongue darted out to wet his lips. She shifted her weight from one foot to the other and reached up to scratch her ear. She'd never thought it would be so difficult to have a conversation with Keiran, and yet here she was, with no idea what to say.

"Just nervous, I guess," she finally mumbled. "About tomorrow."

He smiled, shifting the strap of his weapon from his shoulder and placing the device down on the bed. Moving over to her, he took hold of her arms.

"We've got everything covered," he bent a little to look at her properly. "You just need to do your thing at the compound then meet us when it's all done."

She nodded, avoiding his gaze. Yet with him this close, she could see his face in her peripheral vision everywhere she looked, which only made trying to evade the awkward conversation worse. At the end of it all, she did want to keep seeing him.

Leaning forward, Keiran placed a gentle kiss against her cheek, squeezing her arms as he stepped back again. Unlike usually, when Georgianna would have leaned into him, this time, she found herself moving away. She couldn't do this; she couldn't keep pretending that she was fine with casual when she wasn't. It was only making things more confusing.

"Are you coming to mine tonight?"

She frowned and chewed on the inside of her cheek.

"I don't know." She tried to think of a reasonable way out of it and couldn't. "It's not a good idea."

"Why not?"

"I don't know, I just…"

Georgianna looked away. She went and sat on the bed, tracing her fingers carefully along the barrel of the gun he'd put down.

"What's going on with you? I've not seen you for days and now you're being all weird."

Weird was hardly the word she'd give to it. She'd maybe been a little more emotional, but seeing as Keiran had his wonderful reputation with women, surely this wasn't the first time a girl had realised she wasn't happy keeping their relationship at just sex.

"I dunno, I've just been thinking and… and my

brother said some things..."

"Your brother, huh?" He nodded in understanding as he took a seat next to her. "So, am I about to get my face beaten in or do I need to provide a grass symbol before the week is out?"

Georgianna glanced at him. So, this definitely wasn't the first time someone had had an issue with the just-sex arrangement. Only maybe it hadn't been the girl he'd been sleeping with, but her family that had the problem.

"I think he's more likely to beat me up than you."

Keiran whistled.

"Well, that's a relief!" He mockingly brushed the back of his hand against his forehead. "Dunno what I'd do if I had to go up against a horse rearer."

Georgianna smacked his arm.

"This isn't funny!"

Keiran sighed. Moving a little closer to her, he slung his arm carelessly around her shoulder. Georgianna wanted to be angry at him for mocking her brother. Halden was only trying to look out for her. However, she was almost impressed that Keiran remembered what he did.

"Okay, so what did your brother say?"

She scraped her front teeth over her bottom lip as she glanced at him and away. If she was going to tell him and sound like an idiot, she might as well get it over with.

"He accused me of liking you," she mumbled.

Keiran gave her a look of mortified shock.

"How dare he?" he mocked. Georgianna rolled her eyes. He could at least try to be serious.

"He doesn't think you and I just having fun is..." she paused, trying to think of the right words. "He thinks I'm kidding myself. He said I was being childish because I thought you and I just having fun would work... that I should stop being with guys for fun, and instead think about the future."

Keiran looked at her, eyes narrowed, and hummed out his thoughts for a moment.

"So he wants the grass symbol," he answered.

"No," Georgianna defended quickly. "He just thinks that I should... I don't know, it's ridiculous. But he's wormed in and... and I don't know."

Keiran reached out and hooked his finger underneath Georgianna's chin, turning her to look at him.

"You're not happy with things the way they are now?"

When he put it like that, she didn't know what to say. She loved how things were now between them. Not right this second, because it was awkward and embarrassing, but in the more general sense, yes, she did like what they had. She just wasn't sure she liked that he also had the same thing with other women.

"No," she mumbled before her eyes widened in panic. "I mean, yes, I do. I like how things are between you and me, but..."

"But..."

She looked down at her knees.

"I think I want it to be just you and me," she murmured. "I want to..."

"You want to be together, properly," he finished.

Finally looking up at him, she shrugged a little. Clasping her hands tightly in her lap, trying to stop herself from fidgeting, she found herself drumming her fingers nervously against the backs of her hands.

"I... maybe."

Keiran nodded slowly. He stared past her, his tongue darting across his lips again. She held her breath, wondering whether he was about to tell her that this wasn't what he wanted, that he couldn't be just with her. Only, when he looked back at her, he smiled and leaned forward, pressing a kiss against her lips.

"Look, we've got a whole lot of shit to deal with tomorrow," he said as he brushed a lock of wavy blonde hair back from her face. "How about, you stay at my place tonight, we free some dreta tomorrow, and then we'll discuss what this relationship stuff entails?"

Georgianna's mouth dropped open. Had he just agreed to it? He hadn't walked out. He hadn't told her that he wasn't interested. He wanted to talk about it. Staring at him blankly, she blinked and shook her head.

"Yeah, yeah that sounds good." She smiled.

"Good," he answered. "And tell your brother that who you have sex with is not a conversation to have with siblings!"

He leaned forward, planting another soft kiss on her. This time, instead of being worried, instead of leaning away, Georgianna felt her lips smiling against his. She leaned into him until he pulled back.

"I'll see you in a bit, alright?"

She nodded, not moving from her place on the bed for a few minutes, even after Keiran had left, the sound of his boots against the stones fading through the echoing tunnels. That hadn't gone nearly as badly as she'd thought it would. Oddly enough, it made her feel a little better about the next day too. She knew where she stood, and by the end of the next day, she would have two of her friends standing there with her, almost free.

31 Back Before Sunset

When Georgianna awoke that morning, it was with a knot in the pit of her stomach. She didn't think she should really be worried, they had everything planned, but knowing that just one thing going wrong could mean the whole plan falling apart, she had tossed and turned through nightmares until Keiran woke her. Each time she apologised and slowly fell back to sleep, only to be revisited by the same horror of seeing Keiran and Wrench up on the execution block in Javeknell Square, of Landon and Nyah being killed as Wrench tried to remove the collars from around their necks, of Taye being dragged off to Lyndbury by Maarqyn and other faceless Adveni.

It was still early when Georgianna gave up trying to sleep, far too early to actually get out of bed, but the knot in her stomach would not let her drift off again. Instead, she lay motionless against Keiran's body, listening to his ~breathing and watching the rise and fall of his chest beneath her hand through the shadows.

By the time Keiran finally woke, she had not only suffered her nightmares, but each scenario had played itself through her conscious mind a dozen times. So Keiran's first act of the day was not to get dressed, but to talk Georgianna through the plan again so that she could see how they would get out of it if something were to go wrong.

Georgianna was set to visit the compound late in the morning, before sun-high. At sun-high, Nyah and Landon would be ready to run. Taye and Keiran had put aside their sniping at each other long enough to figure out the quietest route through the dwelling quarter, which would also lead them closest to Oppression City where Wrench would be waiting.

Once in Oppression City with Wrench, Keiran and Taye would keep a look out while Wrench removed the collars. Only when that was done would they move onto the new location at the southern edge of the district, where they would wait for Georgianna.

Georgianna didn't particularly like the fact that Nyah and Landon would have to travel so far with the collars still attached, nor did she like that they would be waiting for her in the same district the collars would give off as their last location. However, it was too late to change the plan now.

Taye banged on the wall of the shack not ten minutes before they had to leave. When he entered, it looked like he'd not slept a minute in days, yet he seemed alert and ready to go. Georgianna could only imagine he'd been pacing down in the Carae for hours, waiting until a decent time when he'd be able to come up to meet them.

"You ready?" he asked, looking at Keiran as he began wringing his hands, his heel bouncing against the ground.

Keiran nodded, tugging on his second boot and reaching out, grasped the strap of Georgianna's bag to hand to her. Keiran had already tucked two small guns into his belt, where they were covered by his dark shirt. Georgianna wished that he was taking the tyllenich with him, but it would be almost impossible to hide and a coat in the mid-heat weather would only raise suspicion.

Georgianna slung her bag over her shoulder, giving Taye a quick, tight hug before turning to Keiran.

"You..."

"No," he interrupted. "None of that 'be careful' crap."

She gazed at him in surprise. He took her face in his hands, thumbs brushing gentle, rhythmic strokes across her skin.

"I'll see you later." he told her, with a self-assured nod.

He tipped her head up, a soft kiss that felt almost innocent as he looked down at her, his forehead against hers.

"Go save some buryd guy's life."

Georgianna nodded against him, squeezing his waist in her fingers for a moment. Then she left, not daring to look back.

Every step of the walk sounded like the beating of hooves in the migration, pounding and echoing through the tunnels. She kept her gaze on her feet, trying to clear her mind from what was going to be happening in the city. She needed to appear normal, couldn't give anything away to the guards. If she showed up acting suspiciously, they'd know for certain that something was going on. The problem was, the harder she tried to think about other things, the more the plan filtered into her mind. As she walked, her only salvation became that the Adveni had no mind-reading technology, at least, not that she knew of.

When the sun finally blinded her as she stepped out of the tunnels, she shielded her face and took a deep breath. This was it. Keiran and Taye would be setting off. Wrench would be in the Oprust district making sure the coast was clear, and that he had everything set up for the cinystalq removal. Nyah and Landon were probably trying to act normally, just as she was, so nobody would suspect what was about to happen.

The compound looked more ominous than ever, a mass of dark stone against the bright backdrop of mid-heat. With every step Georgianna took towards it, her trepidation grew until she had to curl her hands into tight fists just to stop them shaking. She had to stop; she had to think about other things.

Pausing just before the gates, she closed her eyes, focusing on the first thing that came to mind. Oddly, though she'd figured her thoughts would jump to Keiran and their conversations in the thick of the nighttime, the only face that came to her was that of her father. She took a deep breath. She had to calm down because her father needed her. Her brother and Braedon needed her to be flawless.

She stepped through the gates, but before she'd gone five steps, Edtroka appeared out of the guard station.

"Med," he greeted with a formal nod.

"Morning," Georgianna smiled forcefully. "How's it going?"

His jaw tightened a little and he shrugged.

"There was a fight last night," he explained emotionlessly. "We have three injured."

She nodded, gazing up at Edtroka with narrowed eyes. Maybe he was just in a bad mood because of the fight, not that he'd have to do anything about it. Guards didn't intervene in fights within the block. They simply let it play out until the Veniche inside either broke it up themselves or one of them ended up dead. It wasn't like there weren't a hundred more Veniche to take their place. She grimaced, unable to believe she'd even had the thought.

"Well, I should get in there then," she agreed.

Following him down the path and through the heavy doors into the compound, she placed her bag on the table and let Edtroka search through it. She submitted to the usual hand check to see if she was carrying anything on her and even gave Edtroka a smile as if hoping to cheer him up. Throughout the whole ritual, Edtroka did not say a word.

"Call when you want letting out," he finally told her as he pushed the block door open.

Georgianna nodded, she knew the routine, yet he insisted on telling her every time she visited. Stepping into the block, she looked around curiously for the men who had been injured. People were milling about in the free space within the block. Others, as she walked past, remained seated in their cells. All the cell doors were open, as they usually were, but she supposed some people just felt more comfortable in their own small space.

"Hey," she said to a passing man. "You know where the injured guys are from the fight?"

The man glanced over his shoulder and pointed down the row of cells. Thanking him, she patted his shoulder before moving on. Walking down the length of the block, she found one of the men in a cell, looking like he was in quite a bit of pain.

"Hey, you okay?" Georgianna asked. "It's uh, it's Geiy, right?"

Geiy nodded, not opening his eyes until she was stood in front of him. Groaning in relief, he moved a bloody hand from his leg where a shard of metal was sticking out of the flesh.

She tried to keep her face impassive at the sight of the metal protruding from Geiy's leg. She knew from experience that if she let on how bad the injury was, the patient would only become more scared than they undoubtedly were already.

"Geiy, I'm going to be right back, but I need to check on the others, okay?"

He grimaced and nodded, returning his hand to the wound, holding the skin as close together as he could.

As it turned out, Geiy's injury was the most urgent so she returned to him quickly. One of the other men had little more than bruises, and the other was going to lose his thumb no matter what she did.

Geiy's injury was mostly superficial. The metal hadn't gone nearly as deep as she'd thought and hadn't hit any important arteries. She cleaned out the wound, stitched it up, and gave him two pills, one to stave off infection and one for the pain. It would be difficult for Geiy to keep the wound as clean as Georgianna would have liked, but the Adveni medication would hopefully hold off infection long enough for it to heal a little.

She went to the unlucky man who would lose his thumb next. It was hanging on by so little skin that Georgianna had no choice but to cut it all the way and sew the wound closed over the stump. He was passed out by the time she'd finished, even though she'd given him a pill for the pain at the beginning. Luckily, he had a friend in the cell with him, who promised to look after him and give him the antibiotic when he awoke.

It was as Georgianna was smearing salve onto the third man's face, the dark bruises forming under his eye and along his jaw, that she heard the conversation going on in the next cell. For a few minutes, she paid it little heed, but with nothing but the sound of her patient's breathing to listen to, the words drifted innocently through the cell and into her consciousness.

"That's what I heard," a man was saying. "The guards are all riled up about it."

"Yeah, you heard. From who?" a woman asked. "Who tells you anything, Owain?"

"Jurou. He was by the door while they were talking about it," Owain replied.

Georgianna gave her patient a smile and a roll of her eyes as she gathered up another two fingers of salve, reaching towards his face.

"What do the Vtensu care about a drysta escape? Just more fuel for the fire," the woman replied cynically. "Anyone who thinks they can get out is deluded."

"You don't get it, Nori," Owain insisted. "It's that girl, the blonde they sold not long ago and some other guy. Apparently the owner is some big shot."

Georgianna's fingers froze, not two millimetres from the man's face, her heart giving one resounding thump before it stopped dead. She could hear the huff as all her breath left her body, her legs trembling against the flimsy matt on the bed.

Nyah.

"Well, if it's true, she'll be back here by sunset," Nori answered.

Not two moments later, the woman called Nori passed in front of the cell, not even glancing in to see Georgianna frozen in shock. The Adveni knew. They knew that there was to be an attempt to get Nyah and Landon out. Georgianna swallowed the lump in her throat. She'd forgotten where she was, forgotten what she was doing until the bruised man clicked his fingers in front of her face.

She shook her head quickly, taking a deep breath as she smoothed the salve haphazardly onto the bruises and rubbed the residue off onto the side of her leg.

"You alright there, Med?" he asked.

How could they have known? There had probably been more than one blonde sold from the drysta yard, but it was too much of a coincidence that they would be escaping today. It had to be Nyah. Georgianna nodded, glancing at her patient and attempting a smile. It came out more like a grimace and she quickly grabbed up her bag.

"You're all done. I've got to go!"

She was already half-running through the cell block as she dug the tsentyl from her bag and pressed her finger and thumb to opposite sides of the cube, sending the signal so that a guard would let her out of the block.

It took Edtroka a few minutes to reach the door and unlock it, something that Georgianna didn't usually notice. Tapping her foot impatiently as she wrung her hands together in front of her body, she was barely able to force the reassuring smile onto her face as the thick metal door opened with a resounding scrape. Perhaps if she hurried, she would be able to get to Keiran and Taye in time. If she ran north from the compound towards the Adveni quarters, not returning to the tunnels, she might be able to catch them before Nyah and Landon left the house. If they couldn't see their back-up, surely they wouldn't run.

Submitting to the search was torture, trying to stand still and not look like she was screaming obscenities in her head. She had to get back, she had to warn them. She didn't know how an Adveni had found out about the escape and she didn't care: she just needed to make sure that they weren't caught.

By the time she stepped out of the compound and into the bright sunshine, it was already past sun-high. Not by a lot, but it was definitely too late to call off the escape. They would already be on the move, Nyah and Landon would have already made a run for it. That was, if they hadn't been caught already, the moment they stepped out of the house.

With the fear that her friends were already on their way to the compound burning through her body, she couldn't wait until she reached the tunnels before breaking into a run.

32 Running into Oppression

Her sides were in a stitch, the muscles in her legs beginning to burn as Georgianna sprinted through the tunnel back towards the main line. The rumour she'd heard in the compound had set her mind racing. Not that what she had heard between the two prisoners could really be considered a rumour. There was far too much truth to it, too much information already known. It was no hunch the Adveni guards had—they knew about the escape. They knew who was escaping, which could mean they also knew who was involved.

The tunnel travelled underneath the expanse of open ground between the city limits and the compound, and then the eastern side of the city. It ran directly beneath one of the broader streets, where a number of large Adveni buildings had been erected, holding everything from shops to military training facilities. Javeknell Square, where it ended, formed the buffer between the Adveni districts and the Veniche, a place where rebels and criminals were executed for their crimes. The Adveni made a spectacle of it, important men giving speeches about the importance of their laws. Georgianna avoided it as often as possible, as did many other Veniche, but she had seen enough to know that Javeknell Square was not where you ever wanted to end up.

With her thoughts passing to and fro within her head, Georgianna considered checking the square for any news, but she quickly dismissed the idea. Prisoners were always taken to the compound before being executed, the Adveni taking their time in asking questions and getting all the information they could before they killed someone. Belsa, especially, were kept for days or weeks at a time before being taken to the square. If they were lucky, or if they cooperated, they were given the rope, a quick death. If they held out, however, or if they were especially important, like Beck would be, they were collared.

Georgianna knew that it involved a cinystalq collar, but she'd been told that it was stronger, worse, specifically designed to make a death as long and as painful as possible. Georgianna had never seen anyone collared, but she had heard enough to know that its barbaric brutally was something she did not want to witness.

Once she hit the main tunnel and was heading north, she had to stop running. The number of people walking along the line made it impossible to run unhindered. Georgianna walked as briskly as she could, weaving in and out amongst the people, dodging into any small gap she could find to overtake those who were happy to meander at a leisurely pace.

She glanced over her shoulder continuously, chewing on her lip and the inside of her cheek as she scanned for Adveni around her. Agrah soldiers walked the lines regularly looking for those who would try to pick pockets or ambush people using the tunnels, or simply to get from one place to another, and Georgianna couldn't risk running into one of them now, not when she could barely keep her breath on an even keel.

The first tunnel heading west was quieter than the main line, and Georgianna broke into a run. She dodged around people as she ran, occasionally bumping shoulders and tripping over her own feet. Furious calls pursued her.

The sun was blinding after the tunnels' darkness, despite the tall, oppressive buildings. Once she stood outside one of the western tunnel entrances, sometimes known as the Camps Line, it took Georgianna a moment to gather her bearings before she set off down the street, still having to avoid the crush of bodies as she went.

What if they were already caught? What if she was running into a trap? She knew that she shouldn't be thinking the worst, but she couldn't stop herself asking the questions over and over, not when people she cared about were involved. Nyah and Taye would be hauled to the compound. Keiran and Wrench strung up next to Landon as a warning to those who would attempt the same.

The building Keiran and Wrench had decided on for removing the collars was further north in the district, closer to the Adveni dwelling quarters so that they could reach it quickly and get the Adveni off their tail. However, Georgianna took a sharp turn east, running along the street that ran parallel to one of the tracks leading out towards the camps. It was still early, but maybe they'd made faster work of the tracking cinystalq collars. Perhaps she was overreacting, everything had gone according to the plan and though the Adveni knew of the escape attempt, they had acted too late to catch anybody.

All along the street, Veniche were returning to work after being given a short time to get something for their lunch. Georgianna darted between them, slipping through large crowds in the hopes that the sheer number of people going about their daily business would stop anybody giving her a second look.

The building she wanted was old and rundown, the Adveni not paying enough attention to the disused buildings in the Oprust district to attempt fixing them up. Georgianna slipped down the gap between the building and its neighbour. She brought her hand down to her hip, moving her bag further behind her.

Coming to the thick wooden door in the middle of the side wall, Georgianna finally paused. With her hand on the handle, she took a few deep breaths, steadying her nerves. If Adveni were inside, if they knew enough of their plan to know whoever turned up here could be involved, she had to look like this were simply a mistake.

Georgianna took another breath, holding it behind pursed lips as she turned the handle, pushing the door carefully open. Dust from the uneven wooden floors billowed and swirled at the burst of new air, catching in her nose and making her sneeze. Then she stepped into the shadows.

33 Lies in the Dust

Georgianna stepped into the bare room, pushing the door closed behind her and locking out the shards of light that had thrown themselves across the floor. The glass pane in the door was so thick with dust and grime that only sparse drops of reflected sunshine sprinkled across the wooden slats.

Her heart was racing, thumping so fiercely in her chest that she could feel the pain of it below her breast, her breath coming in quick, shallow pants that she couldn't control. The building stood far enough away from the main street so that the bustle of activity in the district was dulled to a deafening silence. Only the sound of her breath and her heart hammered through the void.

She glanced behind her towards the door before she

looked around the room again. From the looks of it, nobody had been here in months. She knew Keiran had been here before, he had to have been to have told her where to go, but the layer of dust on the floor looked as undisturbed as fresh freeze snow.

She called in the quietest whisper:

"Hello?"

Slow, nervous steps led her across the bare room, further into the small, dark building. Everything was silent, nothing disturbed, and she could only hope that it meant the Adveni had at least not known about this meeting place. She was just about to turn around and head back towards the door when next to the wall, in the shadows, a movement caught her eye. It shifted, bright eyes gleaming at her through the dark, and after a moment of staring at her with a suspicious gaze, a body materialised as if out of the brickwork.

She jumped almost a foot into the air, covering her mouth with both hands as a scream threatened to spill from her lips.

"George?"

Georgianna took a step backward, then another as the man remained in shadows, a dark silhouette framed by brick. The voice was so familiar, yet impossible. She'd not spoken to Landon in a long time, but he was almost a decade younger than the man she had heard. There was no way they could sound exactly the same.

Another step and she would be at the door. She reached out, grasping through the gloom for the handle. They could see her, but they remained hidden in shadows. It was a trick, it had to be. Her fingertips hit the handle and she grabbed it, wrenching the door open. She turned away, foot already outside before he stepped towards her.

"Georgie, wait!"

"Don't call me Georgie."

The words came before she had to think about them, ingrained into her through years of mockery. He refused to stop using the name, even though he knew how much she hated it. Sometimes she'd wondered if he only did it to annoy her. Other times, she didn't even have to wonder.

She didn't dare move. She couldn't even look at him. The lump in her throat exploded in a desperate breath of air. She wanted to scream, to run away or crumple into a ball, because there was no way in this world or the next that the man stepping towards her, staring right at her, could be Alec Cartwright.

"Lec?"

"Hi George."

His hand settled on her, his thumb making a small, gentle circle against her shoulder blade. Her entire body trembled as a sob fought to break free, and she finally turned her head.

He was older. Seams of worry and work that had never been there before lined his face. His hair was longer, dishevelled and uneven. Either his clothes were too big, or he'd lost weight. Both his sleeves were rolled up past the elbows and across his tanned skin she could see the numerous marks of abuse in different stages of healing, many more than she had ever seen on one person, including Jacob Stone.

Still, his eyes were the same beautiful, bright, heat-sky blue they always had been. His lips curved in the same lopsided smile.

Georgianna took a hurried step backward, breaking the contact between them. She couldn't believe what she was seeing. They had never found his body, but after months of looking for him, months of asking questions of the right people, the Belsa had pronounced him dead. There was no way someone could vanish so completely.

"Alec," Georgianna breathed, her hand still pressed to her lips, fingers trembling against her skin. "You're… You were…"

"George…" he urged.

Georgianna took another hurried step back away from the ghost of the man before her.

"You were dead!"

It came out in a hailstorm of confusion and emotion. Alec frowned, and Georgianna wanted to hit him for not being surprised by the news that everyone believed him dead, or at least not showing it if he was. How could he not have found anyone to tell them? How could he not have let them know? In two years, nobody had known he was alive. Georgianna wanted to scream at him that the Belsa had held a fucking funeral.

"I'm not."

Georgianna wanted to punch him even more.

"I… I thought it was Landon. I heard Cartwright, I assumed…"

Alec stared down at her, a tightening in his lip, but he didn't say anything.

"Ho... How did you even get there?"

"It was fast, George," he explained, stopping a few feet from her. "One minute, I'm on a scout, the next..."

"Ashoke?"

"Dead," Alec answered immediately. "And yes, he is, I saw it."

"You were never in the compound! I know. I looked for you! So how?"

"I was sold privately. I was in the compound for all of an hour before I was marched out again, this collar already around my neck. Ash' killed our owner's brother. This was... payback."

He stepped forward again, but this time, she did not back away. He reached out, his fingers drifting down her arm in a cautious comfort. Georgianna let out a sob, and stepping forward, in a way she had not done in almost two and a half years, flung herself at him. She dropped her bag and wrapped her arms around his shoulders, every breath leaving her chest with a moaning sob of relief.

"Suns, Lec," she gasped into his shoulder. "I... I..."

Alec's arm wrapped tightly around her waist, holding her body up against his. Her toes only just reached the floor as she buried her face into the crook of his shoulder. His other hand came up, fingers lost in her hair as he held the back of her neck protectively.

"It's okay. George, it's alright," he murmured.

Georgianna pulled back and looked up at him, her eyes

wet with tears. He was worried, that much was obvious, but he was smiling. Shaking her head, Georgianna let out a low laugh. She brushed the heel of her hand across her eyes, forcing herself to calm down. As the tears were brushed away from her lashes, she caught sight of his neck. There were scars that wove like spiderwebs across his skin, but no cinystalq collar.

"I thought… I was…"

Her gaze swept across his exposed skin, looking for fresh marks. There was a tan line where the collar had blocked the sun from reaching his skin, there were older scars, but nothing that could have been less than a few days old. However Wrench did it, he was good at removing a cinystalq collar without any damage to the wearer.

"You panicked!" he answered knowingly.

Georgianna nodded.

"You knew I was involved?"

"Nyah," he nodded. "By the time she told me, it was too late to stop you."

Finally glancing away from him, Georgianna's smile fell, her eyes narrowing in suspicion. Why had nobody else come out? Alec had confirmed that it was her, so why were they all still hiding? She turned herself full circle, peering at every corner in the hopes of seeing another of her friends hiding in the shadows. All too quickly, her gaze landed back on Alec, the only one with her in the small, dark building.

"Where are the others?" she asked, looking at Alec curiously.

Alec narrowed his eyes a little, his nostrils flaring as he

looked down at her. It was almost as if he was surprised that she'd asked where the others were, like he hadn't known that they were supposed to be here.

"Keiran and I left to check that the path was clear while Wrench moved on to Nyah's collar," he answered slowly. "He told me to come here and check that there were no Adveni about."

All the relief Georgianna had felt at the sight of Alec was slowly slipping away. The warmth of excitement dripping from her body through her fingers and toes, leaving her body cold. While Alec was safe, the others weren't. While they stood here hugging, the others could be in the middle of being dragged off to the compound.

Georgianna pulled away, wrapping her arms around her stomach as she rushed forward through the small building to look out of the grimy window. Not even bothering to cover her hand with her sleeve, Georgianna smeared her hand through the dirt, clearing off a small space to peer through into the alley. Apart from the distant activity on the main street, it was deserted.

"George, what's going on?" he asked. "I thought this was the plan?"

"No," Georgianna muttered, not turning back from the window. "No, I was meant to meet all of you here."

Sighing, Georgianna closed her eyes, taking a breath before she turned back to Alec. He stared back at her, his eyes narrowed and his lips pressed into a thin line. Creases lined themselves between his brow as he stood resolutely still. Georgianna stepped away from the window, leaving a small beam of light shining through the patch she had cleaned away.

"The Adveni know about the escape," she brushed the dirt from her hands. "I heard people talking at the compound. They knew too much to be guesses."

Even through the darkness, Georgianna could see Alec's eyes widen. Before Georgianna could even move, Alec had turned and was heading for the door. Georgianna leapt across the space towards him, reaching the door as his hand settled on the handle.

"Alec…"

"No, George, we have to go back!" he said sternly. "We…"

"And get yourself thrown back into Lyndbury?" she demanded, a vicious force to her voice that she hadn't meant to be there. "If I'm right, every Adveni in Adlai could know who you are, 'Lec!"

He glared down at her, and for a moment she could only think of the last time they'd spoken before his capture. They'd been angry at each other back then too, saying things they didn't mean, or maybe did mean, but hadn't intended to sound as bad as they had in the heat of the moment.

She watched as he took a slow breath.

"We have to go back for them," he repeated. "Nyah has information."

"We'll get them, but we have to…"

He released the handle, grabbing Georgianna's shoulders and turning her to face him. This was the part where he'd order her down, just like he'd done before, where he'd called her stupid and immature. She knew that face, she'd seen it too many times. Not just on Alec, but on her brother too.

"You don't get it!" he said slowly. "Nyah has information I need. Maarqyn helped build the pillars, George. I've spent two years getting that information and Nyah has some of it!"

Georgianna's mouth fell open, her eyes widening in surprise. With those words, she knew why Alec had never fought to be freed, why Beck had kept the secret that he was alive. Alec was gathering information for them, he had chosen this.

"George, we can destroy them!"

"You can't!" Georgianna cried quickly. "They stop it... Without them..."

"Without them, the Adveni wouldn't dare set off the Mykahnol. It's their last defence! Even they can't stop it if the pillars aren't there."

Georgianna didn't know what to say. If Alec was right then destroying the pillars could make the Adveni too scared to even consider going through with their threat. They could build more, she assumed, but it would take time, time the Veniche could use to fight back.

"Information or not, Alec, you have that information too, you can't be..."

Georgianna stopped, her jaw falling as she looked away from Alec, a thought that wouldn't go away finally slotting into place.

"Si knew," she said.

Alec looked quickly away from her, his mouth opening and closing but no words coming forth as he took a slow step back. Georgianna remembered that look, the way he would avoid eye contact when there was something he couldn't say. Before his capture it had been things about his wife, details that he didn't feel right sharing with someone he was sleeping with, like he was betraying her. Now, however, Georgianna glared back at him, knowing that he couldn't tell her because someone had told him not to.

"Si knew about the pillars, didn't he?" Georgianna demanded. "He was meeting with you, he kept talking about 'taking them down'."

Alec frowned, shaking his head quickly as if it didn't matter. Right now, she supposed, it didn't, but Georgianna still glared back at him, waiting for an answer. It all fit inside her head, it all made sense. Si hadn't been able to tell Jaid where he was going because nobody knew that Alec was alive. Beck had wanted to know what Si had found out because it was information about the pillars and their destruction. Everything was fitting into place.

"I was meeting with Si," Alec murmured finally. "Passing him the information I gathered from Maarqyn. The last time we met, Maarqyn had others in the house, they heard us. They chased him and I... I have no idea what happened."

"Si was left out in the sun for three days," Georgianna answered. "Jaid got him back to the tunnels, but he's not the same."

Alec groaned under his breath and reached up, rubbing

his hand across the back of his neck. Georgianna gritted her teeth.

"So all this for some information?" she asked. "People knew you weren't dead and they... your brother?"

"He doesn't know."

"He was captured!"

Alec had been a master at hiding his emotions, even when they were children, but nothing could hide the pain in his face now. His lips parted, as if he was about to speak, but there was nothing.

Stepping back, Georgianna looked down at her boots and the imprints they had made in the dust. Shaking her head, she wrapped her arms protectively around her stomach. Alec stared past her.

"And Beck said he wouldn't help."

"George, he has been helping!" he argued. "He sent Si to meet with me."

"No," she corrected. "He wouldn't help us get you out. I asked him. It was before I knew about you, but I said Maarqyn's name. So he knew there was a Belsa in that house. He said no."

"He couldn't, not if we wanted this information."

Glancing up, Georgianna shook her head. This was ridiculous. They needed to make sure that the others were safe, not stand around discussing the lies of the Belsa commander.

"I'll go!" she finally nodded.

Alec placed his hands on her shoulders.

"No! We both..."

"I'm less suspicious, Alec!" she argued sharply. "You're an escaped drysta, not to mention a Belsa. I can go to see if they're still there."

Alec didn't like it, she could see it in his face. Even after all this time, she could see that he was trying to think of a way to argue, to tell her something that she would have to accept. Though Alec should have known already that Georgianna was stubborn enough not to listen to him.

Finally, he released her shoulders and nodded.

"If you're not back within the hour, I'm coming after you."

Georgianna gave him a small smile as she returned his nod. She knew Alec would not stay put for long. He was too loyal, too caring. He wouldn't be able to sit back and do nothing while other people got hurt. They were too similar to each other in the end.

Pressing her hand to Alec's jaw, Georgianna pushed herself up onto her toes and planted a gentle kiss against his cheek. She would be back soon, she was sure she would. Alec had calmed her nerves, if only a little. The others would be fine. She stepped back, giving him a final smile before pulling open the door and stepping out into the sunshine.

34 THE PRECEDING VOID

Stepping out of the alleyway and onto the street, she didn't even notice it at first, the way her steps quickened the further she went. Through the Oprust markets, her gait lengthened, her stride more purposeful as she weaved through the crowds and made her way between the rows of stalls. Her gaze darted around constantly, cautious and suspicious. Any of the people in the street might be an Adveni. They could look so similar that if they tried, they would fit in perfectly. Dressed in the right clothes, any person in the market could have been posing as Veniche.

There was one thing Georgianna still couldn't work out, and that was how they had been discovered. She couldn't think of anyone who had known the details that would betray them. Maybe Taye had told someone, one of his friends down in the Carae who would do anything for a price. Georgianna couldn't imagine anyone in the Belsa would have sold them out, even if they'd overheard something, but maybe it was possible.

Frowning as she turned the corner onto the correct street, Georgianna's gaze swept through the crowd, looking for anyone who was watching the surroundings. All down the street the market was at its peak, lines of stalls covered in different wares, their vendors yelling the wares they were offering over the general craze of people wandering from one stall to the next. In amongst them, people with the odd item or two to sell set up in any space they could find, their calls to buy unable to match those of the experienced vendors. Through the crush of the market, it was impossible to spot anything out of the ordinary. Even if there were Adveni lying in wait, Georgianna wasn't sure that she could have spotted them.

She assumed Keiran had figured she wouldn't have been listening when he, Taye, and Wrench were making their plans. Georgianna wasn't involved, so she hadn't needed to pay attention. She had anyway. So, continuing down the street, she was able to recognise the two-storey building that they'd talked about.

Even as Georgianna approached, she could see the moss green sign with bronzed letters hanging in the window, but nobody ever slowed to take a look inside. The Adveni owner wanted too high a price for its use, and so the building had remained empty since it had been built. It was a perfect choice for what they'd needed. Once inside, nobody would bother them and it stood halfway down the busy market road, making it difficult to approach with a large force.

Now, standing in front of the gilded wooden door, she was glad she had paid attention as she took one last glance around what she could see of the street. Pushing the door open, she slipped inside, closing the door softly behind her and stepping further in.

One of the windows was broken, glass scattered over the floor. It was an inconspicuous place to meet, not to mention that it had a second floor, meaning that they could keep an eye out over the crowd on the street.

She couldn't hear anything but the bustle on the street outside. Through the broken window, voices and footsteps filtered in like they were right next to her. Georgianna moved through the building towards the back, taking hold of the rail nailed into the wall beside the stairs, and took the first step upward.

The wood creaked beneath her foot, causing Georgianna to pause. What if they thought she were an Adveni and moved out? No, Taye wasn't stupid. If Keiran and Alec had been sent out to look for Adveni, Taye would have been the one watching from the window. He would have seen her coming. He would know she wasn't Adveni.

Each step creaked loudly, the dust muffling her footsteps doing nothing to stop the groan of the disused wood under her weight. With every step, Georgianna paused, listening for sounds from upstairs. If there were anyone here, surely she would have heard it by now? Still, she heard nothing. There was nothing for it. She jogged up the rest of the steps, coming around the banister and onto the open second floor.

Nobody.

Taye, Nyah, Keiran and Wrench were all gone, already moved on to their meeting place, she could only hope. If not, they were on their way back to the compound. She couldn't believe that. If they'd been taken, she could only imagine that the Adveni would have left people to see if anyone else showed up.

Despite finding no one inside, Georgianna could already see that someone had been there. Smears and patches of wooden flooring gleamed in the sunlight through the dust, round marks where knees had rested, imprints of asses where they had sat perfectly still while Wrench had done his work. In a corner of one of the large glass windows, a gap had been rubbed clean to look down on the street below.

As she moved further across the floor, her steps slow and cautious, Georgianna paused as a glint shone out from one of the corners. It was only for a moment, a reflection of something, but with the rest of the room so utterly bare, she crept forward to investigate.

It wasn't a weapon, she knew that much already. Not only would she have seen the bearer, it was too close to the ground. Stepping closer, Georgianna let out a relieved sigh as she realised what she was looking at.

She crouched, slipping her fingers around the polished, dark metal, and lifted it from the floor. The cinystalq collar was lighter than she'd have thought. They always looked so heavy, so solid, but now, with wires hanging from the broken end, it was almost delicate.

DEAD AND BURYD

A second collar lay in the corner, its broken and mangled innards hanging out just like the first. They had to have escaped. The Adveni would have taken the two collars if they'd been caught. Nyah was free, just like Alec. She would be joined with Taye, and even if she had to live the rest of her life in hiding, she would be happy.

Georgianna couldn't quell the smile that had slowly spread across her lips. She would return to Alec, telling him that everything was okay, if the others hadn't reached him already. They could take the information about the pillars to the Belsa and this would all be over.

She wasn't sure what it was that had her moving over towards the window, perhaps the chance of seeing one of them moving down the street, having only left moments before. Georgianna stepped closer to the glass, looking through the small patch that had been rubbed clean, probably by Taye or Keiran as they watched the proceedings, or Wrench while he'd been waiting for the others to arrive.

Standing up on her toes to look down at the street, Georgianna swept her gaze over the crowd in the hopes of seeing one of them, but she couldn't see anyone she recognised, not even the familiar colour of their hair or the shape of their stance.

She was about to turn back. She would drop the collar back into the corner and return downstairs, slipping out onto the street where nobody would pay any attention to her. She would make her way through the people, back to the building where Alec was waiting. She could already picture it. Keiran would have arrived by that point, angry and worried that Georgianna hadn't been where she was meant to be. Taye and Nyah wouldn't be able to keep their hands from each other, the promised joining ring already on Nyah's finger. Wrench would be badgering Alec for more information on the pillars, but Alec wouldn't be listening, his face glowing in relief that she'd not done something stupid. She could already see it. It was so vivid, so real, that she was already leaving when she heard a cry of pain coming from the street below.

Georgianna spun back to the window. She pressed her hand against the glass as she leaned closer to look. A woman was on the ground up the street. A space grew around her as she huddled over, clutching her neck.

The space, empty of people, continued to spread. People ducked out of the way and pressed themselves against walls. Five bodies dressed in black armour tramped down the street. Georgianna turned to look the other way. Five more armoured men were moving in from the other end of the road. Their weapons were raised. They pushed people out of their way, never breaking their stride. The elite soldiers of the Tsevstakre were unmistakable and people knew to get out of their way. Whoever didn't move was forced to. The soldiers' unparalleled efficiency often ended in brutal results.

Georgianna didn't even think about the fact she still held one of the collars in her hand. She turned and sprinted across the second floor. She was halfway downstairs when she knew she would never be out of the building before they spotted her. The Tsevstakre were the best, hunters of the Adveni. There was no chance of getting past them.

She turned and leaped back up the steps. Flinging herself across the room, she opened the door in the corner leading to the roof. All Adveni buildings had them. Georgianna had never really understood their use, but as she wrenched the door open, her foot on the bottom step, she heard it. Footsteps above her were coming across the roof. Edtroka had been right: Maarqyn was an important man, high enough in the Adveni ranks to order a full assault for the recapture of his escaped dreta. Two or three of the Tsevstakre would probably have done the job. They were trained well enough to make up for two or three Agrah soldiers. From what Georgianna had seen through the window, he had at least ten on the ground with more above her. It was a full scale attack under his orders.

Her breath wouldn't come. Her throat felt tight, a large lump slowly wedging itself into place as she retreated back into the centre of the room. There was nowhere to go. She was standing in a building with the broken cinystalq collars of two escaped dreta.

She was trapped.

35 The Lightning Commander

Flinging the cinystalq collar across the room, Georgianna flung herself around the corner of the banister, jumping down the stairs two at a time. Already, through the window, she could see the path clearing towards the door, the Tsevstakre sweeping people away like columns of dust. She grasped the handle with both hands, wrenching it towards her. It was a risky move, but if there was the smallest chance she could duck into the crowd, she had to take it.

Sunlight hit her, a smack in the face as she stepped out into the street. She took one step, then another. But the moment her hope tricked her into thinking that she'd made it away safely, a large hand clamped down on the back of her neck.

Georgianna squealed, floundering to get a grip on the hand that held her as she was pulled out of the crowd. Before her, people were drawing back with horrified expressions on their faces. They quickly turned their backs, running like rabbits in search of their warrens when the hunters came through the brush. Only when they were far enough away did they turn to take another look, staring open-mouthed.

Shaking her head, trying to wrench herself however she could from the grasp of the man who held her, Georgianna was suddenly set upon by two more Tsevstakre. Grabbing her arms, they held her splayed for the whole market to see.

"Get inside!" a man ordered as he stepped forward. Waving his arm to the Tsevstakre on either side of the building, six men in black moved forward, filing through the door, weapons raised.

The man giving the orders stepped towards them, coming to a stop in front of Georgianna and the men holding her. Georgianna gave another squeal as her head was pulled sharply back to look up at him. He was a giant of a man, the black armour only adding more girth to his already generous bulk. She wished that all that was hidden under the armour was fat and disused muscles, but she knew better. This man was nothing if not deadly: able to kill with a snap of his wrist.

"I know you." A slick grin slipped over his lips. "You were in the compound. A medic, if I am not mistaken."

She gritted her teeth. The man on her right gave her arm a painful twist, forcing her to cry out. Unable to turn her head from the grasp on her neck, Georgianna could only glare at the man before her.

"You're not," she answered.

"And what would a medic be doing here?"

"I didn't know the Adveni had claimed the Oprust as their territory," Georgianna snapped back and was rewarded by another twist of her arm. "I was called." Grimacing, she pushed her arm the other way, trying to relieve the tension. "I was told there were injured here."

The man looked at her for a moment, lips curved into an uneven smile. His gaze drifted quite deliberately from her head to her toes before he settled on her face again.

"And you came without any supplies?" he asked in amusement. "You must be incredibly talented, Medic."

She gritted her teeth, even as the man on her left also decided to try convincing her to answer. She squeezed her eyes tightly closed as she tried not to make a noise that would give away her pain. She hadn't even thought about the fact she'd left her bag with Alec back at the other building.

"No one," a voice said from behind her.

The man's attention turned to the Tsevstakre that had just come down the stairs. Reaching past Georgianna and the others, the Tsevstakre held out two cinystalq collars for the commander to take. He reached out and grasped them with agile fingers, turning each one over in his hands. His smirk faded, his eyes narrowing and his jaw tightening.

"Take her inside," he ordered darkly.

Tugged backward by the neck, she struggled and tried to

hit out, but was held fast by the three men. The effort was fruitless. She was pulled inside, the soldiers working together to move her back until the man holding her neck could step aside and she was pressed to the wall, pinning her in place against the warm brick.

"Where did you find them?" the commander asked.

"Upstairs, Volsonne," one of the men answered. "There is nothing else."

The commander frowned and indicated the door. Georgianna glanced to the side and saw four more Tsevstakre coming down the stairs.

"Check every street, every building in this district. I want them found," he barked. "If you kill them, I'll shoot you between the eyes."

Georgianna fixed her gaze on the floor, trying not to let them see the fear that passed through her expression. What if Taye and the others hadn't reached Alec? What if he was still in that building, just waiting to be found? What if they came back here looking for her? She'd been so sure moments before, but now all her certainty was dripping away.

Approaching footsteps brought her gaze up onto the commander's black armour. He brushed the two Tsevstakre aside, forcing them to step back yet keeping a grasp on Georgianna's wrists.

"Tell me, Medic, do you know who I am?" he asked.

Georgianna paused for a moment. There was no point in lying to him, was there? Not about this.

"No," she answered.

"My name is Maarqyn," he explained.

Georgianna couldn't stop it before it was too late, the flicker of recognition that widened her eyes. She quickly gritted her teeth, taking a sharp breath in. She'd never seen him. Perhaps she'd been expecting some middle-aged man, knowing his importance. He looked like a fighter, just like the others.

"Ah, so, you do know who I am," he said, raising an eyebrow. "Well, let me ask you this then, do you know my two dreta?"

Georgianna narrowed her eyes for a moment and shook her head.

"Oh, now, I don't think that's true," he suggested, stepping forward. "How about I ask that one again? Do you know Nyah? Or perhaps Alec?"

"No," Georgianna breathed.

"Really?"

"I said no," she answered.

Maarqyn let out a short laugh and glanced at the man on Georgianna's left. Taking the cue, he began twisting Georgianna's arm until she had to lean forward to relieve the pressure, her knee buckling beneath her. For a moment, Maarqyn left her there, one knee bent towards the floor, before she was tugged back up, her shoulders slammed back into the brick.

Georgianna glared at him as he held up the collars towards her. Rays of light and shadows bounced from the smooth, curved surfaces, and as Maarqyn turned them, Georgianna noticed a symbol she'd not seen when looking at them before. Three green lines intersecting near the base curved outward from each other, like the trident her father had used to fish when she was a child.

"These collars belong to my dreta," Maarqyn hissed. "I want them back, and you will tell me what I want to know."

"I don't know where they are!" Georgianna cried back, pushing herself furiously away from the wall only to be whipped back into the brick again.

"We'll see about that," Maarqyn answered.

Glancing over his shoulder, Maarqyn frowned, then turned to the two men. He watched them almost absently for a moment before, having finally made some kind of decision, nodded.

"Take her upstairs, we'll see what she knows!"

Georgianna squeaked in fear, but Maarqyn ignored her as he turned and walked back towards the open doorway. He stopped just inside the door to converse with one of the Tsevstakre on the street. Georgianna was sure that she saw him reach out to take something from the other soldier, but she was tugged roughly towards the stairs, and as she was turned away from them, couldn't see what it was that Maarqyn had been handed.

* * *

By the time Maarqyn finally came up the stairs, Georgianna's wrists had been bound before her, and she had been forced to her knees between the two Tsevstakre. Maarqyn tapped a Cinystalq collar repeatedly into his palm as he approached, his eyes narrowed.

Georgianna watched him, trying to keep her fingers from shaking in fear. Was it her imagination, or did that collar look different to the one she'd picked up from the ground? There were no coloured wires spilling from the open ends, no damage at all as far as she could see. Her gaze flickered from the collar up to Maarqyn's face as he stepped closer, nodding to the men on either side of her. Both men took a step away from her, leaving her on her knees in the centre of the floor. She looked helplessly at each one, but neither acknowledged her, their eyes fixed forward. One, however, had the smallest of smiles on his face.

"Are you sure you would not like to change your story?" Maarqyn asked slowly, tapping the collar harder into his palm.

"My story?" she asked.

"That you were called here as a medic," Maarqyn replied slowly.

Georgianna paused, and slowly shook her head.

Maarqyn stepped forward and took hold of the two sides of the collar, pulling them deftly apart. Georgianna shifted on her knees, trying to move herself back, but Maarqyn was faster. Georgianna lifted her bound hands towards her neck, shaking her head.

"No, please!" she begged. "Don't!"

Maarqyn took no heed of her pleas, swatting her hands out of the way, and clamping the collar around her neck in a single movement. A vibration rumbled through her skin, a cold shiver that travelled down her spine and settled in her stomach.

Barely pausing, Maarqyn stood up straight and reached into his pocket, pulling out a tsentyl. He swiped it open, holding it in one palm as he glanced down at Georgianna.

"Where are my dreta?" he asked.

Georgianna, touching the collar tentatively with her fingers, looked up at Maarqyn quickly and shook her head.

"I don't know," she whispered.

Maarqyn touched the tsentyl. The shock that travelled through her body seared like lightning collected and released on command, shooting through her body to the tips of her fingers and toes. She screamed, falling forward. Her hands hit the floor. Another shock reverberated through her skin. She slid forward onto her elbows.

"Where are they?" he asked again.

Georgianna gasped and carefully brought her head up.

"I don't know."

Another bolt of lightning ripped a cry from her. Maarqyn kept the shocks coming. Two, three, four, he sent one after the other in quick succession. Georgianna balled her hands into fists, gritting her teeth together. Her body shook and trembled against the dusty floor until finally the last echoes of the shock faded into the memory of pain.

"Come on, Medic," Maarqyn sneered. "We both know you were involved."

Georgianna carefully pushed herself up until she could look at him. For a moment, she simply stared at him, her breath rattling through her tightly clamped teeth. Maarqyn was smiling, a sick, amused smirk that didn't reach his eyes.

The tsentyl lay open in one hand, his thumb hovering over it, ready to shock her again.

"I came here because I was called," she breathed.

"And yet you have no tsentyl to prove it, no supplies to treat an injured person?"

His thumb pressed down and Georgianna was back on the floor, writhing and screaming.

"Where are they, Medic?" Maarqyn shouted over her screams. "Tell me where Alec and Nyah are. I will let you go."

Unlike before, now Maarqyn didn't remove his thumb from the tsentyl. He kept it pressed to the surface, administering shock after shock to Georgianna's trembling body. Her throat was raw from screaming. She couldn't think, couldn't focus on any thought other than the pain and making it stop. She clutched at the collar, trying to pull it from her neck, but it only sent the shocks through her hands instead, shooting in the opposite direction as well.

"They're gone!" she screamed finally. "I was looking for them!"

The pain, while not gone completely, dropped instantly. Old tremors still radiated through her skin, but no new assaults came from the collar. Each breath seared in pain down her throat into her lungs as Georgianna lay on her side, staring across the dirty floor.

Maarqyn paced for a moment before he crouched down, taking hold of the collar and yanking her up from the floor.

Georgianna yelped, clutching at his wrist and trying to keep the pressure from her neck. Maarqyn pulled her close, glaring at her and ensuring she could see his thumb hovering over the tsentyl.

"Gone where?" he asked.

It was over, Georgianna knew that. There was no point in denying now, not when she had admitted that she knew about the escape.

"I don't know," she breathed.

Maarqyn's thumb moved to press the charge, his fingers slipping from the collar so that he could shock her again. She shook her head desperately.

"I promise, I don't know!" she cried. "I was meant to meet them and they weren't here!"

She couldn't tell them about the second meeting place, not when Alec was probably still waiting for her.

"Please! Please, I'm telling the truth! I knew about the escape, but I don't know where they are now!"

Maarqyn stood up straight, brushing the dust from his arms. Georgianna watched him in desperation, her gaze fixed onto his face as he looked down at her in disgust. He finally glanced at the man on her left.

Holding out the tsentyl, he handed it to the Tsevstakre before rubbing his hands together.

"Keep shocking her while I see if the others found any tracks," he stated as if telling the man to make sure his breakfast didn't burn. "She's going to Lyndbury anyway. They won't care what state they get her in."

Georgianna's screams had begun before Maarqyn's foot hit the first step downstairs.

36 Hopeless Apparition

Georgianna was no longer sure whether the shakes travelling through her body were from the torture administered from the cinystalq collar, or fear at what was coming. Each press of the tsentyl sent electric agony through her, snapping and licking at every nerve, jolting each limb into spasms. She tried listening for the sound of footsteps on the stairs, but could hear nothing over her own desperate screams.

Each shock, though lasting only seconds, had effects that continued on and on. With each administration, the aftermath took longer to wear off, her hands constantly trembling against the floor. She tried to lift herself between shocks, braced against the floor on her knees and elbows, though even those didn't hold up fully when the next shock came.

Georgianna didn't hear anything, but one of the guards

must have, because one reached out and nudged the other. The shocks stopped long enough for Georgianna's cries to fall to a whimpering that allowed her to hear boots on the stairs.

"Volsonne?" one of the guards asked.

Glancing up just enough to see Maarqyn heading towards her, Georgianna received a kick to the stomach from the Tsevstakre Commander, sending her recoiling on her side.

"They're gone!" he snapped furiously. "Get her downstairs. We need to sweep up here for evidence, see if we can find out who else was involved."

Maarqyn snatched the tsentyl from one of the guards before stalking away downstairs to the other men he'd brought with him.

Dragged to her feet, Georgianna stumbled down the stairs between the two guards, hitting the wall as she found herself unable to right her steps in time to make the turn. The Tsevstakre behind her reached out, grabbing her arm and flinging her sideways, sending her down the last two steps to the dirty floor.

"Wait with her outside," Maarqyn ordered, barely looking at them between conversing with one of the other Tsevstakre. "I need to get the others back here."

Georgianna was pulled to her feet, dragged by her arms. She tripped and stumbled, and was finally flung against a wall outside. Sliding down it, she collapsed over her knees as a length of thick rope was attached to the binding around her wrists. He kept hold of the other end. He stepped away, holding a conversation in Advtenis with one of the other Tsevstakre positioned outside.

Staring across the street, Georgianna watched the Veniche people staring at her, murmuring to each other. Her gaze swept dejectedly through the crowd, knowing that nobody would help her here. There would be no rebel force to surge forward and fight for her freedom. She was one person, and remembering Beck's words about Alec, she knew that one person was not worth the risk of many. No one even knew that she'd been caught. She would be in the compound before anybody even considered organising a plan.

Her gaze had passed him by a couple of faces before Georgianna realised that the expression the face held was not one of curiosity, but horrified pain. Her breath caught in her chest. She checked the Tsevstakre, distracted in conversation, before she sought him again. He took a few moments to locate. There were so many faces staring back at her that finding the one she wanted, while her head spun and pounded in pain, took concentration she just didn't have.

Finally she saw them, Keiran's blue-grey eyes staring back, his teeth bared as his lips pulled back into an angry snarl. Georgianna shook her head quickly, urging him to run, but he was moving closer. Edging through the crowd, he watched the Adveni as he came closer to the wall she'd been placed against.

Georgianna tracked his movements, glancing at the Adveni guards whenever Keiran slipped behind other onlookers. In a panic as she looked back and couldn't see him, her breath stopped, and she searched the crowd desperately.

"George."

She jumped, the voice was so close that she expected him to be standing right next to her. However, when she looked to the side, there was nobody for at least ten feet. Even the faces in the crowd were not Keiran's. Georgianna let out a quiet moan, resting her head back against the brick. She wanted to see him. Maybe she was hearing things. Maybe she'd never seen him at all; he was just an apparition to calm her desperate mind.

Then, inch by inch, a set of fingers edged around the corner of the building and tapped against the brick. Georgianna turned her head and looked at the two guards, but it seemed neither of them had noticed. With a moan, she pushed herself up straight.

"Keiran?" she breathed. "They knew! In the compound, they knew."

Behind the wall, Keiran let out a growl. At the edge of the crowd, Georgianna spotted a boy watching him, his eyes narrowed curiously as his gaze flickered between Georgianna and Keiran. She gulped.

"You have to go," she whispered. "They know there was help, I've not... I've not said who."

She paused, her breath rattling through chattering teeth. She didn't want to say it, she didn't want to be left alone, but she knew that Keiran couldn't be caught up in this. He hadn't really wanted to be involved in the first place. He'd done it for her.

"Keiran, please go."

Georgianna glanced again towards the guards.

"George, I…"

"My father… Please, Keiran, you have to tell him."

Glancing around the wall again, Keiran paused a moment longer, his gaze locking with Georgianna's. His expression was pained, angry, and Georgianna wondered who exactly he was angry at, whether it was the Adveni, or Taye for getting them involved in this in the first place. Perhaps he was angry at her for getting caught. She was certainly angry enough at herself.

"Go," she urged.

"No, I could get…"

"Keiran!" she breathed.

Keiran ducked back behind the wall far enough that only his hand remained, fingertips pressed so hard against the brick that they turned white. She turned her head and looked forward, taking a glance out of the corner of her eye at the guards. They were both watching Maarqyn as he stepped out of the doorway, giving orders to four men on where to search.

"I'm going to the compound," Georgianna breathed. "You'd be killed. Go, please."

She didn't dare look towards the corner again. She didn't dare risk that one of the guards might notice.

"We'll get you back," the whisper came. "I'll get you out, I promise."

Georgianna was tugged sideways along the wall, a quick and vicious snap of the rope binding her. The guards were staring at her. For a moment Georgianna feared that they had heard the last of the conversation. However, their glares remained on her, not one of them looking towards the alleyway Keiran had hidden himself in. She realised that she was the one they wanted.

One of the Tsevstakre came forward, hauling her to her feet with a grumble in Adtvenis.

They turned, dragging her along behind them like an animal being led to slaughter. She chanced a look behind her. Keiran, and the fingers around the edge of the wall, were gone.

Hanging her head, she was glad that the Tsevstakre hadn't spotted Keiran, that he had managed to get away, but she had never felt so alone and helpless. While Alec and Nyah were free, each corner turning them to safety, she was being dragged to the compound with Maarqyn, the very man they had escaped. Every step leading her to being buryd alive.

* * *

"You know, Med," Maarqyn taunted as they finally began climbing the steps out of the tunnels. "I am now two dreta short."

Georgianna glanced at him, narrowing her eyes. He watched her, a crooked curve of his lip growing in amusement.

"Yes," Georgianna answered.

His grasp tightened painfully around her arm, his step slowing as he tugged her body closer to his. Transferring his grasp into his other hand, Maarqyn's fingers trailed across the small of her back, sending a shudder of revulsion through her.

"Seeing as you so kindly helped bring about my current situation," he murmured into her ear. "Maybe you would like to help me rectify it? What do you say, my little bird?"

A coarse and vicious chuckle spilled past his lips, sending a wash of warm breath over Georgianna's skin. She gritted her teeth, focusing on her feet as they passed over the sun-baked ground.

She didn't want to think about the fact that Maarqyn might see fit to buy her from the compound. She wanted to believe that she would be staying in the compound, a convicted criminal to be kept locked up, not somebody's slave, not Maarqyn's plaything. Though the knowledge quickly resurfaced that Nyah had committed a crime and been sold, the same as Alec, a man who would have been sent to his death. Maarqyn was powerful. It seemed that when he wanted something, he made sure that he got it. How else would he have been able to buy Alec privately before anyone even knew that he'd been captured, or purchase Nyah after an assault on an Adveni. For Maarqyn, most likely, Georgianna's situation was nothing more than something to be laughed at, Adveni rules to be brushed aside as if it were nothing at all.

The fingers, that had been so tauntingly gentle at the base of her spine, knotted into her hair, giving a swift yank that pulled a surprised cry from her, tugging her head back.

"I asked you a question, Ven!" he hissed. "Would you like to rectify my problem?"

Georgianna gasped through gritted teeth, glancing at him through the corner of her eye.

"No."

He released her hair by shoving her head forward, making her stumble a step. He kept a tight hold on her arm, preventing her from falling to her knees. When she looked back at him, his expression was livid.

"After I'm through with you, little bird, you will do anything I choose."

He didn't speak again and Georgianna made no effort to dissuade him from his decision. There was no point. Maarqyn was decided. Georgianna was to pay for the loss of his two dreta and no matter how hard she argued, it would do no good.

Like the dead, the buryd didn't get an opinion.

37 The Inmate and the Influential

The cell Georgianna was pushed into was one of three that stood alone from the other blocks. Built next to each other, one wall of bars opened up the cell to light from a thin corridor that Georgianna knew from experience led out towards the yard.

A couple of times when visiting the compound, she had been led to these cells instead of the block. A fight had broken out in the yard, meaning that these cells were the closest place an inmate could be locked and left until she arrived. The cell she'd been put in, the furthest from the yard, had a dull, brown bloodstain on the concrete, a large pool where she remembered she'd been unable to stop the bleeding in time.

There had been next to no discussion or ceremony before she was shoved into the cell, the barred door slamming closed behind her. For a few minutes she had stood against the bars, listening to the conversation between Maarqyn and the Adveni guard. They continued speaking in Adtvenis as they walked away and despite being unable to understand more than a few words of the discussion, she listened until their voices faded down the corridor.

After that, when the only sounds were the distant movements of the block and yard, Georgianna took a seat on the edge of the bed, twisting her wrists within the ropes in the hope of scratching the skin beneath the rough binds. Each time she tried, almost able to get her fingers underneath the rope, it only scratched the skin on the other wrist. She gave up, resting her elbows on her knees and lowering her head into her hands.

Her fingers traced the rounded edge of the cinystalq collar still clamped around her neck. She twisted it, searching for the ridge that indicated the join in the metal. When she was sure she'd twisted it all the way around at least twice, she finally left off. The collar was made to such perfection that the join was indistinguishable from the rest of the device. Next, her thumb swept along the smooth surface, searching out a marking that she had seen on Nyah and Alec's collars. She couldn't find it and, unsure whether she felt relief at that fact, she sighed.

She had never seen an inmate of the compound with a collar clamped around their neck. From what Jacob had said, the collars were expensive, and as the inmates wouldn't be going anywhere, the guards probably saw little point. However, the fact that they'd not removed it already terrified her. What if, like Alec, she would be sold within hours of her capture? Would Maarqyn be able to organise her sale so fast? He had done so with a Belsa. It wouldn't be surprising if purchasing a medic was well within his grasp.

Closing her eyes, she wanted to picture her father's face. She wanted to see Keiran or her brother, some image that would give her comfort. Instead, the only face that she could picture was Maarqyn's, leering over her in the hot sun. She shook her head. She rubbed the heels of her hands into her eyes, but over and over, Maarqyn's eyes were the ones that glared back at her.

When she finally opened her eyes, a pair of black, heavy boots stood in the corner of her vision. Slowly, she lifted her head, her gaze locking onto the dark expression of the guard, Edtroka.

Georgianna opened her mouth, but she couldn't think of a single thing to say to him. She didn't know why she wanted to apologise. He was an Adveni, a guard to the compound that would be her prison until they saw fit to sell her on.

"Edtro…"

"It's Guard Grystch," he answered coolly.

Georgianna looked down at her knees.

The door slid open, the metal grinding against the concrete. She flinched, but didn't move as Edtroka stepped into the cell, closing the door behind him. For a moment he simply stood staring down, but finally he reached into his pocket and pulled out a tsentyl. He swiped it open and Georgianna finally looked up at him.

"I'm sorry," she muttered.

"Sorry?" he asked, letting out a snort of derision. "Apologies are a little late, Ven, after the crime has been committed."

"No, I mean…" Georgianna shook her head. "To you. You think badly of me."

"My opinion of your actions are neither relevant nor warranting apology."

With the tsentyl lying open on his palm, Edtroka glanced between Georgianna and the device, his expression not softening any.

"You admit that you were a part of the escape by two dreta from their Adveni owner?" he asked.

Georgianna nodded slowly.

"Who were you acting with?"

"No one."

Edtroka let out an impatient breath, grasping the tsentyl tightly in his hand as his gaze fixed, unwavering on her. Georgianna, unable to stand the way he looked at her, broke the gaze and stared at the wall. Edtroka snorted lightly and lifted the tsentyl.

"The trackers in the cinystalq collars worn by the dreta Alec Cartwright and Nyah Wolfe, owned by Commander Maarqyn Guinnyr, began moving at sun-high," Edtroka commented slowly. "A time in which you were inside this very compound."

Chewing on her bottom lip, Georgianna fixed her gaze

on a single brick in the wall. She didn't want to answer him, she didn't want to risk that anything she said might give them a hint as to who else was involved, even though they clearly already knew that there were others.

Edtroka crouched suddenly, smacking the flimsy mattress next to Georgianna's leg.

"Med!" he snapped.

Georgianna looked back at him, sitting up straight and putting as much distance as she could between them.

"You won't help yourself by keeping their names," he told her.

"There is no benefit to me giving you names," she answered. "Not for me. We both know that I will rot in this prison or be sold to an Adveni."

Edtroka watched her for a moment, his expression that of a hunter staring down his prey. Finally, when Georgianna did nothing but look back at him, he pushed himself to his feet. He began pacing, tsentyl in one hand and the other coming up to run his fingers over his short hair.

"You were useful, Med!" he murmured finally, a sadness to his voice that Georgianna had not expected.

She blinked, chewing on her bottom lip. The other guards would have been crueller than Edtroka was now, but she almost wished she could have had one of them asking the questions.

"Will I be sold?" she asked quietly.

Edtroka glanced at her, his jaw tightening before he quickly looked away and continued pacing.

"I have no control over that."

"That's not what I hear," she whispered. "I was told you are one of the guards that sells on the yard. You stopped my sale to that man before."

"Because you were not an inmate!" Edtroka snapped. "My control over the dreta on the yard is limited, Med. My influence does not stretch as far as Maarqyn or other volsonnae."

"But you could organise a sale before that?" she begged. "You could do it privately. Please Edtroka, do not sell me to him!"

Edtroka lunged forward in a motion Georgianna could only describe as a predator moving in for a kill. He didn't hesitate. Every movement of his body was fluid and skilled. He reached down, grasping her face by the jaw and tightening his hold under her chin, pulling her seamlessly to her feet.

Whatever humour had once lit the guard's eyes at their banter was gone. Cold eyes narrowed and the almost delicate features of his face contorted in fury.

"Whatever you expect of me, Med, you will forget it," he ordered in a venom-filled snarl.

Georgianna flinched, unable to turn her face from his tight grasp. While Edtroka had often seemed cold and surly, she had never seen him with as much anger as his voice held. She realised in that moment how deeply she had insulted him by asking for his help. Being on relatively friendly terms with a medic allowed into the compound to treat inmates did not extend to him helping a prisoner.

"I'm... I'm sorry," she stammered, gazing desperately

up at him. "I didn't…"

"You would do well to get used to the idea of Maarqyn owning you," he sneered. "He pays a hefty price, far more than you are worth."

Georgianna's legs hit the side of the bed before she even fully realised that he had released her. The force at which he flung her back sent her onto the thin mattress with a heavy bump, her head only just missing the wall as she rocked back.

"Confirm, you are Georgianna Lennox, Kahle Tribe."

"Yes," she whispered.

Edtroka pressed something on the tsentyl.

"You were involved in the escape of two, legally owned dreta."

Georgianna paused.

"Yes."

Another tap of the device.

"You will not name other conspirators in this crime?"

Georgianna didn't even need to answer before Edtroka pressed something on the tsentyl. She shook her head just the same.

"You will remain as an inmate of Lyndbury Compound unless it is seen fit to sell you," he informed her emotionlessly. "Get up."

Georgianna carefully got to her feet. Reaching into his pocket, Edtroka tugged out a small knife like device. He grabbed her wrist and slotted the end of the item into the bind holding the rope fastened around her wrists. Turning it twice in one direction, then once in the other, the binding slid open and off into his hand. Edtroka unwound the rope from her wrists, wrapping it around his palm.

He stepped closer to her, his hand coming up towards her. Georgianna flinched, eager to step away from him, but with the backs of her calves pressed against the bed there was nowhere to go. Edtroka curled his index finger, hooking it underneath her chin and pushing her head back with a jerk. Georgianna kept her face towards the ceiling, but looked down at him through her lashes as he leaned forward, a breath between them as he twisted the collar around her neck.

"Stay still," he said.

Georgianna didn't dare move. She had seen the burns those who had once worn collars had been scarred with. Having only known those who had the collar removed by Wrench or another Veniche who had the skill to get the device off without killing the wearer, Georgianna had never seen one removed properly by an Adveni. Edtroka moved the device this way and that, one hand still holding the tsentyl, which he pressed instructions into with his thumb. His dark eyes narrowed in concentration, finally void of anger as he focussed on the task at hand. His lips set themselves into a thin line, his cheek pulled in as his jaw moved, chewing on the inside flesh. Finally, after what seemed like an age of watching his face through her lashes, Georgianna heard the cinystalq emit a sharp whistle and click open. She hadn't felt a thing.

Edtroka stepped back, turning the collar in his fingers almost absently.

"Inmates are expected to be ready for count at sunrise and sunset," he ordered, turning and unlocking the cell door.

He pushed the door open, standing to the side as he allowed Georgianna from the cell. The door slammed behind her and Edtroka's hand slipped around her arm, holding tightly onto her elbow as he led her through the corridor down towards the block. The heavy door she knew so well was fast approaching. Georgianna glanced at the guard she had felt she might have been able to be almost friends with.

"If you have injured," Georgianna muttered hopefully. "I can still help. With supplies, I can…"

"You are an inmate, not a medic," Edtroka answered. "You should get used to that."

He placed the odd-looking key into the lock and turned it. He exchanged the key for the black card and Georgianna watched as it intricately etched itself with blue lines when pressed to the device next to the door. The door creaked open, and finally, Edtroka stepped back.

Georgianna could feel at least a dozen sets of eyes on her as she looked one final time at the Adveni guard. His expression, cold and distant, gave no impression that they had ever known each other at all. Her hopes of keeping any semblance of her old life slipped away.

Georgianna stepped into the block for the first time without her medic bag hung from her shoulder. Without a tsentyl to request her release, the door closed behind her.

38 FROM THE OUTSIDE IN

Each day became like the last, a slow monotony that did not change nor falter. Every day the guards came in twice to do the inmate count, every other day they let them out into the yard. Past that, there were only the events between the four walls of the block, which luckily were few and far between.

Georgianna learned quickly that there was a certain hierarchy within the compound walls, and that the best way to survive was to stay as far under the radar as possible. A pair of brothers, Ta-Dao and Vajra, had asserted their dominance. Ruthless and efficient, the men acted like the elders of a tribe, though Georgianna had heard that they had previously been outcasts, travelling alone before the arrival of the Adveni.

Hearing the stories, Georgianna heeded the warnings to

stay off their radar, to make herself as invisible and inconsequential as she could. Keeping a low profile, however, was harder than it seemed when she already had a reputation.

While Edtroka had told her the truth when they last spoke, that she was no longer a medic, but an inmate of the compound, within the walls of the block the other inmates were not so keen to forget that she had ever been of service to them. She was not called by the guards to help prisoners, or soon-to-be dreta, but the other prisoners were quick to call on her expertise when needed.

There wasn't much Georgianna could do. Without supplies, she couldn't sew wounds or even treat a virus. There was nothing to be done but to patch things up as best she could and hope the guards would pay enough attention during count to give injured prisoners the treatment they needed, a hope that was often dashed.

Since the day he walked her into the block, Edtroka had refused to look at her. Each day during count she would watch him, waiting to catch his eye. However, even when he was the one reading off their names, he turned his head the moment he reached her. The other guards were not nearly so affected. A few of them seemed genuinely amused that the medic who made such an effort to visit the compound was now one of their permanent residents. She received more than one taunt or amused smirk as they passed her on count, or as the prisoners were led out towards the yard.

She waited in constant fear that this would be the day she'd be taken back for more questioning, that they would demand Nyah and Alec's whereabouts, or the people who had helped free them. It never came. The longer she remained in the compound, the more sure Georgianna became that Maarqyn wanted to question her himself, that he was waiting until he owned her and he could torment her in any way he pleased.

Every night, once the doors had been locked after count and most inmates returned to their cells, she lay on her bed, staring at the ceiling, trying to figure out what she had missed. Someone had to have betrayed them. That was the only answer she could come up with that made any sense. There was no way the Adveni could have known without being told. She had wondered once or twice whether Nyah and Alec had been talking and Maarqyn had overheard them, but why would Maarqyn have let them run if he already knew? Was it an attempt to capture more Belsa? Whatever roads her thoughts took her down, they never led to any answers.

The days were slowly getting shorter, the heat not quite as unbearable as it had been before. The air, previously so dry and unforgiving, began holding the promise of wind, maybe even rain. While the other inmates were praising the relief the cooling weather brought, Georgianna could not help but feel depression as the heat began coming to an end.

Every year around this time, before the Adveni anyway, the Kahle would be getting ready to leave Adlai, travelling south to Nyvalau where they would live out the freeze. Since the Adveni had arrived, fewer people travelled. Most were forced to suffer the harsh northern blizzards in Adlai. The lucky few who were allowed to travel petitioned for passes from the powerful Adveni volsonnae.

Georgianna loved the trail. She adored the cities, yes, but there was something about waking up in a different place each morning, seeing the expanses of the land. Trapped in the compound, despite being on the edge of the city, that land only seemed that much further away than it did when working in the centre of Adlai. She couldn't help but wonder whether her family would try to make the journey. There was nothing keeping them here; she would be buryd whether they went on the trail or not, but not knowing whether they were already packing to move on was pulling Georgianna down a little more each day. Even though she couldn't see them—and she hadn't seen them nearly as often as she should have when she had the chance—she had liked knowing that they were close.

Only one thing kept Georgianna's spirits up each day, that in the weeks since their escape, Nyah and Alec had yet to be caught. Georgianna didn't recognise a single face among the new inmates brought into the compound each week. Whenever the doors opened to bring a new inmate into the block, Georgianna breathed a silent sigh of relief that she did not know the person standing before her. Wherever they were, Taye, Keiran and Wrench had gone undetected, and Nyah and Alec were free.

* * *

"Medic! Hey, Medic!"

Georgianna pushed herself up off the bunk, running her

hand through her hair as she stepped out of the cell she had claimed as her own, moving to the edge of the upper-level balcony. It had taken a lot to gain her own cell, but her medic stills, as limited as they were without supplies, had been enough to bargain with. She leaned over the balcony to see Dhiren, one of the other prisoners, looking up at her hopefully.

"How many times?" she asked, her eyes widening in accusation.

Dhiren thought about it for a moment, or at least pretended to, before he shrugged his shoulders and grinned lopsidedly.

"Please, George," he whined.

She rolled her eyes and stood straight. Barely glancing back into her cell, she made her way along the upper walkway towards the steps. She didn't have much, only a few bits and pieces other inmates had given her for medicinal purposes. She didn't think anyone would bother trying to search it in the hopes of finding anything. There were others in the block who would have much more interesting things than she did, having been here a lot longer.

Coming to the bottom of the stairs, she was greeted by Dhiren, who took hold of her wrist and began tugging her through the block. She tripped but caught herself, falling into step beside him.

"What did you do this time?" she asked, glancing sideways at him. "Or is this another 'request'?"

Georgianna couldn't see any bruises on his face, nor the evidence of blood pouring from a wound. However, Dhiren wasn't exactly one to come to her to help someone else. Not many of the inmates trusted him enough to send him to fetch her, except maybe Ta-Dao or Vajra.

"Kinda personal," Dhiren explained, leading her around the corner towards the next row of cells.

She had met the famed brothers once since her permanent arrival into the block. Vajra, having decided that he liked the idea of controlling the flow of medical care within the block, however limited it was without supplies, had sent for Georgianna. While the message had been relayed to her as a request, the look on the inmate's face made it incredibly clear to her that this was not the sort of request you denied. In fact, it was best to consider any "request" made by either brother as an order, given with a smile that would quickly disappear if you refused. Georgianna still worried that her single occupancy cell had been influenced by the brothers. Though, if it had been, they had not demanded repayment.

Once Georgianna had reached his cell and they had exchanged the briefest of pleasantries, he had offered her protection and luxuries in return for her answering to him and his brother, Ta-Dao.

Georgianna had declined as politely as she could. She could tell that, despite the fixed smile on Vajra's face, he didn't approve of her answer. There was no doubt in Georgianna's mind that it was only a matter of time before he made the request again.

Dhiren, she knew from other prisoners, was clasped within the hands of the brothers, though Georgianna couldn't exactly see why. He was a bulky, well-built man, but from what Georgianna had seen of him when he came to her in the hopes of her treating a wound, Dhiren was naturally funny and kind. Unfortunately, his reputation for carrying out the punishments from the brothers made him vastly disliked amongst the other prisoners. Georgianna hadn't asked him how he had come by his situation, but when she had taken the chance of asking another inmate, she had been greeted by a perplexed stare. There were no rumours to be heard of. Whatever had happened between Dhiren and the brothers, nobody outside the little circle knew about it, and Dhiren was not telling.

There were easily a hundred Veniche in their block, though Georgianna had never taken the time to count the number of cells. She already knew that some people shared, whether through choice or by force. Dhiren however, she knew, had his own cell in one of the corners of the block.

Dhiren stepped aside, letting Georgianna enter first. She took a few steps in, turned, then jumped in surprise when she saw that Dhiren had taken no time at all to drop his trousers. He stood before her bare from the waist down.

She was a medic, she was used to seeing people naked, but the ease with which he did it, when any inmate could walk by, had caught her off guard. Blinking, she looked away for a moment.

"Are you shy?" he asked, amusement ringing through his voice, his head cocked to the side.

Georgianna looked back at him and snorted.

"I've seen much worse on much better," she claimed,

earning a chuckle from Dhiren.

The cut on his upper thigh wasn't bleeding too heavily, and even as Dhiren took a seat on the bed, letting Georgianna sit next to him for a better look, it didn't seem to be causing him a lot of pain.

She grabbed a cloth from the basin, drenching it with tepid water and gently cleaning the wound. Dhiren did grimace as she pulled the cloth across the slice of flesh, but other than that he seemed relatively comfortable. She frowned. The wound was relatively shallow, but what was puzzling her was why it was so straight. She couldn't imagine someone making such a straight, even wound with a glancing attack, and if it had been more premeditated than that, it would have been deeper.

"How did you do this?" she asked.

Wringing the blood from the cloth, she rinsed it through and returned to him, taking a seat. She looked at him suspiciously, only then glancing towards his trousers. There was no slash in them that she'd noticed.

"Usual way," he answered, looking at her with an expression that clearly told her not to ask.

She pursed her lips, but shook her head, cleaning the wound off again before wringing out the cloth a final time.

Glancing at the wound, she chewed her bottom lip. Blood had oozed up to the surface, creating a thin but vibrant line, yet there it stayed, not forced up by more blood. From what she could see, it was a simple cut that would need little more than cleaning as it healed.

"Do you have anything I can wrap it with?"

DEAD AND BURYD

Dhiren glanced around, leaning over and reaching under the bunk, pulling out a ratted shirt. There was a long slash running through one of the arms of the shirt, and looking at Dhiren now, she could see the scar where the slash had gone through flesh as well.

"Knife?"

They weren't allowed knives, nor any weapons within the block, but Georgianna knew that many prisoners had been able to fashion something, if only to protect themselves. Even Georgianna had managed to trade treatment for a thin metal knife that she kept hidden in her cell or tucked into her clothes.

Dhiren reached under his blanket, pulling out a knife and holding it handle first towards Georgianna. Taking it, she flinched when she realised it had blood on it. Not a lot, but it wasn't old. Whoever had injured Dhiren, he'd managed to inflict some pain himself.

Georgianna used the knife to cut a deep nic in the edge of the shirt. Then, grabbing each side, she tore a strip from all the way along the bottom, finally using the knife to cut through the other hem. It wasn't the best, and certainly not clean enough, but it was the best she had in here and she hoped it would be okay on a shallow wound.

"That was a good shirt, too," Dhiren lamented, shaking his head and taking back the knife.

She glanced at him as she sat down, sliding her fingers under his knee just enough to get him to lift his leg from the bed. She lay the strip over the wound, tugging the rest of it underneath his leg so that she could tie the ends together.

"When you sleep, take that off, it'll heal better with some air," she explained, picking up Dhiren's trousers and tossing them over his lap.

He gave her a nod and lifted his closed fist to his chest in a mock Adveni salute.

"Will do, Med." He rolled his eyes at the glare Georgianna threw his way. "George."

She placed the knife on the bed next to him, tapped his knee and stepped out of the cell, moving back through the block.

Inmates glanced at her as she passed, but as she'd most recently been seen with Dhiren, she wasn't all that surprised. She gave people small, reassuring smiles, but didn't linger as she returned to her cell, climbing the steps to the upper level and along the walkway.

She didn't notice it at first, stepping into the cell. Taking a seat, she didn't notice anything different until she slumped down onto her side and the sound of rustling paper crinkled beneath her head.

She sat up immediately, and seeing nothing on the mattress, she wondered if she had imagined it or if it had come from one of the cells close by. But as she went to brush her hair back behind her ear a note slipped from between the locks of wavy hair.

Picking it up from the mattress, she turned it over in her fingers. A small wax seal covered a small fold, holding the paper closed, and while it was nothing fancy, just a couple of drips of candle wax, she could only wonder where an inmate had gotten a candle, not to mention why a note should be so important as to seal it. Had they placed the note in the wrong cell? She turned it over again. In rough, slim handwriting, a letter G was scrawled near the bottom corner.

It wasn't difficult to open without tearing it. The wax came away without a fuss. When she pressed it back, wondering if it had been a secure way to seal it, the wax didn't stick to the paper again.

She brought her legs up and tucked them underneath her, leaning back against the wall as she carefully unfolded the note. As each fold came up blank, she began to worry. Surely, she thought, if someone had gone to the effort of putting it on paper and leaving for her to find, it had to be something important that needed explanation. Finally, as she opened the last fold, the paper laying flat between her hands, she found three short lines scrawled onto the paper in the same thin handwriting as had been on the front.

She stared down at the paper in her hands. She recognised it now, at least she thought she did. The paper was the same as in her notebook. On one corner, where the sheet had been torn out, she saw a small scribble of her own handwriting.

Chewing on her bottom lip, the paper in her lap, Georgianna's desolation slowly melted away at the sight of those words. His last words to her. His promise, unbroken.

I have too much time on my hands.
Be ready.
K.

ACKNOWLEDGEMENTS

I would like to thank my editor, Kevin Booth, for his amazing work and support in shaping *Dead and Buryd* into what it is now. My gratitude also goes to Mia Holappa for the beautiful cover.

Kim and Rhian, you have both been there for in-depth discussions, rambling, ranting, and everything in between. I would not have come this far without you.

Mostly, I would like to thank my family, friends, and authors I have met on the journey to self-publishing. The unwavering support and encouragement I have received has been overwhelming.

Every day you push me to go further and dream bigger.

Thank you.

ABOUT THE AUTHOR

Chele Cooke is a Sci-Fi/Fantasy independent author based in London, UK.

Chele is an English-born writer based in London. With a degree in Creative Writing from the University of Derby, Chele has been writing for over a decade, both original fiction and fan fiction. She has a number of original short stories, which are available to read free online.

Self-Publishing her books, Chele is a member of the Alliance of Independent Authors.

For more information about Chele, the "Out of Orbit" series, promotions, giveaways, and future releases, sign up to Chele's mailing list at

http://eepurl.com/vgmVL

or visit

www.chelecooke.com

Made in the USA
Charleston, SC
18 September 2013